OPEN GATES

The P.J. Stone Gates Trilogy

BOOK 3

AVA WIXX

First Edition: October 2025
Published in the United States of America by
Wicked Wixx Press.
The Wicked Wixx Press Logo is a trademark of
Wicked Wixx Press.
Originally published under the title
Open Gates: 2013

Cover Art, Ava Wixx Logo, Wicked Wixx Logo, & Interior Book
Graphics by Lindsay Tiry of LT Arts
Trilogy Logo by Jordan P. Fremgen

Print ISBN: 978-1-955950-48-0
Kindle ISBN: 978-1-955950-49-7
EPUB ISBN: 978-1-955950-50-3

For more information visit: avawixx.com

Content Warning

Coerced sex, gun violence, attempted murder, murder, teenage dumbassery, and probably a few other things I forgot about because it's been over a decade since I wrote this book.

Never laugh at live dragons.
~J.R.R. Tolkien

Chapter 1

My mind kept playing the same scene over and over in an endless loop.

Bryn's father abruptly appeared directly behind him. The Rider inside of him shone so brightly it eclipsed his host's features. He met my gaze, grinning down at me. In that instant, understanding slammed into me.

"No!" I screamed, my heart fisting painfully in my chest. I reached for my fire magic, but it was too late—all too late. I watched, completely helpless to stop it, as Bryn's father gripped his head and twisted, snapping the neck of his only son. The sharp crack shot through my skull and pierced my eardrums. "No!" I heard myself scream again as Bryn's hand slipped from my grasp, his body collapsing lifelessly to the ground.

Life over. My Life is over.

"Life over. My life is over," I mumbled, the words tumbling from my mouth without my permission. Not that I really cared since everything ceased mattering the instant Bryn's life ended.

"Your life isn't over. You are still alive. Your heart did not stop beating when his did." Khol's deep voice barely registered within my subconscious. "Please, my little queen. We need you—*I* need you—just—please."

"My life is over," I mumbled again.

Staring blankly ahead, I made no move to stop Khol from pulling me into his arms. I remained limp and impassive within his embrace.

The low drone of the local news station buzzed in the background. "President Wexington is minutes away from making some major announcements in regards to the current state of the union. There have been rumors that he has some radical new changes in mind to better keep the public safe. The President has never been shy about pushing controversial platforms, and it looks like now he is going to…"

"Shit. Things are getting worse. We need to do something!" Jeremy exclaimed in frustration.

But what could I do? I'd just lost my reason for living *and* fighting. "Bryn," I whispered. Even when we hadn't been together, Bryn had always been my reason for everything. I knew that now with the kind of certainty that only comes after having lost something.

"Your baby," Khol rumbled, pressing his cheek to the top of my head. "It could be his."

Those words pierced through my armor of numbness

and I instinctively drew my hand up to protectively rest over the small bump in my abdomen. *Or maybe I'm just imagining that I'm finally showing a little?*

Thoughts of Bryn as a child rose unbidden to the forefront of my mind. He smiled at me, his blue eyes dancing with mischief as his black tousled hair fell across his forehead. If only I could go back in time...if only...

"You have to fight for your baby, if nothing else matters, he should." Khol pushed on, probably sensing that he had made a small amount of headway. "You're our queen."

Anger raced through my system, quickly overtaking my indifference. I stood abruptly, facing Khol with fire burning at my fingertips. "I don't wanna be anyone's queen, and I'm not—not anymore. That all died— everything died with Bryn." My lower lip trembled as hot tears slid down my cheeks. *I liked it better when I was feeling nothing.* I dropped to my knees. "I can't—I just can't—it hurts too much." I was angry, so angry that Bryn had been taken from me permanently this time, and there was nothing I could do about it. *Absolutely nothing.*

Khol's green eyes sparked with fire as he looked at me. "So make them pay for what they've done. Make the Riders suffer. Don't let them go unpunished for what they did to him—to you."

My anger spiraled down into a focal point of determination. *Khol is right.*

"Yes," I growled. "Every last one of them will suffer for what they've done."

I will do whatever it takes to avenge Bryn, because everything I've ever done has been for him.

And it always will be.

Always.

I tilted my head back, roaring my fury to the heavens.

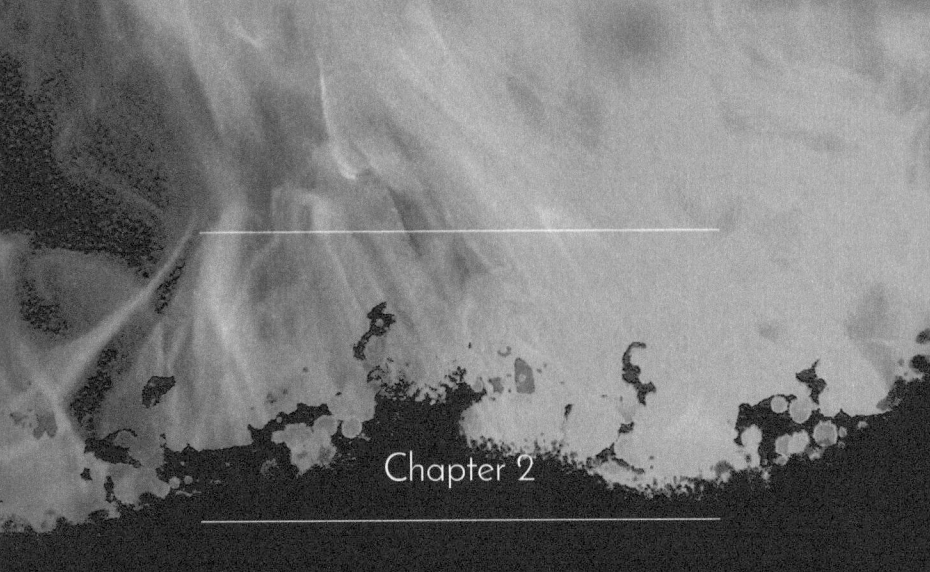

Chapter 2

"What do you hope to find here?" Khol rumbled against my ear, his breath tickling my sensitive skin and eliciting a small, unwanted shudder from me.

Of course, Khol already knew, he wasn't fooling me. Despite there not being a mental connection between us anymore, Khol probably figured out my motivations before I realized them myself. He simply wanted me to admit them out loud.

"I wanna find the Rider bastard who killed Bryn and deliver him to the same fate." My voice came out an inhuman growl, which almost made me flinch...almost. I peered out from the shrubbery I was crouched behind, turning my full attention back to the office building across the street. I was attempting to go unseen, although I wasn't putting much effort into it.

"You mean Bryn's father?" I blinked rapidly, ignoring

Khol's question. "Do you think Bryn would want you to kill his father?"

I clenched my fists, barely holding my fire magic at bay. "Well Bryn isn't here to let me know what he would want, is he?" I ground my teeth together, my jaw aching.

"He'd want you to find a way to save his father. Or have you completely given up on discovering a way to evict the Riders from their respective hosts?" Khol exhaled heavily, the hot air ruffling my hair. "What about Jenna? Have you already written her off as well?"

I slid my eyes shut, counting to ten before turning to meet Khol's judgmental gaze. The calming tactic always failed to work for me. "I'll save Jenna. I won't lose her too. As for the rest—"

I abruptly stood, sprinting across the street towards the office building. *The time for talk is over.* I knew Khol would follow me regardless of his opposition to my tactics. He would follow me anywhere. I was his queen *and* the woman he loved. Too bad I wanted to be neither of those things. *Sucks for him.*

I slipped around the back of the building, not bothering to pretend I was hiding any longer. With the current government issued security cameras on almost every corner in the United States, I knew my prey was already well aware of my presence. I could have just popped in dragon style to see him, but I guess somewhere along the line I had developed a slight taste for the dramatics. I wanted him to see me coming, and to know that there was nothing he could do to stop me. I hoped

Riders could feel fear in the manner humans did, because I wanted to witness that fear in the eyes of the Rider who inhabited Bryn's father's body just before I killed him. The image wouldn't keep me warm at night, but it might stop the endless loop of Bryn's death scene from playing in my mind.

I burst through the back door, coming face to face with Bryn's father. He just stood there, waiting for me, horror and expectation shining from the Rider's features within him. I smiled to myself. He knew why I was there, and that there was nothing he could do to stop me. I raked a hateful gaze over him from head to toe. I used to think Bryn and his father had the same features, but now I realized I was wrong. They simply had shared the same large build, and black hair, but that was where the similarities began and ended. For the millionth time I wondered who Bryn's real parents were, and how he had ended up being raised by those we all thought were his real family. Not that I would probably ever find out. Unless one day I finally gained full control of my queenly dragon powers. *So yeah...I'll probably never know.*

"Been waiting for me I see." I smirked at Bryn's father, raising my hands up to hip level while letting my fire magic rise into my palms.

His eyes briefly flicked down to the means of his eminent demise before he met my gaze. "I knew you were looking for me, and I knew you would find me."

"So you know that I've come to kill you then? Good to know I don't have to explain it to you first." I raised my hands, about to set him ablaze, when Khol stepped in behind me to whisper in my ear.

"Think about this. Please."

"I have thought about it, and I'm done thinking, Khol." I let my fire erupt from my palms, and it quickly engulfed its target—the man that raised Bryn as his own. He screamed as the white-hot flames hovered over his skin, kissing it gently at first, before curling its unyielding fingers into his tender flesh. It blackened quickly, and the Rider inside screamed along with its host, trapped and dying inside the prison of burning blood and bone.

I watched with grim fascination as Bryn's murderer burned alive. The scene was almost macabre, and yet the stench of charred flesh intermingled with the agonizing screams, instead of acting like balm to my pain, caused me to suddenly feel sick. A wave of nausea slammed into me, sweat trickling down my spine. I forced myself to remain facing the scene until the scorched body dropped to the ground, still smoking. He was dead, and so was the Rider inside of him. Satisfaction was fleeting as guilt settled in its place. Maybe I could have saved Bryn's father. *Collateral damage*, I rationalized. *He had to die.*

"There's no one else in the building," Khol said when I finally turned away from the ashes that used to hold not one, but two lives. "They must have hoped that once you killed him you would be satisfied. They clearly sent him to his death."

"And he went like a good little soldier? Just like that? That must mean they finally realize what a threat we really are, and they gave us what we wanted, hoping to appease me."

"Or they just don't want to be bothered anymore." Khol wrapped me in his arms, shifting us out of the building just as a thick black smoke began to pour from the ceiling.

I blinked a patch of woods into focus as the familiar feeling of weightlessness passed. "What the hell just happened?"

"It was a trap," Khol murmured, his hands running up and down my arms as if to reassure himself that I was still in one piece.

I chuckled darkly. "Not a very good one."

Khol bowed his head, his breath hot on my neck. "A few more moments and we both would have been dead. That smoke was highly toxic, even to a dragon such as myself. If I hadn't gotten a faint whiff of the fumes before we inhaled them, then it would have done its job. It would have paralyzed us, leaving me unable to shift us away before they blew up the building. I smelled the accelerant mixed in with the poison. But I'm merely guessing."

"Oh."

Khol whirled me around in his arms, forcing me to meet his angry fire backlit eyes. "I just tell you we were moments away from death and all you can manage is an *oh*?" His face softened as he studied me, the flames in his eyes fading to their normal iridescent dragon green. "I know you still hurt, my little queen. But you can't afford to be so reckless with your health—with your son's health."

Bringing up the safety of my unborn son never failed to hit me straight through the heart. I brought my hands up to protectively cover the bump in my belly. "Sometimes I don't know who I am anymore," I whispered, wishing I could take the words back even as I said them. The last few months, since Bryn's death, I'd worked hard to cultivate an impenetrable outer shell. I didn't want anyone...not even Khol to know how soft my insides still were.

Khol ran his warm hands through my hair, letting them fall onto my shoulders and then roam down my back. "I'm here for you." His magic slid into me, igniting desires in my body that my shattered heart despised. He brought his lips down slowly, giving me a chance to back away, before he captured mine, sliding his tongue in to fully sample my mouth. His raw spicy flavor washed over my taste buds, and I moaned as he pulled me closer to him, the hard expanse of his body surrounding me with magic and heat. I sank briefly into the pleasure he offered me, or really the escape, but as his hands began to boldly roam my body, I remembered myself.

I wrenched out of Khol's scorching embrace, slapping him across the face with as much force as I could muster. He didn't even flinch. "What do you think you're doing? Have you forgotten yourself?"

He took a step back, his gaze not shying away from my glare. "No..." His eyes held a fathomless sadness that I'd never seen in their depths before. "I didn't forget myself, I was merely trying to help you remember who you are."

My face muscles jumped with tension. "That part of me died along with Bryn."

Khol crowded in close to me again as he took me by the shoulders, shaking me slightly. "Not one part of you died with Bryn, except his claim as your *Anam Cara*. I need you to stop pretending that you lost all your emotions when he died. Come back to me...please."

I squeezed my eyes shut and turned my head. "I was never yours. I chose him."

Khol's voice dropped into a low growl, his frustration palpable. "And now he's dead. You're a female dragon, full-blooded. If I had followed the dragon ways, the minute he was dead I would have claimed you for my own, no matter your thoughts on the matter. You would not have felt the grief that has been drowning you—"

My eyes snapped open as I stared at Khol in horror. "You would even dare to suggest that I simply bond with you and forget all I had with Bryn? He was the love of my life!"

"The love of your *old* life. But you have been reborn as only the second ever dragon queen. I would never ask you to forget him—just to move on. You can't keep going on like this—this empty shell of your former self. I'll say it again—come back to me." Khol's eyes pleaded with me. But I couldn't accept what he was saying. I just couldn't.

I closed my eyes again, shaking my head slowly. "I'm sorry. I can't."

Khol leaned into me, his voice a low inhuman rumble. "I won't wait forever." Before I could open my eyes once more, he was gone.

Dropping to my knees, I swallowed over and over in an attempt to combat the sudden dryness in my throat. *What does he mean by he won't wait forever? Will he claim me for his, regardless if I want it or not? Or does he mean to leave me?*

Panic slowly shimmied up my spine, spreading throughout my system. The real issue was if I stand to live with either option. I needed Khol, even in my current state I could see that. But what if he would only stay with me as his *Anam Cara*? Did Khol actually expect me to move on with him after everything that happened with Bryn? How could Khol even still want me? He knew I chose Bryn. How could he truly accept me as his *Anam Cara* knowing he was my second choice? But then again, love makes us all do stupid things sometimes...even us dragons.

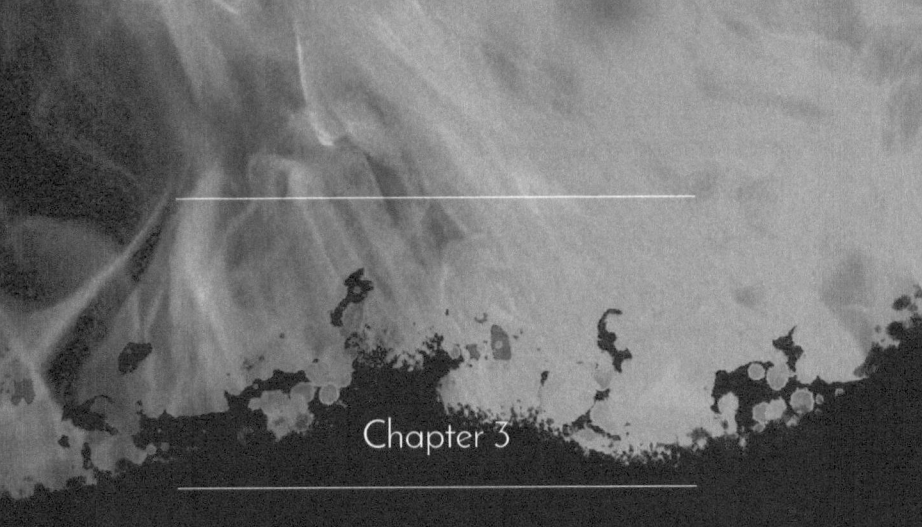

Chapter 3

Bryn loomed over me, naked and ready to finally give me what I needed. Him.

Despite the raw hunger in his eyes, he hesitated. *"Peej—we shouldn't—why won't you just—"*

"Let you go?" I snarled. *"Never. I'll never let you go. You promised always and I'm here to collect."*

Bryn's pupils noticeably dilated farther as he stared at me with wonder. "Always," he murmured, and as the word left his mouth, I could almost see the acceptance wash over him. He finally understood. He finally realized he belonged to me and when he promised always, there would never be any going back. We didn't need to be mated as dragons for that to be the truth between us. Being mated to him would merely be an added bonus.

He brought his lips back down to mine in another onslaught of need, and in one quick motion he came to find his home inside me. I cried out as the pleasure of feeling him again rippled through my system. "I love you, Peej. Always." Bryn's voice was a guttural sob as he began to build a blistering pace.

My magic—my new stronger magic, flowed up to wrap around us in a sweltering embrace. I instinctively knew that this time, our mate bond would be complete...the real deal. No words were needed between us like when Khol had claimed me. Bryn's soul and mine were linked together on a much deeper level.

I cried out at the pure joy of knowing he was finally and completely mine.

Gasping for air, I sat up, devastation caused by the crushing knowledge that my dream, a bittersweet memory of one of the last times Bryn and me had been together, would only live on inside my mind. I would never again see Bryn anywhere beyond the confines of my memories, no matter what else I told myself.

I slipped from my sweat-drenched sheets, the cool night air refreshing. I padded across my small room to sit at the old desk that sat haphazardly in the corner. With a trembling hand, I switched on a reading lamp, the soft glow of the light illuminating a scattering of newspaper clippings and articles. Sitting among them were the sapphire earrings Bryn had given me for my birthday. It seemed like lifetimes ago when things had been so simple. I couldn't stand to wear them anymore—their presence reminding me of how I would never again receive a gift of any kind from Bryn. Their glittering blue facets were pale reminders of the emotion-filled depths of his mesmerizing eyes—eyes that I would never again gaze into.

With a growl of frustration, I shoved them under some of the clippings on my desk, letting my gaze scan over the articles, my mind taking in bits and pieces of phrases and titles. "Senator Bill Wexington to be sworn into office as President today... New laws passed to mandate... Our Leader speaks out against claims he's going against the constitution by passing his latest Executive Order ... Shooting at Movie Theater, 20 Dead, is stronger gun control needed?... Micro chipping people for their own safety?...The President denies a constitutional crisis ..." It went on and on, my head swimming with the disturbing words.

A light knock on my door drew my attention as it slowly creaked open. Jeremy's sleep tousled hair stood up at odd angles, which if I was in any other mood might have made me laugh. "Hey, I saw your light on from under the door. Can't sleep either, I see." He gave me a tentative smile as he moved further into the room.

I blinked wide eyes up at him. "My God, we've stepped right into an Orson Welles novel, haven't we? Why didn't I notice it before?" I motioned at the mess of papers on my desk. "Have we already lost?" Much to my horror, my face crumpled up and I started to babble. "We have, haven't we? I mean our families are all dead...Bryn is dead...Jenna has a Rider in her...the Riders are controlling the world and no one even seems to care." A guttural sob wrenched from my chest. "Even if we manage to beat them, what happens if there's ever another threat? I mean, how are we supposed to perpetuate our lines now?"

I hadn't allowed myself to think about the very real fact that even if we won this battle, we were destined to lose the war. Our world would be left vulnerable after the span of Jenna and Jeremy's lifetime. We could make do without Guardians because dragons would suffice, and I was still a Seer, even though I wasn't human...but we wouldn't have another Gatekeeper or Speaker after Jeremy and Jenna died. How would we manage then? And even if we all lived forever...how could just one team keep the entire world safe? I dropped my face into my hands. "It's hopeless...completely hopeless." I suddenly felt like a once naïve child seeing the severities of the real world for the very first time.

Jeremy wrapped his arms around me in a comforting hug. "Don't say that—don't even think it. It's not hopeless. Nothing is completely hopeless. Just don't give up, okay? Don't give up."

"What if I already have?" I whispered into the soft fabric of Jeremy's t-shirt.

A large warm hand ran down the back of my hair, one that was definitely not Jeremy's since both of his arms were still wrapped tightly around me. "Leave her with me," Khol said in a low cajoling tone. And as Jeremy relinquished possession of me, I went from feeling like a child to a baby being passed from one adult's care to another's.

When Khol's embrace engulfed me instead of Jeremy's, my skin felt the sudden jolt of Khol's powers, and I reacted instantly, an acute awareness of him settling into every molecule in my body. For the second time in twenty-four hours I thought about how much I hated the part of me that could still react to Khol in the way any female dragon most certainly would. My body was a traitor completely unaligned with my heart. My need to feel a male's touch should have been vanquished with Bryn's dying breath.

"Khol," I said his name with warning.

"Shhh... just let me hold you."

"But it's never just holding me with you, is it? It's never *just* anything with us."

Khol's chest rose and fell as he inhaled deeply, and I sensed he was weighing what he would say to me next. "That in itself should tell you something." He inhaled deeply a few more times, signaling whatever he was about to say would probably be something I wouldn't like. "I know you want it to be his, I'm not deluding myself on that subject, but what if the baby you are carrying is mine? What will you do if it's mine?"

I was right. I didn't much like what he was saying. At all. "No—I can't—I just can't even think about any of that. Not now."

"Then when?"

"I don't know," I croaked, trying not to cry yet again. "Would you really leave me?"

Khol pulled me away from his chest so he could meet my gaze. His eyes were blazing as bright as any bonfire. "I was angry before—upset. I would never—*could* never leave you. It's not in my genetic makeup as a male dragon to leave the one I love. You should know that by now."

I nodded numbly, unable to put any kind of response into words. Did it mean more than I was willing to admit that just the thought of him leaving caused me utter agony? Probably, but of course I wasn't going to let myself admit that either. There had been a time when I contemplated choosing Khol over Bryn, but then again, magical means had been used to strengthen my bond with Khol. A bond that had to exist to begin with to be strengthened, I hated to admit.

"I'm not Bryn," Khol added, causing white-hot anger to race through my veins.

"I know that!" I screamed, pulling away from him. "What the hell is that even supposed to mean? As if I could ever forget and confuse the two of you?"

Khol's illuminated eyes met mine steadily. "Because he left you. I won't." He continued to stare into my eyes. "I'll never leave you, no matter what I say. Bryn left you even though he said he never would."

"Shut up!" I screeched. "You have no right to say such things!"

"You mean the truth? I've never spoken anything but the truth to you, regardless of whether or not you choose to believe it."

My fire magic erupted from my hands, coursing up my arms. "Stay back!" I yelled instinctively.

Khol pulled me into his arms without fear, my flames causing no more harm to him than they did to me. "You can't burn me. And even if you could, I would walk through the fires of hell just to hold you."

My anger fizzled along with my flames as I sagged into him. "I hate you."

"And even if that were true, I still wouldn't leave you, my little queen."

The rollercoaster ride of my emotions, combined with the burst of fire magic left me drained and dizzy. My eyes slid shut against their will. Khol lifted me up, placing me back on my bed, and covered me with my comforter. His heated lips skimmed my forehead briefly just as sleep pulled me under.

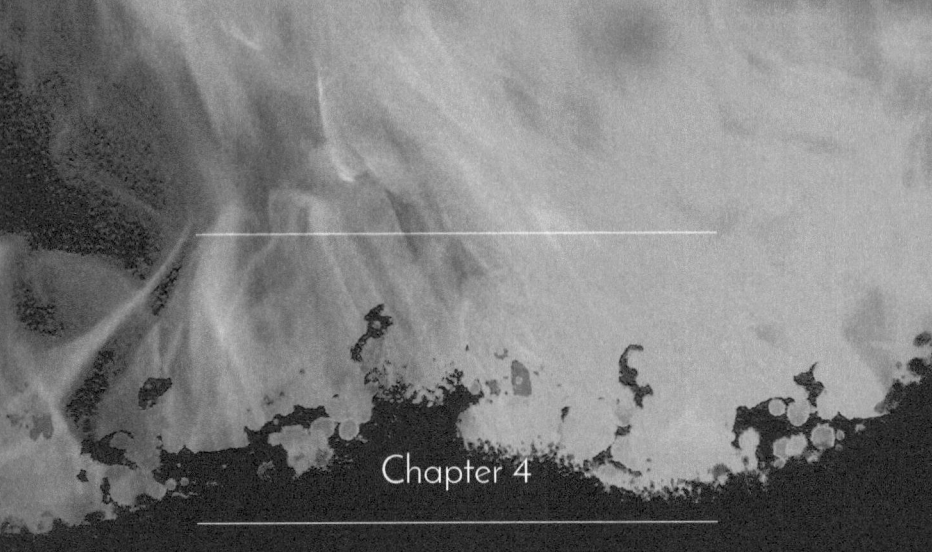

Chapter 4

J eremy hunched over, his head hanging forward against his chest. "There has to be something else that we haven't tried yet. There has to be."

"I don't understand, my birth mother said that there was a way to save her—a way to evict the Riders from their human hosts. Why can't we figure it out?" I ground my teeth together, my jaw aching.

"Give it up." The Rider inside of Jenna sneered. "I'm here to stay. The only way you're getting rid of me is if you kill her, and I know that's not going to happen."

I bit the inside of my cheek, turning away from Jenna and the Rider inside of her. Lately the Rider seemed to have more and more control of Jenna's body. I hoped and prayed it wasn't a sign she was giving up.

"Where's Khol?" Jeremy demanded. "Why isn't he here helping us?"

"He's searching through some ancient archives of some

sort, hoping to find any kind of information that might help us."

Hope sparked to life within Jeremy's gaze. "Yeah? Does he think he might know of something?".

"I hope so," I muttered, moving towards the door on Jenna and her stowaway's makeshift prison.

Jeremy didn't follow me out of the room. He was more of a glutton for punishment than I was, apparently. I'd given up on trying to actually talk to the real Jenna, and my visits were now limited to attempting to remove the Rider from her body. So short torture sessions really. I was determined to not lose Jenna too, but a part of me felt like I already had.

"My queen."

Startled by Macon's voice, my gaze landed on him standing in the dim lighting of the narrow hallway, worry in his eyes. I raised my hand to my chest as it thrummed a staccato rhythm. "Macon, you startled me."

"How is she?"

Biting my lip, I studied him for a moment before responding. Did Macon love Jenna? I knew he had deep feelings for her, and that he cared about her, but as a male dragon, if he loved her, really and truly loved her, he would never love anyone else. I hoped for Macon's sake he didn't. "She's the same."

His head dropped, his vibrant red hair falling into his face. "There has to be a way—"

"We'll find it. I promise." A sense of determination and

hope that I wasn't really sure I actually felt anymore vibrated in my voice.

"Okay," Macon croaked before he disappeared dragon style.

Heaving a huge sigh, I contined down the corridor. I didn't really know where I was going but I knew I wanted to put some distance between Jenna's Rider and myself. I idly wondered how Khol's search was going—

I staggered, gasping as my vision blurred only to refocus on a completely different scene. My hand was touching the cool stonewall in the corridor where I knew my body still was, but my mind was trying to supply me with an answer to my question.

Khol sat at a large wooden table, completely covered with papers, scrolls and a ton of dust. As he finished with the parchment he was currently reading, he tossed it aside, running his hands through his loose hair in obvious frustration. It wasn't often that Khol wore his hair down, in fact one of the only times I'd ever seen it free was—

"What are you doing?" My voice shook with nerves as he dipped his head to hover where his fingers had been minutes before. "You said touching and kissing only."

His eyes, completely filled with flames now, met mine as they looked up the line of my body. "I didn't say where I would kiss you."

Understanding skittered through my mind, pushing past the shock his words caused. I hadn't considered...I just assumed he would continue to use his fingers. "Oh God!" I screamed when he kissed me long and deep in a way that I'd never experienced before. Bryn had wanted to do this for me, but I had been shy, despite everything else we'd done. And boy was that a mistake. I definitely didn't know what I was missing.

Khol's head moving between my legs was erotic in a way I never would have imagined. His shoulder length hair had fallen out of the gumband securing it at the nape of his neck, and the silky strands tickled my thighs while he focused on giving me pleasure. The man definitely knew what he was doing, of course he'd had plenty of time to perfect his technique on who knew how many partners, a fact I really didn't want to contemplate.

Clutching at the bed sheets and finding that not enough, I arched up and dug my nails into Khol's shoulders, which caused a low growl of approval to erupt from deep in his chest. I fell back onto the bed, my muscles coiling tight, my heels digging into his muscular back, and then his power rammed into me, heightening everything I was feeling times twenty. Too much. It's just too much. I shattered into a million pieces of pleasure all the while screaming Khol's name until my voice gave out, followed by my body. Spots danced before my eyes, leaving me half blind.

"That was—that was—" My brain was too jumbled to find the right words.

"I'm not done yet," Khol growled, dipping his head to start in on me again.

"No!" I screamed in alarm, meaning it and yet not.

Could somebody die from pleasure? I was pretty sure I was about to find out.

Blinking away the erotic memory, I mentally chastised myself for letting my mind even wander in that direction.

All my new queenly dragon powers needed was a hint of me wanting to see something like that, and because I still couldn't control them, the next thing I knew I was whisked away to be shown whatever I was thinking about. And yet, no matter how hard I concentrated on wanting an answer to the Rider dilemma I got nothing.

My skin prickled in awareness signaling Khol's eminent arrival. When he appeared in front of me, my face heated at having to see him so soon after my current vision/memory of us together in such an intimate situation. When his fire backlit eyes met mine with heat, I knew that somehow he had felt my vision. "But how? Our connection was broken—"

"It appears things are changing…again," he said gruffly, stalking towards me.

"Khol, no," I rasped. Just the mere sight of him, the way his muscles rippled as he stalked me, had my body yearning to betray my heart and mind again. *Do I really expect more from myself?*

"I just want to touch you, hold you—you never complained when you allowed me before." A knowing male smile tipped up the corners of Khol's mouth.

I was backed into a corner…literally…with nowhere else to go. If only I had control over my dragon shifting power I could just pop out of here. *Please. Come on. Just work for once. Take me back to my room. Or I don't care—take me anywhere but here.* Of course, nothing happened. "Khol—"

The rest of my words were swallowed up by Khol's

fierce kiss. His tongue breached the defense of my lips and teeth to deftly take control of my mouth, and I drank down his spicy flavor with an almost reverence. Every time I tasted him it was like he aged closer to perfection just a little bit more. I let out a small moan as his power completely enveloped me, seemingly pushing itself into every pore in my body, making me vibrate with sexual tension.

"That's right my little queen, give yourself over to me," Khol rumbled, his talented mouth burning a path down my jaw and neck.

"You can't claim me," I muttered around a moan.

"Not until you want me to," Khol grated, his fingers digging into my skin.

Did he really think it would be that easy? I pressed myself more firmly against his hard body, moaning again. *Yeah, he probably does.* "Khol," I said in an effort to chastise him.

The familiar weightlessness that accompanied shifting ran through me just before Khol dropped me onto his massive bed. Not giving me time to pause and question what was happening, Khol ripped first my clothes off and then his own.

"No!" I exclaimed, scurrying back on the bed in an effort to escape him.

"I said I wouldn't claim you—until you want me to— but short of that everything else is on the table." The flames in his eyes burned hotter with each word.

"No." I shook my head vehemently. "Just—no."

Khol crawled towards me from the foot of the bed and I found myself admiring the way his muscles rippled and flexed. My eyes dipped briefly between his legs, and when I saw how much he wanted me physically, my body became more pliant even though I wished for it to be otherwise. Khol grabbed my ankles, yanking me closer to him on the bed, and then roughly pushed my thighs open, shoving his head between my legs. "This is what you were thinking about, and this is what I'll give you."

The past and the present intermingled as Khol's dark auburn head began moving between my thighs. I arched up, lacing my fingers through his hair, wanting to push him away, yet unable to when he really set in on my delicate flesh.

Oh God, yes! Mmmm... I mean—no. No, no, no. I think. In the recesses of my mind, I realized if I let Khol continue to lead me down this path, he would be inside me, claiming me as his *Anam Cara* before I left his bed.

"Reciprocate!" I blurted out as my body coiled tightly for release. I obviously wasn't thinking clearly, and was grasping at straws, but—but maybe if I gave Khol pleasure it would buy me some time, keep him from claiming me... at least for the moment.

Khol stilled, causing me to squirm shamefully. His eyes met mine with question, and yet an intense yearning.

I answered his question before he could ask it, motivated by wanting him to finish what he had been doing. "Yes! It means what you think it does. Just no claiming." My pregnancy hormone addled brain obviously felt like I'd been depriving myself too long.

Khol's large hands squeezed my thighs briefly before he slid up the length of my body. "As you wish," he murmured with a sly smile.

Huh? Wait. What? And who did he think he was, Westley from *The Princess Bride*? "What are you doing?" I asked, utterly confused as he flipped around—*oh!* I was going to 'reciprocate' at the same time he continued doing what he was doing. *Another first for me.*

I didn't think it was possible, but as Khol positioned himself above me, my blood boiled hotter, my skin aching with need. I arched up to touch him with my tongue as he resumed his ministrations. *Oh yes, I'm gonna definitely enjoy this.*

Only later would I stop to consider that while I was within Khol's embrace, and while we were pleasuring each other...not once did my mind turn towards Bryn. Not even for a second.

Chapter 5

A strong, steady heartbeat playing rhythmically under my ear pulled me from my fitful sleep. For an instant, barely a moment in time, I allowed myself to luxuriate in the warmth and comfort of Khol's naked body intertwined with mine. His massive frame made me feel tiny and safe, like nothing could hurt me while I laid encircled within his muscular arms.

I had somehow kept him from claiming me as his *Anam Cara*, but I had also allowed myself to temporarily get lost in him...all of him. And while I was lost, I found that being with Khol helped to ease the pain of losing Bryn. Did that mean I'd used Khol? Probably. But somehow I didn't think Khol minded all that much. I had to wonder though, how long would Khol permit me to use him in that manner before pushing the matter of becoming his *Anam Cara*? How long would he let me to lose myself in him to hide from my pain?

"For as long as you need, my little queen," Khol's sleep addled voice rumbled from underneath me.

I ignored the fact the connection between us that let him read my emotions seemed stronger than ever. At least on his end, because I still wasn't getting anything from him on my side. "It's not fair to you."

His fingers idly twirled the ends of my hair. "I'll be whatever you want me to be, for however long you need me to be."

I bit the inside of my cheek, sending up a silent prayer of thanks that I didn't have to look Khol in the eyes for this conversation. Somehow it made it easier for me. "So you're okay with not claiming me?"

His chest heaved under my head as he sighed deeply. "No. I don't think okay is the right word for it but...I'll survive."

"I'm sorry," I blurted out. "I don't wanna hurt you—I've never meant to hurt you and yet I keep doing it over and over again—hurting you." Tears gathered at the corners of my eyes.

"If you were anyone but you I would never have fallen in love with you. And of course you hurt me...that's what you do because you're young, and impulsive, and you're always following your heart." Khol paused as if to gather his thoughts. "I just keep hoping one day your heart will lead you to me. Just like mine led me to you."

When he was like this—so open and vulnerable, it was difficult to not let my heart get involved, despite the pain I still felt over Bryn's loss. It was when he was demanding and possessive that made it easy for me to pull away from him. "Khol—" I started, but he didn't let me finish.

"I know now is not the right time—of course it never seems to be the right time but—" He lifted me away from his chest so he could gaze into my eyes. His face appeared so young in that moment—young, and hopeful, and absolutely beautiful. "I love you. And I need to tell you not just so I'm sure you understand, but to unburden the weight those words put on my soul." He stroked the back of his knuckles down the side of my face. "I love you," he repeated, his gaze locked with mine.

The tears that had been pooling in my eyes finally spilled, leaking down my cheeks. "I love you too—just not the way you want. Bryn was the love of my life, and whether you wanna hear this or not, he took a part of me with him when he died. I'll never be able to be what you want me to be to you."

"For now," Khol whispered softly.

"No. You need to listen to me, Khol. Never. I'll never love you the way I did him. I'm sorry. I wish I could. I really do. More than I really wanna admit—because it would be so easy. It's just I can't. You need to truly believe that."

"I don't want you to love me the way you did him. What you shared with Bryn was fleeting, like a shooting star streaking across the sky, hot and bright but gone too soon. I want our love to be like the sun itself." I shook my head numbly, wishing I could just make him understand. "We are fated to be together—fated to be *Anam Caras*. I'm sorry that you had to love and lose him, truly I am, but he was the love of your old life. I am the love of this life and beyond. Loving him prepared you to love me."

Unable to find any words that would be a sufficient reply to his, a sob burst from me, ripping the air from my lungs. A part of me wanted to believe him—to believe that one day his love would fill the gaping hole in my chest. But even wanting that felt like a betrayal of what I'd had with Bryn. You don't ever move on from a love like that. You count yourself lucky for getting to experience it at all and then close off your heart to all others.

"It doesn't matter what you believe now, my little queen. Even at your lowest you can't deny that you seek me out for comfort. What we did here in my bed means more than you're willing to admit." He slid his hand up to rest on my belly. "And he still could be mine." He dipped his head to deliver me a brief scorching kiss before disentangling himself from me. He rose quickly, leaving me there completely breathless, nestled down in a stack of pillows, staring after the magnificent sight that was his naked body.

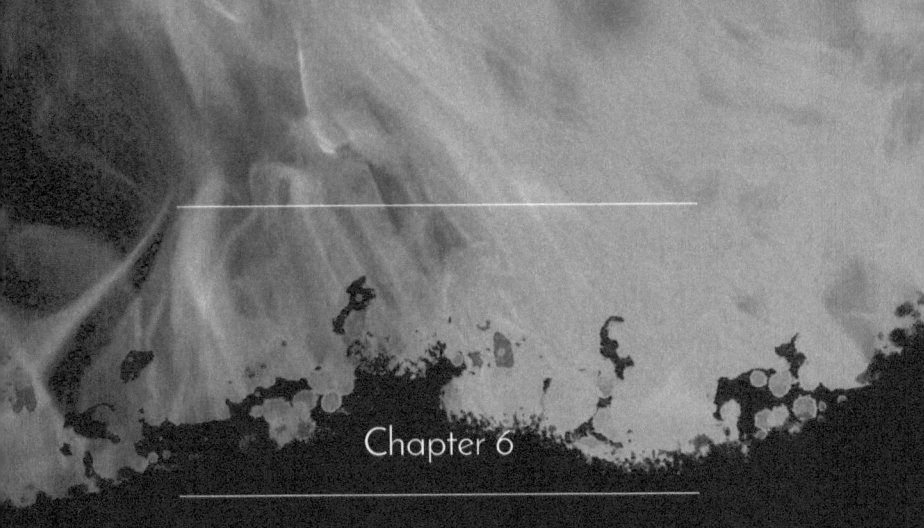

Chapter 6

"Jenna! No!" I screamed as she crumpled to the floor. The red ruby dangling from my dragon pendant glowed brightly, pulling at the Rider's vapor-ish form that hovered above Jenna's body. The Rider screamed out in pain and terror before seemingly disappearing into my necklace with another flash of brilliant red light.

I rushed forward, pressing my shaking hand to Jenna's neck, searching for her pulse. Seconds that seemed like hours passed by and still I searched. *Is she breathing?* I bent over her face to check, noticing something I hadn't before: her eyes were open and lifeless, glazed over in the sightless manner of death.

"No!" I screamed. "No! The Rider's gone! I got it out! You're not supposed to be dead! You can't be dead!"

"P.J.! Wake up!" I sat straight up in bed, blinking Jeremy into focus.

I'm in my room. In bed. None of that was real. "A nightmare...it was just a nightmare," I mumbled with relief.

"About Jenna? Are you sure it wasn't a vision?" Worry pinched Jeremy's already exhausted features. *He rarely smiles anymore.* He used to be such a happy-go-lucky type of person when I first met him. *I ruined that too.*

"No, it couldn't have been," I said, swiping at the sweaty tendrils of hair sticking to my face.

"It couldn't have been, or you don't want it to have been? Tell me," Jeremy grated, reaching forward to grab me by the shoulders.

My eyes widened slightly as I met his panicked brown depths. "I—I—I don't know for sure," I stammered. I owed him the truth at least.

Jeremy's hands slipped from my shoulders and he turned away from me. "Tell me what you saw. I need to know."

"I don't wanna talk about it, Jeremy. Please don't ask me to."

He chuckled darkly. "That bad, huh?"

"Yeah," I whispered.

Jeremy dropped to the ground as if he was a marionette that just had its strings cut. "I just don't know what to do anymore. I keep telling you not to give up—not to lose hope, and yet I think I already have."

"We have to keep on going. With or without hope, we just need to keep on going." Not the best words of encouragement, but I was fresh out of pep talks.

My skin prickled with awareness just before Khol appeared in my room. "We need to talk," he said without any preamble.

"About what?" I asked grumpily. "I was kind of planning to try and get some more sleep."

"It's of the utmost importance." Khol eyed Jeremy. "And I need this to be a private conversation."

"There's nothing you can't say in front of Jeremy if it's—"

"It's all right," Jeremy interrupted, rising to his feet and shuffling towards the door. "I'm gonna try and get some sleep myself. Maybe things will look better in the morning."

As soon as Jeremy was gone and the door clicked shut behind him, Khol came to me in a blur of speed. "I shared your vision with you."

My heart stumbled within my chest as I shook my head in denial. "It was just a nightmare. It had to be." But the truth was, I already knew it was a vision. I was getting better at distinguishing the subtle flavor that set them apart from everything else.

Khol dipped down to his knees, resting his large hands on my legs as he stared up at me with excitement dancing in his eyes. "The future is changeable. Your birth mother knew that. Your vision doesn't mean Jenna is definitely going to die, by receiving it we stand more of a chance of stopping it, just like—"

"The school shooting!" I exclaimed, launching to my feet. "How could I possibly forget?" I nibbled my lower lip as I began to pace the small space in my room. "But how, I didn't really get much information from that particular vision..."

Khol stood and spun me around to face him, his hands running down my arms to take me by mine. He left what felt like a trail of fire in their wake and I melted into his touch. "You got more than you realize." I looked up at him with expectation, waiting for him to clue me in. "The necklace—the stone—it pulled the Rider out of Jenna's body—"

"And killed her!"

"We just need more information." Khol's hands had moved to my back where they kneaded at the tension there. I bit my cheek to keep from groaning in pleasure. "But now we know where to start looking."

"We do?" I murmured, swaying towards Khol as he increased the pressure of his massage.

"Yes." I could hear the smile in his voice, which was good because I had somehow come to lean on Khol's massive chest. "My family archives. The necklace is a family heirloom, there has to be information about where it came from. Once we know that then we can follow the trail."

"Mmmm..." I groaned as his fingers worked on a particularly bothersome knot by my shoulder blade.

Khol's chest pleasantly rumbled, sounding almost like a cat purring. "You need to get some good rest. I'll take care of everything, my little queen. I'm here for you."

My brain was complete mush, and I struggled to keep

focused. "Are you doing something to me?" My face heated. "I mean magically. I really shouldn't be this calm after what I just had a vision about."

"Shhh…" Khol murmured. "You and your baby need to rest. It's not good for either of you for you to worry needlessly. Your vision gave us a piece of very good news. We know where to start looking therefore we have something to be happy about. Rest now, I said I'd take care of everything else."

"Makes sense to me," I said around a yawn. *Wait.* He didn't answer my question exactly. "But are you doing something magically?" I interrupted myself with another yawn. "To me?" My eyes fluttered shut and I luxuriated in Khol's touch. Maybe he was right, maybe a little bit of sleep would do wonders for my unborn son and me.

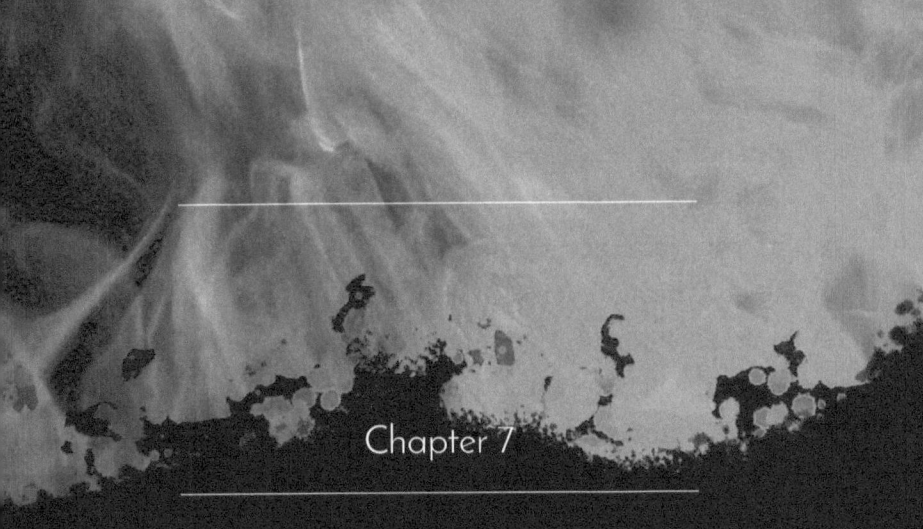

Chapter 7

President Wexington's fist slammed down on the desk with enough force to make the entire piece of furniture shake in protest. "Why is she not dead yet? And why is the stone not in our possession?"

A tall skinny man called Ethan grimaced at his master's outburst. "The red dragon known as Khol figured out our plan."

"Then what is your backup plan?" The President demanded before Ethan could say anything else in way of explanation. "That stone—if they figure out what they have in their possession—well I don't think I have to tell you what it means for all of us."

Ethan swallowed down his nerves as best he could. "Yes, I'm aware. But the good news is that it appears the stone has been in their hands since their queen was at your son's school. It bodes well that they haven't figured it out yet, maybe their race is just as we suspected, too stupid to figure out that they hold the key to evicting us from our residence here."

"It's something we can't risk!" the President bellowed. "Fix your mistake, get me that stone, and kill their queen. She and the stone are the only hope any of them have. If we remove both of them then none of them, not even the dragons, will be any real threat."

"Yes. I understand," Ethan responded in a shaky voice. "I won't fail you like the others. I know what it would mean for me."

The President grinned an unpleasant smile, which was little more than him baring his teeth. "Good. Then everything is understood. Leave me, and don't return with any more bad news."

Ethan left the oval office pale and shaking.

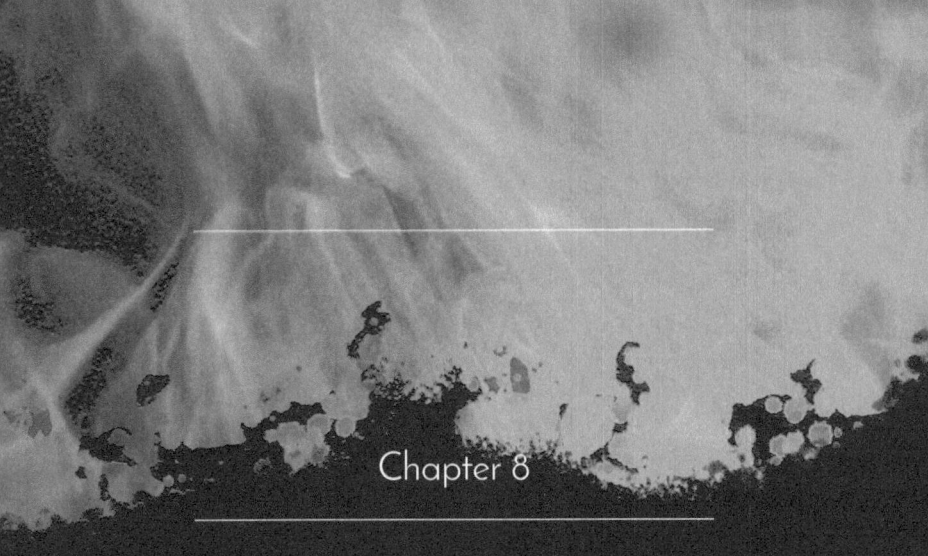

Chapter 8

Waking up alone, after experiencing the intimacy of sleeping in the arms of the person you love, has to be one of the worst things about losing someone. When Bryn was still alive, and we weren't together, I would wake up missing him, but there was always the hope that one day I'd be in his arms again. Now...well that hope had been dashed forever. Never again would I feel the press of his hard body against mine as he curled around me in his sleep. Never again would I wake up entangled in his limbs, his unique scent being pulled into my lungs with every breath. I'd never hear his sleep-laden voice first thing in the morning, the way its scratchy tone abraded my ears, yet was somehow pleasant.

I shivered, and curled into a small ball under the covers, even though I wasn't physically cold, just emotionally bereft. My thoughts flowed from being in

Bryn's arms to being in Khol's. Waking up to Khol hadn't been the worst thing in the world. In fact, it had been pretty amazing. He had a way of making me feel safe and treasured. And it's not that when I was with Bryn I didn't feel that way too, but it was just with Khol...there was something comforting in the way he seemed to always know exactly what I needed, even when I didn't.

Maybe it was my pregnancy hormones, but being taken care of in the manner Khol did—I liked it. I'd always felt that a woman should be able to take care of herself, which I still do, but it was also nice to know that I could depend on Khol. The only thing I hated to admit, especially with Bryn being dead, was that when Bryn left me, no matter the noble reason behind it, he had made me feel as if I couldn't depend on him completely. Some part of the trust between us had been broken. In the end it hadn't mattered. I'd chosen him for my *Anam Cara*, but I couldn't deny that where Bryn had lacked, Khol excelled.

My skin hummed with the awareness of Khol's eminent arrival. Did he know I was thinking about him? Or was he sensing my emotional turmoil?

"My little queen," Khol rasped, appearing out of my line of sight to slide in behind me, his arms encircling me. He pulled my small frame tightly against his muscled chest, inhaling deeply as he pressed his face into my mass of sleep-tangled hair.

I burrowed deeper into the covers and Khol's warmth as I let my eyes slide shut. "Don't you have research that you should be concentrating on?" I mumbled.

"I'm taking a break," Khol murmured, nuzzling me. I knew he was really here to comfort me. Khol's large hand slid under the covers, around my hip, and came to rest on my slightly protruding belly. "How is he?" Khol asked, tenderly. "Can you feel him moving yet?"

I brought my smaller hand to rest over his. "I'm not sure I'm far enough along for that to happen yet. I really don't know."

"Do you need anything, my little queen? Are you comfortable? Hungry?" Khol slowly rubbed my belly, and my whole body quivered deliciously as his magic skimmed lightly over my skin.

The truth was, I didn't know what I'd do without Khol if I ever lost him. Since he stepped into my life he hadn't left my side, no matter what was going on between us. His devotion to me was almost overwhelming. Here was a man that would do anything I asked of him, and yet I couldn't bring myself to give him the one thing he desired most from me...my heart. I almost—almost wished I could push Bryn out of my mind. I felt disloyal for even considering that, but I couldn't help the longing I had to just be content. I knew Khol would do everything in his power to keep me content, if not make me happy. *But could I be happy with Khol? Truly happy?* I mentally shook myself. How could I be thinking about being happy when the world was in the current state of chaos? Maybe I hadn't grown up or changed as much as I thought I had, because apparently I was still capable of being completely shallow and selfish.

"Khol," I said, squirming away from his tight embrace. "We need to find the answers to the necklace stuff. It's selfish of me to get so wrapped up in myself."

Khol gently pulled me back against the hard expanse of his chest. "There are times when being selfish is completely acceptable. For instance, when you need to recharge yourself so you can be at full mental and physical capacity to deal with the problems at hand. You're not helping anyone if you continue to unravel."

I ground my teeth together. "I hate it when you do that."

"What?" Khol asked with amusement.

"Make your side of things sound completely logical."

Khol chucked against my ear causing goose bumps to race across my flesh. "It's not that hard to do when logic *is* on my side."

"I miss him, Khol. And I'm sorry that you have to hear about it, but I just don't have anyone else to really talk to." I rolled onto my back, gazing up into Khol's pensive face. His eyes swept over me, and his lips quirked up slightly.

"He was your best friend. Of course you miss him. I'm not asking you to forget him. And I know I can never replace him, but I can be something new to you... something incomparable."

I reached up to run the tips of my fingers along the side of his jaw. He was so beautiful, and so familiar to me now. It was as if I'd known him my entire life. "As you keep saying...it's just..." I flicked my gaze away from him. "...I don't know. I can't seem to sort my feelings out."

"No one's asking you to," Khol paused as if to consider what he would say next. "I'm just asking you to let me love you."

I sighed in frustration. Khol made it sound so simple. *If only.* "But I know what you really want Khol, you want—"

"Yes, for you to be my *Anam Cara* and for you to be happy. Because being my *Anam Cara* would make you happy." Khol cupped my cheek and brought my face back towards him. He dipped his head, skimming his lips over mine. Even the slight contact had me reacting to him. My hands slid into his hair on their own volition. My eyes closed in preparation for a deeper kiss from him. A kiss that never came.

My eyelids fluttered back open reluctantly, and I registered Khol studying me, his expression expectant, and yet strangely wistful somehow. "What are you doing?" I whispered, annoyed.

"Waiting," he rumbled, his voice dipping low.

"For what?" *He needs to just kiss me already.*

Disappointment flashed in the depths of his dragon green eyes. "I guess I have longer to wait." He stood abruptly and disappeared.

I sat up, my weight on my forearms as I swore under my breath. "What the hell was that about? What was he waiting for exactly?" But of course no answer was forthcoming.

I grumbled and huffed before sliding back down into the comforting fluff of my bed. More sleep...that's what I needed.

~

"PEEJ."

"Bryn!" I joyfully exclaimed, hurtling myself into his waiting arms. I immediately started to sob when my face was pressed into his chest. "I know it's a dream, but I miss you so much Bryn."

His arms tightened around me. "I've missed you, too." He inhaled and exhaled before speaking. "This isn't a regular dream."

"Yeah, okay," I mumbled into his now wet shirt.

"What I mean is that it's really me. I mean, yeah, I'm dead, but I'm still here in your dream."

"Dream you isn't allowed to talk about you being dead," I said with irritation.

"Okay, yeah, maybe I'm not saying this right, but I'm visiting you in your dream, Peej. This is really me."

I pulled back enough so I could meet his gaze, but I didn't want to lose the contact of his skin on mine. "I wish," I murmured, as I took in the face of the man I'd known practically all of my life. His strong sculpted jaw line and high cheekbones, his full supple lips, his jet back hair that was currently falling forward into his sea storm eyes. How I longed for his image to be more than a memory conjured up by my sleeping mind.

"I don't have much time so you're gonna have to pay attention, Peej." Longing washed over his beautiful features as he brought up his thumb to brush over my bottom lip. "I'm not supposed to help, not supposed to come to you. It's against the rules" —he chuckled darkly— "but when have we ever followed the rules?"

"I'm not really sure I believe anything you're saying, because I think you're just a part of a really weird dream, but I'll take seeing you whether it's real or not."

Bryn smiled, shaking his head at me. "Same old Peej." His expression then smoothed out into serious lines. "Okay...first of all...I need to tell you that I love you and I—"

"I love you, too!" I interrupted, but Bryn brought a finger up to effectively quiet me.

"Just listen, Peej. I really don't have a lot of time." I nodded once, and he continued. "I love you but I'm not an option anymore with me being dead and all. I want you to be happy. He'll make you happy."

"Khol?" I whispered, completely flabbergasted. "You're claiming to have come to me just to tell me you're okay with me being with Khol? More like my subconscious is trying to dream something up...quite literally apparently...to help me with my feelings of guilt for wanting him at all."

"Just listen," Bryn snapped, running his hands through his hair. "That's not the only reason I came, but I had to tell you while I was here. I can't take seeing you so miserable. I need you to be happy, Peej. You still have a life, and I don't." I stared at him in silence as he continued speaking. "A lot of things become clear after you're dead.

And one of them for me is that some things are inevitable. Like you and Khol being together. It was gonna happen at some point no matter the choices either of us made. You're fated, and that's rare."

"No! You and me are fated! You and—"

"Obviously not. If we were fated then we'd be together." Pain and longing rippled across his features briefly. "But enough about that, I can't say anymore, I don't have enough time. What I need to tell you is that you're on the right track with the necklace. But you'll be faced with a choice—a choice that'll be the hardest decision you've ever had to make. Choose him."

"What does that mean?"

"That's all I can say without affecting things too much. You'll know what I mean when the time comes. Choose him. Please, just choose him."

The edges of my dream started to waver and I knew Bryn was leaving me. "Bryn, wait! Why does everyone keep saying they can only give me so much information without affecting things too much? It's beyond irritating! If this is real, or as real as a dream can be—you have to tell me more—you have to tell me—"

All went dark.

Chapter 9

Pissed. I woke up pissed. Completely, and utterly pissed off at the world. I wasn't sure whether my anger should be directed at my subconscious for imagining Dream Bryn into existence to tell me he was okay with me wanting Khol, or if I should be angry at the Real Bryn for thinking I was waiting for his permission. Like if he simply said it was okay I would move on with Khol, no questions asked.

In fact, the whole situation made me want to avoid Khol completely. Hell, if it was Real Bryn, he would know by telling me that he gave his permission he would effectively keep me away from Khol. So maybe he didn't want me to be with Khol after all. Of course, knowing I would figure that out, because Bryn knew me so well, he might figure I'd go against what he said because I would get pissed at him for giving his permission. He could want me with Khol after all. Or...I could just be losing my mind. The last option was probably the most likely.

I kept wishing I had the old, Rider-free Jenna to talk to, and my thoughts kept returning to her all morning. Recently all my visits centered around me trying to figure out how to remove the Rider from her. I didn't have any new ideas to test out—because I so wasn't going to attempt the necklace thing and kill her like in my vision, even if I did know how to work it, which I didn't. But I had to talk to someone, and I needed her, as selfish as that was. I needed her more than ever with Bryn being dead.

After pacing back and forth outside of Jenna's makeshift prison, I finally worked up enough courage to face her for the second time in mere days. But facing her wasn't really the problem—it was facing what was currently inside of her.

I entered the room slowly, my eyes adjusting to the dim lighting quickly as they came to settle on Jenna's still form laying in the center of her big bed, chains wrapped around her wrists and ankles, securing her there. I wasn't sure which was worse, the chains or the bars. I hated having to think about Jenna in the same sentence of either of those things. *I hate it all.* She appeared to be asleep, or a least resting, so I turned to go, my courage waning.

"Wait," Jenna croaked, causing me to stop dead in my tracks with my back to her. "P.J. it's me. Don't go."

I plastered the best smile I could manage on my face before turning back around. It was brittle at best. "Hey. I was hoping to talk to you."

As I slowly approached her, I studied her appearance. The Rider inside of her wasn't shining as brightly, which I'd come to learn meant that Jenna was mostly in control. I was sure the Rider could hear us, but it was as if it was sleeping or resting inside of her, because its eyes were closed. The dual imagery was still disconcerting, but I was more used to it than I liked.

"Yeah?" Jenna gave me a brittle smile of her own. "I hope it's good—or at least about sex or something."

Despite everything, I couldn't help but laugh. "I guess my question is finally answered. You can talk about sex in any situation, no matter what."

Jenna grinned. "What can I say? Some things will never change."

"That's not the only thing." I chuckled, eyeing her new blue do speculatively.

She reached up to run her fingers through her hair, the chains attached to her wrists rattling in the process. "Yeah, Jeremy helped me do it. He thought it might help cheer me up a little."

I came to sit on the edge of her bed, towards her feet, out of her reach just in case the Rider decided to take back control. "And did it?"

"I guess." She sighed. "I don't think I deserve his devotion. He's just—"

"Of course you do. I don't wanna hear you say otherwise."

Jenna's eyes had definitely lost most of their spirit, they seemed dull and lifeless, a muddy brown instead of their usual vibrant deep chocolate. "Yeah, whatever. So... spill it. It has to be about Khol, right?"

I laughed again. "Am I that obvious?"

She answered my laugh with one of her own. "To me you are."

I fought it the best I could but in the end it was to no avail. My face crumpled up, tears sliding down my cheeks. "I miss you Jenna, more than ever."

"Don't," she said harshly. "Let's just pretend...let's just pretend everything is normal." She chuckled hoarsely. "At least as normal as it ever was with us."

I wiped at my tears with my fingertips. "Okay." I inhaled a shaky breath. "So...yeah...I had a dream that Bryn came to me and told me that he was okay with me being with Khol... " My voice trailed off. How was this conversation going to help us pretend that things were normal? *Bryn is dead.* Nothing would ever be normal again.

"Did something happen between you and Khol again?" Jenna clucked her tongue and rolled her eyes. "Wow. That was a stupid question. Of course something happened between you guys. Whenever you're not doing something with Bryn, then you're doing it with Khol. It's been that way since—well, since basically Khol showed up. And now—"

"Yeah, and now there is no more Bryn." I turned my face away from Jenna as fresh tears spilled out of the corners of my eyes.

Jenna sighed heavily. "Sorry. My tact filter was never

very good and with everything—well—I think it's now completely busted."

"It's fine," I rasped, wiping at my face again. "And I'm sorry. It's beyond selfish of me to come here just to dump all my love life drama on you. It's just that I don't have anyone left to talk to. You're all I've got, Rider and all."

"Here's the deal. Even when Bryn was alive, you couldn't seem to stay away from Khol for long, could you? You were in love with two guys, or dragons—whatever— you were in love with both of them. You chose Bryn because he was familiar and safe. But honestly, I think Khol's who you belong with. He just gets you in a different way. Besides, I read a quote by Johnny Depp once that said if you fall in love with two people, pick the second one, because you didn't really love the first one as much as you thought you did."

I guffawed at Jenna. "Seriously? You're gonna throw a quote from Johnny Depp at me? One that he probably didn't even really say, I might add."

"Whether he actually said it or not is beyond the point. To which I'm gonna let him have it because he's just plain yummy..." She gazed off into the distance, her eyes glazing over. "Anyways,"—she shook her head— "you need Khol. You'd probably be dead, or more of a wreck than you are now, if not for him. Think about it. Think about all Khol has done for you since you've met him. What did Bryn really do?"

I bit the inside of my cheek to keep from saying something mean to Jenna, something I was sure to regret later. Then again, in some ways, she had a point. I felt disloyal for even thinking it—but Bryn had left me when I needed him most. Again, I reminded myself it was for a good reason. He thought he was protecting me, but the results were still the same. He had left me feeling alone and abandoned. Khol had been there for me, he'd always been there for me, *and* he accepted every part of me—even my child, even if it turns out not to be biologically his. I could trust in Khol, and I'd always be able to trust in him. Even when everything else was so uncertain, that I still was sure of.

"It feels wrong—to be with Khol after Bryn's death."

"Or because it feels so right, do you just feel guilty?" Jenna asked, a knowing gleam in her eyes.

"When I'm with Khol I can almost forget about Bryn, and that kills me. It's my fault Bryn died, and I can just move on so easily? What does that say about me? Nothing good I'm sure."

"Oh, please," Jenna huffed as she yanked at her chains almost demonstratively. "Bryn's death isn't anymore your fault than me being like this is. Casualties happen in war. You can't react to all of this like if things were normal... because they're not. Find happiness where you can."

"It's not that simple. Khol—"

"Of course it is—you always way over-complicate things. Stop over-thinking, and stop over-analyzing. Do what feels right. Mourning Bryn's death isn't gonna do him any good, and it most certainly isn't gonna do you any good. Just let Khol claim you already and start having hot monkey sex. Or I guess I should say hot dragon sex. At least one of us should be having it. Because the forecast for me isn't looking too good for the immediate future."

"Jenna, everything isn't all about sex. There are—"

"Ummm…yes. Everything *is* all about sex. The sooner you finally accept that—well the sooner you'll figure out all the answers to life."

I shook my head and smiled. "You're beyond help. You know that, right? I think you might possibly actually be a sex addict."

"Says the girl who can't keep her hands off of Khol."

"Hey, I can keep my hands off of Khol." I grimaced. "If I really try to," I muttered under my breath.

Completely unbidden my mind conjured up an image of Khol stark naked. I mentally scanned him from head to toe. He was absolutely gorgeous. Every part of him, from the dark auburn hair on the top of his head, down to his perfectly formed toes. Yeah, I said toes. They were more like a sculpture's feet than a living, breathing male. I suddenly flushed. *Who am I kidding?* I thought his feet were hot, and I hated feet. I mean feet are…feet. *Ewww.* I shook my head to dislodge Khol from it.

I cleared my throat. "I can keep away from Khol, no problem."

Jenna tilted her head back, laughing long, loud, and genuine. I couldn't help but snicker a bit myself. We met gazes and said in unison. "Yeah, right."

Amid a fit of fresh laughter Jenna managed to speak, "The only way you're staying away from Khol is if he decided he doesn't want you anymore. And yeah—that ain't happening."

Clutching at her head, Jenna cried out, the Rider's glow from inside her growing brighter as its eyes snapped open. "No!" she screamed. "Just leave me alone!"

Even though it was still Jenna's voice, and her mouth, I could see the Rider within her moving in sync with her lips. The Rider and Jenna were having a conversation while they both resided in the same body. "You know I won't."

Jenna screamed again and her body fell limply back on the bed. I stood quickly, backing up a few steps, not sure what I should do. I hadn't had the real Jenna to talk to in quite some time. I'd had her for longer than I thought possible, but it wasn't enough. Not nearly enough. I wanted her restored to herself—and we still had so much more to talk about. Not just about me, but about her and Jeremy, and Macon and—

"Well, hello there, your majesty." The Rider addressed me with its nickname for me, a small smirk spreading across its lips. And I now thought of it as the Rider, no longer Jenna. Unlike some of the Riders I'd run across in the past, Jenna and hers hadn't fully merged. It was more like someone with split personalities than anything else.

"I don't have time for you," I muttered to myself, turning on my heel to leave. As soon as I was outside the door, I slid down the wall and let loose the anguish trapped in my heart. *I can't lose Jenna too—I just can't.*

I pulled my legs up into my chest, burying my face

against my knees, and continued to sob. My senses came alive with awareness just before Khol appeared directly in front of me. He scooped me up in his arms without saying a word. He simply held me, his strong heartbeat lulling me to sleep.

Because as usual, Khol knew exactly what I needed, when I needed it.

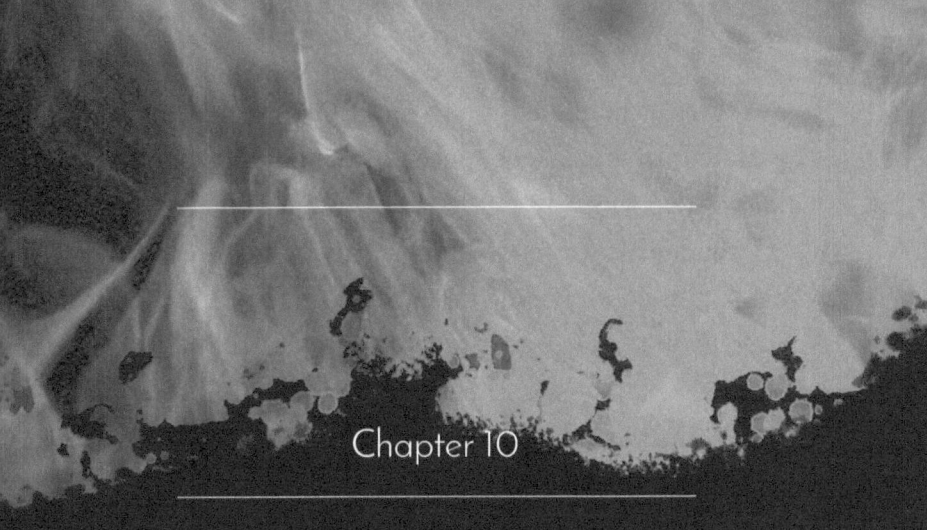

Chapter 10

"**M**y little queen," Khol's deep voice rumbled low, causing me to blink my eyes open balefully.

"What? I'm sleeping," I grumbled.

Khol chuckled. "You sleep with your eyes open now?"

He had me there, but I refused to give in. "Yep. Now go away. I'm sleep talking too, in case you haven't figured that part out either."

"I wish I could let you sleep, and I also wish that I could join you. You make my bed seem much more inviting than it normally is."

"Wait—your bed?" I sat up on my elbows to take in the scenery around me. Sure enough I was greeted by the dark mahogany furniture and rich colors of Khol's room, instead of the purple hues of mine. "Why didn't you take me to my room?" *He never plays fair.*

Khol slid onto bed beside me but remained on top of

the covers as he pulled me to him. "I like you in my bed," he stated simply as he pushed his face into my hair, inhaling deeply.

I shuddered as goose bumps erupted across my skin. Yeah, I didn't mind being in his bed all that much either. A fact I wasn't a fan of. "So why are you waking me up then?"

"We must prepare for a journey."

"Oh?"

"Yes. The trail leading to information about the dragon pendant has grown cold within my archives." He sighed. "We must visit my brother in hopes that he may have what I'm missing."

"B-b-brother?" I stammered. "You have a brother and this is the first time I'm hearing about it?" About a million questions raced through my mind. "Where has he been? Why didn't he come when we needed aid against the Riders? Why—"

Khol slid out from behind me, but not before I could feel the tension in his muscles. "He's my half-brother. And the two of us don't get along. That's all you need to know."

I sat up all the way, staring in disbelief at Khol's back. "Ummm...no. I need to know more than that. Just tell me."

A vision slammed into me, stealing my breath.

I focused in on a small boy, his features were smaller, younger, and his hair had a brightness to it that was almost orange, but still I immediately recognized him as Khol. He appeared to be no more than ten, and I internally chuckled because he was scowling much the same way he did at me sometimes. I then let my gaze follow the path of his glare to an infant with a tuft of jet-black hair being held in the arms of a large man who resembled Khol's adult self. I had no doubt the man was his father.

"This is your brother, son," Khol's father stated with some kind of undecipherable emotion in his voice. His father spoke in a language unfamiliar to me, although beautiful, but my powers translated it easily.

Khol's scowl deepened. "But father, his hair is black."

"Yes, so it is. He is your brother all the same."

Khol crossed his little arms over his chest in another familiar gesture. "We are rua arach, so therefore he cannot be my brother, or your son. Why do you lie to me?"

Khol's father sighed and seemed to draw on the well of patience that all good parents have access to. "He is not my biological son, that part is true. But your mother grew him in her womb therefore he is your half-brother."

Khol's face registered shock as he backed up a few paces. "No, father. Mother would never be unfaithful to you. You are Anam Caras, she could not be."

Pain flashed through Khol's father's eyes. "That is also true, son. Your mother was not unfaithful to me, by her choice." He gritted his teeth and looked at his son with almost pity. "I had wished to spare you from such truths until you are older, but I will not lie to you. Your mother was...violated. This child was an unfortunate side effect."

Understanding registered on Khol's face, which was quickly replaced by anger. "Then kill him. Why do you suffer him to live, father?"

"No, Khol. He is an innocent. A babe. He will not suffer for the sins of his father. His father, the dragon who hurt your mother, he has been punished, he is dead."

Khol nodded with approval. "Good."

"You will treat your brother no differently than as if he was my biological son, do you understand me? If I can love him as my own, then you will accept him as well."

"And do you love him, father, as your own, I mean? And what of mother?" I was struck by how mature Khol seemed for his age. Were all dragons as wise as Khol at such a young age? I don't remember being anything but a normal child.

"Your mother loves him, despite his origins. Females— females are funny in that way, son. And because I love her, I will love him. Learn that lesson well Khol, if you love a female... you will love what she loves...no matter the pain it might cause you."

Khol studied his father as he seemed to mull over his words before he dropped his head in acquiescence. "Yes, father."

I became fully aware of my actual surroundings again. "Damn," I muttered to myself. "I really need to learn how to control my powers or be more careful when I ask questions."

"I wish you hadn't been shown that," Khol grated. "There are some things that are not meant for you to know, and things I don't wish to revisit."

"So that's why you hate black dragons so much, because one of them raped your mother?" It all made complete sense now. Of course Khol would hold some kind of small resentment from his childhood. And obviously Khol didn't have a loving relationship with his brother as his father had wished. Khol said they didn't get along, which lead me to wonder, why?

"Stop trying to analyze me," Khol demanded harshly. "I won't speak of such things. That is all in a part of my past I don't wish to revisit."

"But I wanna know you Khol, all of you." As soon as I said the words, I realized they were true. There was still so much about Khol that was a mystery to me. Sure I knew the most important part, that he was trustworthy, but what about all the rest?

"I can't," Khol rasped. "If you care for me at all, my little queen, you won't ask me to revisit that painful part of my history."

My heart clenched at the raw pain in his eyes. "Fine. I'll let it go." *For now.*

Khol eyed me warily, probably sensing that I only planned to drop the subject for the immediate future. "Please shower, eat, and whatever else you need to do before we leave. You have an hour until I return for you." He then shifted out of his room leaving me alone with my thoughts.

Touchy much? I guess it was okay for him to pry into every little aspect of my life, but not for me to do the same. *Right. That's about to change. I will be getting all the answers I want, whether Khol likes it or not.*

"BUT WON'T the Riders be able to track us here?" I asked, eyeing the lobby of the very modern looking high-rise smack dab in the middle of Manhattan.

"No. The building is cloaked much like my lair is, with dragon magic," Khol responded as he impatiently stared at the elevators.

I hadn't thought about Khol's lands since we left them. *Weird.* They held some very good, and some very bad memories for me. "Is your lair still cloaked, and your lands still protected?"

"Yes, my little queen, my lair is very much still mine and intact. My magic not only protects it from outsiders, but from time itself."

My eyes widened slightly, "You mean...?"

His lips quirked up slightly, his gaze remaining on the elevators. "Yes, it will be as it was when I return. Just as it remained untouched while I slept for all those years."

"Oh." *Huh.* Some of the things that dragon magic could do still boggled my mind. *Will I have magic like that some day? How cool would that be?*

Khol visibly tensed as a set of elevator doors opened, chiming loudly, to reveal a tall black-haired man. The man's green eyes lit up when they landed on Khol, and he strode towards us with purpose. I studied him as he neared. He was shorter than Khol, but stacked with the same amount of massive muscle. He also shared Khol's intense green eyes, but that's where the similarities ended. Where Khol's features seemed as though chiseled by Michelangelo himself, his brother's were more rugged, and his nose was crooked, as if it had been broken one too many times. Where Khol always had an almost serious and intense energy surrounding him, his brother seemed less...formal.

"Khol," his brother said warmly, a smile breaking out across his face. "It's been a long time." He stepped forward as if he might embrace Khol, but Khol backed up, scowling. "Well." His brother laughed. "I see you haven't changed."

"Nor have you," Khol bit out. "What have you been doing all this time? We needed your help. The survival of this planet—"

"I don't care much what happens to the humans. And the planet will be fine. Our kind will go on much as they always have."

I was fully prepared to give Khol's brother the benefit of the doubt, but his response evaporated any chance of that happening. "I was raised human," I hissed, anger coursing through my system.

Khol's brother turned my way for the first time, shock playing across his features briefly. "The queen? I thought it was a rumor..." His voice trailed off as his gaze moved between Khol and myself and then down to my distended belly. A fresh smile cracked his lips. "Well, well, well, is it yours brother?"

"Yes," Khol growled. "But we can discuss everything in private. Not here, out in the open."

"All right," his brother drawled, reaching out to the touch the both of us. Khol slapped his hand away from me, taking mine in his instead. Khol then touched his brother and nodded. I then felt the familiar weightlessness of shifting.

When we appeared in a large, and rather gaudy penthouse, several things were swirling around in my mind. One, Khol had just told his brother that my son was definitely his. Two, Khol hadn't wanted his brother to touch me, even to shift us. And three, the whole dragon acquisitiveness was definitely not a stereotype. *Hello...gold encrusted...everything.* Or maybe it was just Khol's family that dug the over-decorated look?

"So, you knocked up the friggin' dragon queen. Nicely done, brother."

Khol growled, tugging me behind him. "She deserves your respect. She—"

Khol's brother raised his hands in mock surrender. "No disrespect. I guess I've been watching too much T.V. lately. I've been using more human slang. My bad."

I stepped out from behind Khol, shooting his brother a death glare. "Oh, I see. You don't care for humans and yet you like watching T.V.? Well I got news for you—no T.V. if there aren't any humans to film stuff."

"I'm Lorik, by the way. For someone who is all about respect and manners my dear brother seems to have forgotten his." Lorik bowed low with a flourish. "Nice to meet you, your queenliness. And I'd probably do better without that stupid contraption sucking up all of my time anyhow." He winked at me and I fought back my fire magic. It probably wouldn't do anyone any good if I burned Lorik to a crisp before he helped us find what we needed. *But after...*

Khol squeezed my hand. "No burning my brother to a crisp, my little queen. If I've managed not to kill him after all these years then you can put up with him a few short hours." He couldn't hide the slight amusement in his voice, which annoyed me even more than I already was.

"I told you to stop doing that. My thoughts—or emotions—are mine. And I'm not really sure I'm buying that you can't read my thoughts, you word choices are pretty convenient sometimes," I huffed. *Seriously—if he can read my mind, why won't he just tell me already?*

"Ouch. Burn me to a crisp. Really? A bit harsh, don't you think? At least get to know me before you hate on me." Why did I feel like Lorik and Jenna would hit it off famously? I hoped for Jeremy's sake that the two never crossed paths. "It appears we have a lot of catching up to do, brother." Lorik smiled at Khol tightly. "Why does she not bear you mark? If she's—"

"It's complicated," Khol stated with no emotion. "Come, brother, we will talk"—he glanced down at me briefly— "in private."

"Oh, no-no! Hold up! I have a right to be included in your little pow-wow." Did Khol really think to not include me?

"This is family business, my little queen."

I stepped in front of Khol and stood up on my tiptoes in an attempt to look him directly in the eyes. After a moment's hesitation he gave in, meeting my angry gaze.

"You wish to claim me as your *Anam Cara*, I'm carrying your son—" I raised my eyebrows at him in silent question. "And I'm the dragon queen. Do I have to keep reminding you about that? I didn't get this ugly ass hair for nothing, I hope." I tugged at my offending white locks.

Khol's eyes danced with sudden amusement that quickly turned to heat. Before I could react to his abrupt mood change, his lips ensnared mine in a scorching, passion filled kiss. My mind blanked as his tongue deftly took control of my mouth. His large warm hands slid down my back, pulling me tightly against his rock hard chest. But just as abruptly as Khol had taken my mouth with his, he broke off the kiss and stepped around me, leaving me a sputtering, hormonal driven mess. Was that his plan—to kiss me into submission? *Because it's working. Damn him.*

"I won't be long, my little queen." And with that, both Khol and Lorik disappeared, leaving me in his brother's penthouse all alone. Or so I thought.

"Wow. So the mighty Khol has finally chosen who he wants for his *Anam Cara*. Of course it would have to be the queen of us all. I should have known."

I willed my pulse to slow as I turned my startled eyes towards the owner of the voice. She was short and thin, almost childlike in appearance, except for her killer curves. *Killer curves that I do not possess.* She had long auburn hair, a shade or two lighter than Khol's, that hung down to almost her waist. Her pale heart-shaped face and blue eyes were currently studying me as intensely as I was studying her.

"Who are you?" I asked.

"You can call me, Zen." She smiled hesitantly at me. "My dragon name is way too long and complicated. What should I call you?"

"P.J. My name is P.J. so that's what everyone should call me. Khol keeps calling me his little queen. Well, I don't like being called queen and—"

She chuckled. "And Khol doesn't care much for what you want, right? He continues to call you that regardless." She grinned a genuine smile complete with dimples. "Nope, Khol hasn't changed much over the years."

"So what are you, a friend of the family or something?" My eyes were probably lit up with anticipation. Maybe Zen could give me some of the answers I'd been wanting. *Hello, and welcome to Khol 101. Today we will be learning all about the most pigheaded and stubborn red dragon to ever be born.*

"Yep, something like that. But don't get any ideas. Khol would kill me if I spilled the goods on him—quite literally."

My mouth opened and shut a few times like a fish out of water. "Am I that obvious?" I asked, disappointment washing over me.

"Um, yeah. Your whole face lit up like I was an unexpected gift." Zen eyed me warily, her expression becoming closed off. "You hungry? I can get you something to eat."

I gave her a self-deprecating smile. "I'm pregnant. I'm always hungry."

"Right. Well right this way."

As I sat in Lorik's kitchen with Zen, watching her prepare me a bowl of pastinas, my mind rolled around possible ways to get information from her about Khol. "What do you want on your pasta?" Zen asked, pulling me from my scheming thoughts.

"Oh," I said, getting up from the stool I was perched on. I waddled over to the stainless-steel refrigerator and peered inside. "I need some lemon, butter, and parmesan cheese. I should have asked if Lorik had any before I put in my pasta request."

"Hold on."

"What?" I asked with my head still in the fridge, studying the contents. The man—or dragon—did seem to like meat. *Blak!* My unborn son had craved meat in the beginning, but luckily he wanted more carby things now. Just as I turned around and shut the door, Zen appeared in front of me with my requested items. I raised my eyebrows at her.

"I don't think Lorik has any of what you wanted, so rather than rummage through the mess that is the inside of his refrigerator, I thought I'd just pop on over to the store and grab what you need."

"Thanks?" I wondered how she had done that unseen, but as my belly grumbled I decided that I didn't really care. Zen watched me with interest as I added about a tablespoon of butter, half the bottle of lemon juice, and a bunch of cheese to my undrained acini di pepe. It was what I liked to call lemon soup. I'd never come across anyone but me that didn't find it completely disgusting. But I'd loved it since I was a little girl. I don't even remember how the combination of ingredients came about, just that I'd always loved them.

"Please tell me that's a pregnancy thing," Zen muttered. "Because that's—um—that doesn't look very appetizing."

"Actually it's one of my favs," I said, shoving a spoonful into my mouth. "So, how do you know Lorik and Khol?"

"We grew up together."

"Then how come I've never met you before or even heard about you?"

Zen flopped onto a stool across the island from me. "Khol avoids me now. Things got weird between us."

"Oh?" I silently willed her to continue on.

"As you know, Khol used to be a bit of a player." Zen gazed off over my shoulder, her chin resting on her hands. *No, I didn't know that, per say.* But I didn't want to interrupt Zen in case it would prevent her from giving me any more juicy information. "He, of course, was—and still is one of the most sought after red dragons as a desired *Anam Cara.*"

Something I'd never really considered rose up as a question in my mind. How was it that Khol could claim me, force me into an *Anam Cara* bond against my will, and yet no female dragon had ever ensnared him? In fact, on several occasions, especially when I'd first met Khol, he had warned me that younger inexperienced dragons would try to lay claim to me against my will because they didn't know any better. I was finding that I was still a little befuddled by how exactly the bond worked.

"I'm confused," I admitted, my cheeks flaming. I mean, shouldn't I know more about the whole process since I was the queen of all dragons?

Zen's eyebrows knitted together. "About what?"

I bit my lower lip, considering my options. I could just wait to ask Khol to clarify things for me, and save myself the embarrassment, but then again I could lose the opportunity to get more information from Zen if I didn't know the right questions to ask. *Pride goeth before fall, and all that jazz.* "Um, well I'm kind of embarrassed to admit, but—" I closed my eyes and blurted the rest out. "I'm not one hundred percent sure how the *Anam Cara* bond works. Why does it seem like the male dragons have more control over the whole thing?"

Zen's eyebrows rose to almost her hairline. "Because they do." I simply blinked at her with surprise. "You do know that a female dragon can never bind a male dragon into an *Anam Cara* bond without his desire, right? But a female dragon does not have to be willing."

My mouth dropped open. "That's so—so sexist!" I exclaimed, absolutely horrified. *How was it that dragons were a matriarchic society, with a queen and all, and yet it seemed like the males held most of the power?*

Zen laughed bitterly. "Well it's not like any of us made the rules up. It's just the genetic makeup of dragons. There's absolutely nothing any of us can do to change it."

"So what you're saying, is that if you were in love with a male dragon, and you guys—well had sex—all the time—if he didn't want the bond, it wouldn't happen?" Zen nodded in affirmation. "A-aand—" I stammered. "All a male dragon has to do is want the bond, and to say so or want it during sex—sex that doesn't necessarily have to be consensual—and BAM—*Anam Caras?*"

"Yep, that's about it in a nutshell."

"Oh." My mind was racing.

"And that's exactly what happened with Khol. He had sex with many female dragons who wanted him for their *Anam Cara*, but clearly he didn't reciprocate those sentiments. He clearly also never slipped up and wished, even for a second during sex, to have someone as his *Anam Cara*, because if he had then you wouldn't be standing here carrying his child. That happens too, you know, a male dragon can have an idle thought, slip up during sex and end up strapped with an *Anam Cara* he hadn't started out wanting. Although thankfully, when a male dragon is young, and his powers are still weak, he is unable to hold the magic of an *Anam Cara* bond, regardless of his desires. There'd probably be a lot more accidental bondings if that weren't the case." She shook her head and chuckled. "Thank the gods for small favors."

"So why can't he have sex with me without claiming me?" I grumbled under my breath. Apparently, it wasn't so all or nothing like I thought.

"Because when a male dragon falls in love, it's forever. And if Khol loves you, like I think he does, he wouldn't be able to have sex with you without having the unstoppable urge to claim you for his. It's in a male dragon's nature. He can't help it, really."

"Oh," I said again. I hadn't really planned on her hearing that part.

"But the real question is, how are you pregnant with his child and he hasn't claimed you already? Unless his feelings developed after the child's conception? But the even bigger question is—why the hell wouldn't you want Khol for your *Anam Cara*?"

Isn't that the million-dollar question. Something that I didn't think about often—but well—what if I ended up in a bad situation where I was unable to defend myself, and Khol wasn't there to protect me? Any random male dragon could still claim me. Bile erupted into my throat. And what if the child I was carrying really was his? Didn't I owe it to my son to give us a chance to be a real family? I knew without a doubt that Khol would be a good father. And I loved Khol, didn't I? But I still couldn't seem to get over the guilt of Bryn's death. What right did I have to be happy, when Bryn was dead? "It's...complicated," I muttered.

"Is there someone else? Another suitor? Competition maybe? You are the queen after all," Zen pushed.

I dropped my spoon and pushed my bowl of lemon soup away, my appetite smothered by the subject of our conversation. "Not anymore."

"Did Khol kill him? Is that the problem? Or are—"

"Look," I grated through clenched teeth. "I said it was

complicated. Just—leave it at that." I started to stalk from the kitchen but Zen caught me by the arm.

"How can you not want him to claim you? He deserves to be happy," Zen growled at me.

"And why do you care so much?" I growled back.

Her hand dropped away, and she seemed to deflate. "Because if he ends up with a queen—the queen of us all—then at least I can feel as if the better woman won."

Zen's words rolled over me slowly before seeping into my consciousness. "You want Khol for yourself?" I asked numbly.

"I've loved him practically all of my life, but he never wanted anything more than sex from me."

"You had sex with Khol?"

Irrational anger crept up my spine, fanning out into my system. I knew Khol had been with a lot of women over the years, after all, he was ancient, and I knew he must have a past. And I also knew from firsthand vision knowledge that when I had bonded with Bryn, Khol had slept with the stupid redheaded dragon to try and forget about me for at least a little while. But coming face to face with one of Khol's conquests was something else entirely.

"Yes, and because I did, I know he's not lacking in that department either. Why don't you want him for your *Anam Cara*?" Zen continued on, completely oblivious to her imminent danger if she didn't shut the hell up.

Fire sparked to life on my fingertips as I turned my wild gaze onto Zen. "When was the last time the two of you—when did you—"

"Have sex? You sure you want to know?" Zen asked, smirking.

Red dropped down in front of my gaze and flames spread up my arms. What did she mean by that exactly? I thought she said Khol had been avoiding her, or was it that she had been avoiding him? *Like it matters.* "Tell me," I snarled.

"Why does it matter, if you don't even want him for yourself?" Zen taunted. Did she not know how much danger she was in? As if she heard my thoughts, her eyes flicked down briefly to the flames still creeping up my arms. Her eyes widened slightly. "Maybe you care about him more than you're willing to admit."

"Tell me the last time you were with Khol. I won't be responsible for my actions if you don't tell me."

"That's a lose-lose situation on my end," Zen muttered. "Lorik," she called out. "A little help here."

My skin prickled with awareness as Khol and Lorik appeared in the kitchen with us. Khol took me into his arms, pulling my fire magic into himself. "We'll finish our conversation later," Khol said to Lorik. "I need to take care of this first." He nodded towards me as if I was a puppy who needed to be scolded after making a mess on the carpet.

I struggled in Khol's arms. "No, I'm not going anywhere. Zen and me were just having a nice little conversa—" But I didn't get to finish my sentence before Khol shifted me into another room.

"Now what was that about?" Khol asked, sinking down onto a soft couch with me still in his arms.

I turned my face away from Khol, clenching my jaw, anger at him causing my stomach to roil.

"This does not bode well for me, does it?" When I didn't answer he heaved a huge sigh. "This is going to be a long night. I knew I shouldn't have brought you here." His heart beat strongly against my back, a steady rhythm telling me that he wasn't nervous at all. "I didn't think I had to ask you not to burn people alive, especially after having just met them." I knew what he was doing. He was trying to goad me into talking. But even though I knew what he was doing...I still cracked.

"She's not a people. She's a dragon," I said with all the petulance of a five-year-old child. I hated how immature I was being, and yet I couldn't seem to help myself. If I really had a problem with Zen, or any other female for that matter, there was an easy remedy to my problem. All I had to do was let Khol claim me.

"You're jealous?" he asked, amused.

"You had sex with her!" I rose from the couch and started pacing, my nervous energy causing me to want to be in motion.

"I've had sex with a lot of females. But I've only loved one," Khol stated calmly, the amusement still apparent in his tone. I hated how he always seemed happy when I was jealous over him.

"Yeah? Well when was the last time you got naked with

Zen?" Fire licked at my fingertips. "Have you been with her since you've known me?"

A shadow of something crossed briefly behind Khol's eyes, and even though it passed quickly, I was sure I had seen something. Alarm maybe? Guilt? "Zen has been my friend for a very long time. She—"

"She's in love with you! Did you know that? She wants you for herself!" I ground my teeth together trying to stave off a vision of the two of them in bed together. I didn't think I could handle it, and maybe that's why I hadn't seen it yet.

Khol stood, approaching me as I kept pacing, fire sparking between my fingers. "What she wants is irrelevant." Khol paused as he took me by my shoulders, very effectively halting me in place when he pulled my back into his chest. "I want you."

My emotions were so snarled I wasn't quite sure why I was angry anymore or who I was really angry at. I broke away from Khol, whirling back to face him from a few feet away. "I hate how you make me feel—that you make me feel anything at all for you. I crave you all the time, and I hate it." Angry tears slid down my face. "Every time I turn around you're there, and I hate that. But I love it, and then I hate it more that I love it. It feels so wrong that it feels so right wanting you—being with you. Why can't things ever be simple between us? For me? Why does there always have to be so much drama?" I dropped to my knees, tired from my emotional outburst combined with magic use. "Things used to be so simple for me—until you came along—and then nothing was ever the same again."

I inhaled a couple of huge shaky breaths. "Everything keeps pointing at the obvious, that I should just let you claim me. And a part of me wants it. I do. But then with everything else happening around us, what right do I have to happiness? The world is falling apart, quite literally, and my biggest worry is you." I wiped at my blurry eyes. "It's just not right, Khol. I'm so confused, so selfish, so wishy-washy. I can't make up my own damn mind about you, and a part of me wishes you would just take the decision away from me like you once did. Because a part of me doesn't wanna make the decision at all."

Khol studied me with fathomless illuminated green eyes. His features were drawn tightly in thought. "If you want me for yours, now and forever, you must take the final step. You must claim me, and not the other way around."

"Khol, please," I begged, for what I really wasn't sure anymore.

Khol came to me, scooping me up in his arms, and placed me tenderly back down on the soft over-stuffed couch. He knelt beside me, leaning over to kiss me briefly as his large hands ran lovingly over my body. He started to pull away, but then seemed to think better of it, deepening our kiss instead. His hands slipped under my back, arching me up towards him, and I wrapped my arms around his neck, my fingers tangling in his hair. I moaned with pleasure as both his scent and magic enveloped me, excitement coursing through my veins.

It was then Khol did break away, rocking back on his heels to gaze at me with his fire backlit eyes. He stayed like that, perfectly still for a few moments as I held my breath waiting to see what he would do next. Finally he spoke, "I'm still waiting."

"For what?" I demanded, drowning in frustration. This was the second time he'd pulled that 'waiting' crap with me after he'd been kissing me. *What the hell is he waiting for exactly?*

A muscle ticked in his jaw. "I guess I still have more waiting to do." And just like the last time he shifted out of my presence.

As soon as he was gone I hit the couch as hard as I could. *What the hell does he want from me?* What was he *waiting* for? Was I being a complete idiot by not knowing what he was talking about? *Probably.*

Then it finally dawned on me and I groaned for being so clueless. He'd just told me what he wanted. He wanted me to claim him. In his mind he'd already laid his claim, and he wanted me to stake mine. He'd only take things so far with me. He stopped kissing me and was *waiting* for me to continue. He was *waiting* for me to make my intentions clear. I punched the couch again. He was *waiting* for me to pursue him. Khol was trying to turn the tables on me, and I didn't like it much…at all.

Chapter 11

I t felt like days since Khol had left me alone in that room after his proclamation of him *waiting* for me to make my intentions known. In reality, it was no more than a few hours, but patience has never been one of my best virtues. In fact, sometimes I wondered if it's one I possessed at all.

What is Khol doing? Was he making plans about things that I should be weighing in on as well? I mean, last time I checked *I* was the queen, regardless of whether or not I wanted the title. Khol being intent on excluding me from certain conversations wasn't sitting well with me. Not at all. He'd told me it was a family matter, but the way I saw it that should include me. He wanted me for his *Anam Cara* after all, it didn't matter that I wasn't. Maybe I was being irrational, something that wouldn't be unusual for me, but I didn't appreciate double standards...unless they worked for my benefit.

I closed my eyes and concentrated on Khol, focusing on transporting myself to wherever he was. I stood in the middle of the room, my heartbeat thumping in my chest, my attention narrowed down to the task at hand—but nothing, I felt nothing. So far I'd only managed to shift myself less than a handful of times, and with each one I'd been frightened or panicked. And not panicked in the general sense like when Khol had the habit of cornering me but panicked in the way of fearing for my life.

I heaved a frustrated sigh. With all the powers I had running through my body, why couldn't I get a handle on even the simplest ones? I bet adolescent dragons could shift. I bet Khol, when he was a toddler, was shifting all over the place.

But I wasn't going to give up that easily. *Not this time anyways.* I decided to try something different. I narrowed my focus back down but concentrated on the magic I knew I had coursing through my system. I imagined my magic as white-hot light, rising to the surface of my skin, and then surrounding and carrying me to wherever Khol was. My mind fully turned to Khol, and I imagined his spicy scent surrounding me, his heat enveloping me, and his deep voice a low rumble as he spoke to me. I was so immersed in my sensory perceptions of Khol, that I almost didn't notice when the familiar feeling of light-headedness finally washed over me.

Grinning to myself, I opened my eyes—to a room that looked just like—I swore under my breath. *Have they been in the same condo the entire time?* Here I was angsting over shifting to Khol and all I had to do was search the damn condo. I gritted my teeth. It was then I realized that Khol and Lorik were so caught up in a heated conversation, that neither of them noticed my added presence. I ducked behind an over-stuffed chair and tried to make myself tiny. *Be a ninja. I am a ninja. Think invisible.*

"No, I'm not taking her. End of discussion," Khol spat, his voice vibrating with anger.

"You can't go alone. What would be the point? She's the only one Morag might respond to," Lorik said, sounding none too happy himself. "It's too dangerous for you to go alone."

"I won't put her in that kind of danger. Things with Morag may well be different now that the Riders are here. She might listen to me."

Lorik snorted. "Yeah, I'm thinking Morag cares less about what happens to the humans than I do."

"I'll go with him," Zen chimed in. I slapped my hand over my mouth to smother my gasp. *Oh, she's included in the discussion, but I'm not? I'm definitely more family than she'll ever be.* Khol and me were going to have a little chat later. Had she been in the room the entire time, or did she just pop herself in like I did?

"I'm going alone," Khol grated.

"You're not all powerful, brother. As much as you'd like to think you are. Take the queen with you."

A feminine snort reached my ears. "Yeah, okay, and what's she going to do? I don't think she has control over any of her powers yet. Plus, do you really think Khol is going to take her anywhere dangerous while she's carrying his child? I'm surprised he lets her out of bed."

"Excuse you," I snapped, standing up from behind my hiding place, which wasn't a very good one. Seriously, how did no one notice me crunched up behind a chair? "I can do plenty." I met Zen's surprised face with a glare. "If you want, I can give you a demonstration of my fire magic right now. How about that?"

Khol strode forward, coming to stand in front of me, his large frame blocking out my view of Zen. When I tilted my head up to meet his gaze, I noticed he was scowling at me. "I told you this was a family discussion—"

My hands reflexively went to my hips. "And I told you I don't care! Stop trying to run everything!" As Khol bent down towards me I raised my hands up as a barrier, taking a step away from him. "And don't you attempt that kissing thing again to try and get my hormones to distract me! It won't work this time!"

A smug smile tugged up the corners of Khol's full succulent lips. "I beg to differ." He dipped his head to ensnare my mouth, but instead of melting into him like he wanted, I caught his lower lip between my teeth, and bit... hard. Khol made an agitated sound in the back of his throat before he crushed my body to his, his mouth slamming down on mine almost painfully. Khol's power snapped around me, demanding for me to submit to him...but I refused. Things between Khol and me would be on my terms from this moment on. Yes, Khol had stuck beside me through thick and thin since I'd met him, but he'd also been overbearing, and too pushy. It was one thing to feel safe and protected, and a entirely different story to be controlled.

Even as I fought Khol, my hands pushing on the unmovable mountain of his chest, his tongue swept into my mouth bringing with it the coppery tang of his blood. The flavor of it hitting my taste buds seemed to release something primal in me, and a growl of my own erupted from my throat. Instead of continuing to fight Khol, I pulled him to me. *I want more of him...all of him...and I need it now.* And it didn't really matter to me about our little audience either.

I somehow ended up pushed against something hard, a wall I was guessing, with my legs wrapped around Khol's waist, while we made out like two over-sexed teenagers. Of course I technically was an over sexed teenager. So what was Khol's excuse exactly?

My focus shifted—it all reminded me of Bryn too much. Our tree...the way we couldn't keep our hands off of each other when we first bonded. As I began to spiral down into dark thoughts of Bryn and how things with Khol all seemed to parallel our relationship lately, I pushed at Khol's chest again. This time he broke away from me. His fire backlit eyes met mine with heat, and he smiled a very masculine grin as he swept his thumb over the arch above my left eye. "Your eyes, they're like mine."

I didn't need for him to clarify what he meant, I knew he was pointing out that my eyes were filled with flames, just like his were currently. I wasn't exactly sure what it represented to dragons but I did know that with Khol it usually was a sign of how much he wanted me.

I shuttered my eyes from him and turned away. "Put me down," I whispered, not liking how rough my voice sounded.

Khol dropped his hands from me, and I slid down his body, not missing another sign of how much he wanted me. When I was standing again on my own two feet, he leaned back into me. "Don't deny me the sight of things I've long been wanting to see in you. Open your eyes for me, my little queen," he murmured, an edge of anger in his voice.

I squeezed my eyes together more tightly and shook my head. "No. I can't just replace him with you. It's not fair to his memory, or to you." *God...am I really that awful of a person?* How could I just seemingly replace Bryn so easily with Khol? How could I treat Khol almost exactly how I treated Bryn when we were together? None of it was right, and yet I couldn't seem to stop myself.

The implications of my words hung in the air between us, effectively cooling off any lingering ardor for both of us. I could feel Khol's gaze burning into me. "You don't have to keep torturing yourself for wanting me."

"I chose him." I peeked at him through my lashes.

Khol's jaw ticked with tension. "I let you have him. In the end, you would have been mine."

Confusion washed over me. "No," I shook my head. "My magic was strong enough to hold the *Anam Cara* bond after I received my new powers. There would have been no other second chances for us." Sudden dread raced up my spine. "Unless you meant to kill him."

"I wouldn't have taken his life, you know that. But you would have ended up mine in the end regardless." I noticed Khol's knuckles turning white. "Just like you will now."

"You're talking like there were two paths, and in either one..." My voice trailed off, realization dawning on me. "My birth mother..." A lump formed in my throat. Had my birth mother let Khol know that either way I would end up his? Is that where all his confidence about the matter was coming from?

Khol winced, obviously not wanting to divulge the information he'd just let slip. But it was too late. The cat was out of the bag. "Yes. She let me know in the letter that you would come back changed, and that I needed to give you space. She said that even when things seemed final for us, I must be patient."

"But you were so angry when I came back, you were—"

"Of course. You came back and decided you wanted *him* again. It was a hard pill to swallow. But after I reread your mother's message, I realized she was preparing me for exactly what happened. You would choose him, and he would die."

My lower lip began to tremble. "You could have stopped it—you could have—"

"And I'm guessing that's why she didn't give me any specific details, because I would have stopped it, my little queen. I would do anything for you—anything. No matter the pain it causes me. I love what you love, and I protect those things at any cost."

My mind flashed to the vision of Khol as a child and what his father had instructed him to do. *"..if you love a female...you will love what she loves...no matter the pain it might cause you."* Khol really would do anything for me, wouldn't he? I kept being faced with that fact over and over again, but it was still so hard for me to wrap my mind around it. Maybe someone as selfish as me didn't have the ability to comprehend the sentiment. "Khol I—" Khol what? What could I say to all the information he just dropped on me? Was I just fighting the inevitable by not letting Khol claim me? Were Bryn and me doomed from the beginning no matter what we did?

Khol and I just stood there, staring at each other, both warring with our emotions and what to say next. I was torn apart, raw, ripped wide open. I wanted to seek comfort in the very arms that were tormenting me.

A throat clearing drew my attention sharply over Khol's shoulder. "This is better than any soap opera on T.V.," Lorik proclaimed with amusement. "But I have a feeling that it could drag on just as long, so maybe we should—"

"Get back to what we were discussing before we were interrupted," Khol said flatly while still staring at me.

I crossed my arms over my chest and raised my chin up defiantly. "By all means continue. I'm not stopping you." Khol growled, and I resisted the urge to stick my tongue out at him. *Mature I know.*

Zen who had remained suspiciously quiet, chose that moment to speak. "I've changed my mind. I think we should all go." Khol's head whipped around towards Zen, and I grinned in victory. I knew he wouldn't be able to say no to all of us. Maybe I could get over the fact that Zen and Khol had once been bed buddies after all. My stomach clenched at the mere thought of them being together. *So maybe not.*

"No," Khol grated.

"Khol—brother, if we all go, we stand a better chance of making it out of there alive."

Khol turned imploring eyes to me. "Would you really endanger your unborn son? You have no comprehension of what we'll be facing. I might not return." Pain rippled across Khol's features. "I don't want to admit it, but there's a very real possibility that I will—"

"Die?" I croaked, the blood draining from my face as a wave of dizziness swept through my head. "And you think that's gonna make me stay here? Waiting...wondering..." I shook my head vehemently. "No, if anything what you just said convinced me to go." I moved a few steps closer to Khol, raising my hand up to touch him before I let it drop without contact. "Do you actually think that I could handle the not knowing part? Waiting and wondering if I'll ever see you again?"

Khol's jaw clenched and he spoke through gritted teeth. "If you go with me, you could die too."

That time I did reach up to cup Khol's chiseled jaw in my tiny hand. "Then we'll die together."

Khol's eyes slid shut and he turned into my touch as he inhaled deeply. He then brought up his own larger hand to cover mine. "My little queen, I can't—the baby—"

"Khol, I'm coming. I won't be able to handle losing you too." My fingers bit into his face, but not enough to hurt him, just enough to make him aware of my determination. "Where you go—I go. Together we all stand a better chance of survival."

"All right, that's settled then. We'll all go," Lorik said, cheerfully, his voice effectively breaking the moment between Khol and me.

I saw the resignation slither through Khol as his shoulders slumped and his muscles lost their rigidity. "We have much to talk about," Khol murmured, his eyes still shut and his warm hand still covering mine. I knew he was technically addressing everyone, but in actuality he was talking to just me. And he was right, we had a lot to talk about.

Chapter 12

Khol had finally given in, deciding it would be cruel to leave me behind to not know what was going on with him while he risked his life. His decision was forced, something that probably hadn't happened very often in his very long life, and he was pissed off about it. In fact, after Khol informed me, in a rather terse manner, that we would be traveling to see Morag the Ancient, a dragon so old that none could remember a time before her, he left me completely alone...all night. I'd called out for him, putting all the yearning for him in my voice, and yet he still left me alone.

Maybe he thought he was teaching me a lesson. And he most certainly was, just not the one he wanted, I'm sure. I was learning that dragons weren't all that different from humans in their emotions, they just thought they were. He was obviously off sulking. He'd probably convinced himself that he was leaving me alone for my own good, so I could rest. *Like I can sleep with everything I have on my mind.*

We were going to be traveling in Morag's domain, a place that she had spelled to deny dragons of their powers, except for hers of course. We'd essentially be like regular humans while on her lands. I was hoping it wouldn't mean our certain death. Yep...there was only one way I could have found any rest, and it would most definitely involve Khol wearing me out. I flushed at the thought. *Damn pregnancy hormones.*

I was still tossing and turning when Khol's low voice broke into my thoughts. "My little queen."

My heart sped up and I briefly wondered how he had snuck up on me without me feeling him. I usually had a physical awareness of Khol and his powers. "Khol," I whispered into the darkened room.

The bed dipped down as he sat beside me, his hand snaking out to intertwine with my loose hair. "I tried to stay away—" He let my hair drop through his fingers. "But I couldn't. I can never stay away. Not for long anyhow."

I smiled to myself. I used to worry about Khol being too overbearing towards me. Okay, so like half a day ago, but the truth of the matter was I had worried needlessly because I now knew his Achilles heel...me. I was his weakness, and therefore I really did hold all the cards. I was learning that being a female trumps everything when a male truly loves you.

"I can't sleep," I murmured. "Hold me."

Khol slid into bed, taking me into his arms without saying another word. He pulled me against his chest tightly and I sighed contentedly as his spicy scent coiled around me. I loved Khol, I knew it unequivocally in that moment. I'd admitted it to myself before, but I hadn't accepted it until that moment. But it didn't matter...guilt outweighs love. At least for me it did. The guilt of loving Khol, of wanting him as strongly as I did so soon after Bryn's death was eating at my insides. I wanted him to take the choice away from me, but he no longer was giving me that as an option. So instead of turning to face Khol and telling him that I was ready for him to claim me as his *Anam Cara*—that I never wanted to be without him again—I remained perfectly still, eventually drifting off to sleep surrounded by his warmth.

A BABY CRYING roused me from my slumber, its pathetic wail grabbing all of my attention. I sat up, finding the bed empty beside me. My brain was still muddled with sleep as I pulled myself to my feet, drawn towards the sound of the distressed infant. *Whose is it anyways?* As my toes touched down on the floor, I slipped on something sticky. I swore under my breath, reaching for the lamp on the nightstand. I glanced down to see what I stepped in, freezing in horror. Blood. The floor was covered in blood. My eyes trailed up to the sheets, my heart taking off at a gallop when I saw that they were also saturated in the same gore. With trepidation riding me hard, I finally forced myself to bow my head, looking down the line of my body. I raised a shaking hand to my mouth and silently screamed. *My baby's gone. Someone stole him from me.* Was my son the baby that was crying? Was he crying for me?

"Khol!" I screamed. "Help me—help *us*—please!" I suddenly felt like I was drowning, not able to bring air into my lungs. "Please," I gasped, running my hands over my bloody pajamas and flat stomach. "Give him back to me."

"Wake up, my little queen. You're having a nightmare." Khol's worry laden voice penetrated my sleep. I gasped in fresh air, my hands reflexively going to my belly. Heaving a sigh of relief I found my son still inside of me, where he belonged for the time being. Sobs erupted from my chest as Khol cradled me to him, murmuring soft endearments that didn't make sense to my ears. My mind was still lost in my nightmare, the panic from having my son stolen from my body lingering strongly within me.

Then I let myself face the question I was almost too terrified to ask. "Was it a vision or a nightmare?" I croaked, not really meaning to say it out loud. Although it would have been pointless to try and hide it from Khol with how much deeper our emotional connection had grown lately.

"Just a nightmare, my little queen. The flavor was different than a vision, and once your fear subsides, you'll realize the same yourself."

His words comforted me and the last of my adrenaline seeped from my veins. "It was so real—so—"

"I know," Khol interrupted. "But normal. It was just an anxiety dream which is normal after everything that's been happening lately."

I nodded in agreement, my cheek sliding up and down chest, which was damp from my tears. "Yeah, I guess with everything going on—for me to dream about having my baby ripped away from me is about par for the course."

Khol was absolutely right. So many people and things that I adored had been ripped away from me lately, of course a subconscious fear would be losing my unborn child in the same manner. Maybe my subconscious was telling me that I shouldn't go with Khol to see Morag, but then even the idea of not going with him made me feel like he'd be the one ripped away from me.

"I'll never let anything like that happen to you, or your son."

"But you weren't there—in my nightmare—I was alone." Had Khol leaving me alone, even though he had eventually come back to me, been what triggered the nightmare? Was I developing abandonment issues? *Like I need any more issues to deal with. I'm a royal mess as it is... quite literally since I'm the dragon queen and all.*

Khol's warm hand cupped the nape of my neck. "And that's how you know for certain it was a nightmare and not a vision. I would never leave you completely alone."

I knew it was true. Khol leaving me alone in bed for the evening while he went off to sulk was not the same as him abandoning me. I guess it just triggered some neurotic feelings. I hated to admit it, even to myself, but part of my neuroses was Bryn's fault. He'd promised always, and then walked away from me. "I know." And I did know, deep, deep—very deep down.

"He was a child, he didn't know the damage he was causing you. He—"

My body tensed. "Please, let's not talk about him. I can't handle it right now."

Khol's chest heaved under my cheek. "Until you face the unresolved issues Bryn's treatment of you left behind, you won't have closure. And until you have closure you can't move on...with me...not truly and completely."

Well, that was my problem in a nutshell. I was still torn between two males, only one of them was now dead. Instead of Bryn's death bringing closure, a clear choice, it brought guilt, uncertainty, and emotional confusion. I wanted Khol for my *Anam Cara*, but I didn't want to want him. I had chosen Bryn, and for a brief moment in time I had been completely happy. If I bonded with Khol, would I have those same feelings again? And more importantly, did I deserve them? *It's time to stop dwelling.* All I did lately was spin around in emotional circles. I was starting to get on my own nerves so I couldn't imagine how Khol felt. "When do we leave for Morag's?"

Khol's muscles tightened briefly before he relaxed again. No doubt he wasn't too pleased about my subject change nor the subject I was bringing up. "In the morning."

"It's not morning yet?" It felt like I'd tossed and turned most of the night away before Khol had come to me. Surely it had to be morning.

"I'll amend my statement by saying later this morning then. It's morning but still very early." Khol laid down on the bed and I went with him, still pressed tightly to his chest, his arms surrounding me like a cocoon. "Get some more sleep, my little queen. I won't let you have anymore nightmares."

I gnawed on my lower lip. "You can do that? Keep the nightmares away?"

Khol brushed his lips across my forehead. "I can do lots of things, if only you would let me."

"Oh." What else was there to say? I hadn't missed the double, or maybe I should say quadruple meaning to his words. So instead of acknowledging them, at least out loud, I simply snuggled into him as far as I could go, letting my heavy eyelids finally slide shut without worry.

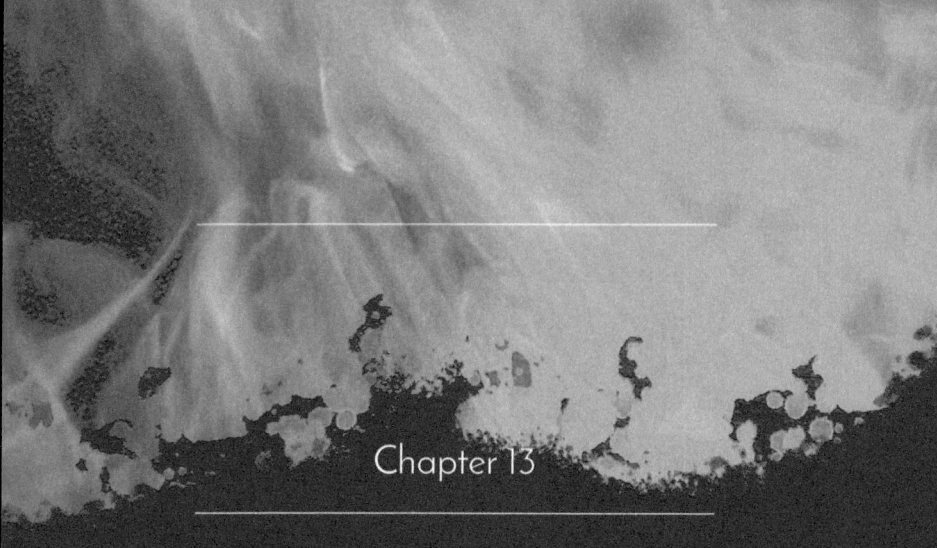

Chapter 13

"I feel so strange," I muttered as I brought my hand up to my forehead with a fluttering motion. I was kind of dizzy, but not—sort of like drunk, but not —almost nauseous, but not quite...so yeah...strange.

"You'll get used to it," Khol stated calmly. "What you're feeling is the aftereffects of having all of your powers denied to you. They're not gone—just blocked. Your system is adjusting to having to function without them."

"It's not like I use my powers all the time though, I shouldn't really need to adjust," I complained. *Okay whined.*

Khol quirked an auburn eyebrow. "You are always connected to your magic, and you have been since the day you were born. Whether you are actively using your powers or not, they're still there, ready at a moment's notice."

Some of the funky sensations caused by me being

powerless started to ebb and it allowed me to take stock of my new environment. I sucked in a shocked breath. "It's absolutely beautiful."

"Damn," Lorik said from behind me, him and Zen had obviously just arrived. "This is going to take some getting used to, this whole no powers thing."

"You said it," Zen chimed in, sounding a bit shaky herself. She sucked in a surprised breath of her own. "Wow. I didn't expect this in Morag's realm."

The three of us, to which I mean—Lorik, Zen, and me, because Khol didn't seem fazed or impressed—stood in utter reverence of our surroundings. It looked like one of those *Home Depot* commercials with the perfect lawn and flowers everywhere. It was as if someone had painted a perfect landscape and brought it to life. Even the sky was a flawless tint of blue with happy little puffy clouds floating by. I'm not sure why but with a name like Morag the Ancient I'd been expecting a desert wasteland or something. It was all so stunning.

"Remember, it's often the most beautiful flower that's the poisonous one," Khol said, his warning plainly directed at the three of us.

Icy fear raced up my spine. Khol was right. Here we were, in Morag's realm, where we were completely vulnerable without our powers and we were standing out in the open gawking at the scenery. Maybe that was the whole point of the landscape, to lull its visitors into a false sense of security. Beauty really is dangerous. I cleared my throat. "Yeah, maybe we should get going then." I glanced around nervously, half expecting for someone appear out of nowhere to attack us.

"Do we know where we're going?" Zen asked distractedly. "Or is our plan to stumble around Morag's realm in hopes that we bump into her, or perhaps until she notices us?"

"She has a point, brother. We never discussed how we would find Morag once we got here. What is your plan exactly?"

"We head due north," Khol snapped.

I whirled around to face Khol, my mouth dropping open with astonishment. "Oh my God, we're just gonna wonder around and hope to run into her, they're right, aren't they?" Something I should have realized about Khol before, because it was so obvious, was that his plans ran parallel to a man asking for directions...it just didn't happen. Khol just hoped to find his way, expected it, in fact, and wouldn't stop to ask for anyone's help. Even I wasn't that careless.

"Khol, answer me, is that your plan?" I had to fight the urge to give him air quotes when I said the word *plan*. If our lives, and the very world, weren't at stake, I might find Khol's actions amusing, and maybe a little bit endearing.

"Due north," he growled under his breath and started walking.

I glanced over at Lorik and Zen who both shrugged their shoulders, trailing after him. I guess they didn't have any better ideas. I rolled my eyes, trudging after Khol—

because what else was I going to do? It wasn't like I had any bright ideas on how to find Morag myself.

"I NEED TO TAKE A BREAK," I huffed, wiping at the sweat on my forehead. "I'm hot, hungry and pregnant lady tired." When I heard Khol chuckle under his breathe I shot a death glare at his back. "Don't laugh Khol, it's a real thing."

"I could use a break," Zen agreed. "We've been traveling for hours and I'm getting hungry. Plus, who knows how long it's going to take us to find Morag, if at all."

"Yeah, maybe why no one has ever returned from seeking her out is because no one has ever found her. Maybe they're still wondering around looking for her. I'm surprised we haven't run into anyone else on the same mission yet." Lorik sounded annoyed despite his obvious attempt at humor.

"We'll look for a place to make camp for the night," Khol responded. "We'll rest and re-energize before starting out again."

I stared at the horizon, blinking back stinging tears caused from the sun. "Is it just me or does it seem like the sun should have already set by now? How long have we been traveling?"

"Time distortion is easy magic to maintain in a realm such as this. It's hard to say how long we've actually been traveling," Lorik grumbled.

"Great." I tried to fight the pout from forming on my face, very unsuccessfully. "What if we've been in here for what equals years in the outside world?" Khol turned to frown at me over his shoulder. "What?" I huffed. "Like I'm the only one that's considered that." When I was met by complete silence, my eyes widened as far as they could go. "Seriously, none of you centuries old dragons had considered that, not even for a second? Don't any of you read?"

Ignoring me completely, Khol slowed, motioning to a circle of trees that provided decent shade from the burning sun. "This looks like a good place."

Still reeling from my dragon companions' lack of foresight, and from being ignored, I stumbled into the shade the trees provided and eased myself down to the ground. The bigger my belly grew, the more my lower back protested. I watched as Khol, Lorik, and Zen sat up camp for us, complete with tents and everything. I marveled at how everything just seemed to pop out of the backpacks Khol and Lorik had been toting around with them. I'd never been camping before so it was all new to me.

Zen was building a fire pit, probably to cook on and keep us warm, if the sun ever went down that is. I would have offered to help her, feeling a little bit guilty that everyone was doing something but me, but I was utterly exhausted and couldn't seem to muster the energy to stand up. It actually wasn't a surprise to me that after a few minutes of watching our camp grow around me, I began to drift off to sleep.

I had a dreamless slumber, thankfully, and I woke up to low murmurs of a heated conversation between a male and female voice.

"I know she's the queen, but are you sure you want her?" I bristled when I realized the female voice was Zen and that she was talking about me. "Or is it just her power that attracts you?"

"I love her. You know what that means for a male dragon," Khol responded softly. Did Khol know I was awake yet? Sometimes he was so good at reading my emotions that I swore he could read my mind and then there were other times that made him seem so adorably clueless. I was hoping this time was the latter because I wanted to get in some quality eavesdropping before they knew I was awake.

"But are you really sure you love her?" Zen pushed. "Maybe you're just finally ready to settle down and she was the first one you felt might be good enough." I didn't miss the hopefulness in her voice. "Now don't get me wrong, I'm not saying you don't care about her, but maybe you don't love her, or maybe you love her, but you're not *in* love with her. The differences can be so subtle, maybe you can't see it."

"You've been having sex with my brother, have you not?" Khol asked bluntly, and I had to stifle back a gasp. I hadn't picked up on any romance vibes between Lorik and Zen. The only thing I'd been getting from Zen was that she was head over heels in love with Khol and wanted him for her *Anam Cara*.

"You know it doesn't mean anything. We care about each other as you well know, but the sex is nothing more than a convenience for us both." *Hmmm...that would explain the no romance vibe.*

Khol's voice came out low and guarded. "I'm sorry, Zen. I never meant to hurt you. What I sought from you, when we coupled, was much the same thing—an easing of my needs, and a convenience of situation. I never meant for you to fall in love with me." A pregnant pause washed over the two of them, and I wondered in that moment where Lorik was.

"As if I had a choice," Zen croaked, breaking the silence. When Khol didn't respond Zen continued on. "She doesn't want you for hers, not all the way as her *Anam Cara* at least. You know I would treat you better. I've always welcomed you into my bed, not denied you, no matter the situation."

Then the unthinkable happened, sounds of kissing met my ears, burning them and causing bile to shove up into my throat. I scrambled up, a strangled cry escaping my chest as I took in the site of Khol and Zen locked in a passionate embrace. Instead of the rage that I expected to feel, anguish washed over me instead. Khol had promised always, just like Bryn, and he too was betraying my trust. Granted, the means were completely different, but the outcome was the same. Half stumbling, I whirled on my heels, dashing as quickly as I could manage in the opposite direction. I had to get away from him—from the second man who was breaking my heart.

"Paige!" Khol called out with desperation, but I didn't care. You don't kiss someone else, especially when they're in the same room, or clearing or whatever, and claim that you love them. Maybe Zen was right, maybe Khol wasn't really in love with me after all. Maybe everything from the beginning was one huge lie, and I really didn't understand anything like I thought I had.

As I crashed through the underbrush, branches and who knows what else clawing at my face and body, I heard Khol in hot pursuit of me. But I wouldn't—couldn't let him catch me. I sent up a silent prayer that I could somehow escape him just before my vision blurred and everything went dark.

I CAME TO ABRUPTLY, the memory of Khol and Zen locked together in a passionate kiss serving as ice water to my system, washing fresh anguish through my veins. "Khol," I croaked. "How could you?"

"Interesting," a feminine voice I didn't recognize said. "Even after losing consciousness and awakening in a strange place, one that could spell your certain doom, your first thoughts still go back to your dragon." I blinked the remaining blurriness from my eyes, focusing in on the owner of the voice. With surprise I realized she resembled Rogue from X-Men with deep brown long hair and a strip of white going through the front. I internally laughed with disbelief, here I was rocking out Storm's hair and she had Rogue's. It made me wonder about the creator of X-Men...was he or she dragon maybe? Or perhaps some other kind of supernatural creature that knew of us?

"Morag, I'm guessing." My voice came out even and sounding a little bored even. The truth was I was too tired both physically and emotionally to be afraid.

"You were expecting...someone more ancient, I presume?" Her lips curled up into a bemused smile. "They always do."

"Yeah, I guess. With 'the Ancient' tacked onto your name like some kind of title what else is someone supposed to think?"

She studied me with her glowing golden eyes for a moment before responding. "You're not what I expected when I made that necklace. And you're not what I expected to find in the next queen. You're so very young, and still so human in many ways."

I figured since we were being all civilized and everything that I'd just cut to the punch. "Will you help me then—I mean us?"

Morag tilted her head, studying me more closely. I felt like she was peering into my very soul somehow. "I'm not sure you have the mental fortitude to wield the kind of power needed to control the rua artair necklace...yet." She chuckled to herself. "Oh yes, you possess the power, but can you handle it without falling to pieces? You're very close to shattering right now as it is." I said nothing, not able to deny that she spoke the truth about me. After a few more minutes of her staring at me, and me beginning to fidget under her scrutiny, she spoke again. "Yes, I will help you. But first there are things that you must know. Things that might very well break you." Morag ran her hands through her thick hair. "Bryn and you are star-crossed lovers and you must come to understand what that truly means."

"Romeo and Juliet were—"

"Fictional and dead. Why do humans romanticize them so? The story is nothing but tragic, and it should show you what it means to be a star-crossed lover in truth. It means pain and agony at best, and death at worst. That is what you and Bryn would always bring to each other, no matter the path."

"Then why did my birth mother place him in my path to begin with? Why did she do that to me if we were destined to suffer because of each other?"

Morag smiled brilliantly at me, nodding her head a few times. "Why yes, that is an excellent place to start. I will answer that question first. My sister did not have a weak, foolish child perhaps after all." She strode towards me, reaching out to take my hand. "This may hurt a little."

Before I had a chance to react to the bomb of Morag being my birth mother's sister, and therefore my aunt, the familiar feeling of being shifted through space caused me to lose focus.

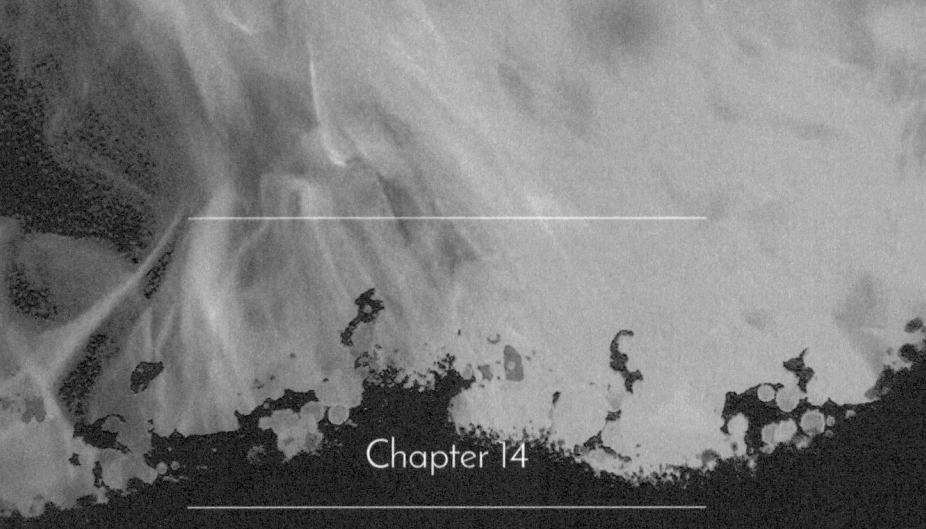

Chapter 14

Loud music assaulted my ears as a weird sense of déjà vu slammed into me. "Where are we?" I asked Morag as I took in the somehow familiar party scene. *Why does it feel like I've been here before?*

"Like I said, this might hurt a little, or a lot." Morag laughed. "But how am I supposed to know, it's never been done to me before. I'm always the one doing it to someone else." She then pushed her palm against my forehead. "You won't remember the you that you are now, when you are the you that you would have been if your birth mother, and my sister hadn't placed Bryn in your path. But don't fear, when I retrieve you, all will become clear."

"What? Wait—" Alarm barely had a chance to register in me before a bright white light engulfed me…and yep…a spike of agonizing pain.

"I CAN'T BELIEVE I let you talk me into this," I hissed.

I played with the hem on my much too long, unflattering dress. I tried rolling it up but then it looked uneven and cheap. When I shifted the entire dress up on my body, I had too little cleavage showing. No matter what I did, I had *way* too much skin covered up. *Little black dress, my ass! How about* big frumpy *black dress.*

"Oh hush. Sometimes it's good to leave a little bit to the imagination. Besides you need to give some of us with short little stumpy legs a chance at getting noticed." She motioned briefly to her legs. "And it's too late now. We're almost there."

I gulped as Ryan's house came into view, framed in the window of Jenna's bright yellow Volkswagen Bug. She parked at the curb, turning to me with a serious expression. "So... what do you think of the new hair color? Too much?"

She had gone from a dark purple color to a shade of red that matched most fire trucks. It would definitely turn heads. I just wasn't sure it would be in the way she wanted. I tried to remain tactful though. "If attention is what you crave, then you definitely chose the right color."

She frowned, her eyes narrowing. "You don't like it, do you?"

"It's not that I don't like it—it's just—well I liked the purple better." And that was very true. I liked the purple a whole lot better.

"But now we both get to be red heads." Her peach glossed lips curled upwards. She really didn't care that much that I didn't like her hair color. Besides, it would probably change by next week. *It's a wonder all of her hair hasn't fallen out yet, seriously.*

"Yeah, but only my shade of red can be found in nature." I smirked.

Why anyone would purposely dye their hair red was beyond me. My natural color was a bright strawberry blonde, to which I had managed to darken to a nice auburn shade through the use of frequent Henna applications. I was still stuck as a redhead, but at least the current darker hue was less traumatizing to my retinas whenever I caught a glimpse of myself in any shiny surface.

We exited her car, heading up Ryan's walkway. All the while I fidgeted with my borrowed dress. I felt like I was wearing someone's grandma's dress, and I suddenly wanted to go home very badly. "I don't think I should be wearing this in public," I grumbled under my breath.

Jenna's annoyed face whipped in my direction. "Okay. I'm done. You look super hot, so stop complaining. I don't wanna hear another word about it." She turned the knob on Ryan's front door, and boisterous voices accompanied by loud music slammed into my chest. When I balked, Jenna took my arm, yanking me over the threshold.

We'd barely made it a half dozen steps inside before she spotted Evan. "It looks like I have a date with destiny." She dropped my arm, heading towards Evan with a huge grin on her face. When he saw her approach, he let his gaze travel over her from head to toe, a grin of his own spreading across his face. I guess he liked what he saw and was going to take her up on her offer from earlier. I turned away abruptly, not wanting to witness anymore. I had already been there and done that with Evan, and I had a twinge of guilt for not letting Jenna know.

I decided to track down some beer to drown my sorrows, so I headed to the kitchen, all the way fidgeting with my dress. I grimaced to myself as I passed a group of guys I didn't know and they eyed my dress speculatively. I smiled, flipping my hair in an effort to draw attention away from my fashion faux pas.

Once in the kitchen I beelined it straight for the keg, filling up a fresh plastic cup. Taking a sip, I crinkled my nose with disdain. "What is this? Some crap light beer? Ugh. At least get a decent light beer, if there is such a thing," I grumbled to myself.

I tipped the cup up, chugging down the rest of the subpar beverage. I decided I would make up for in volume what was lacking in quality. As soon as I was finished, I began pumping the keg for a refill.

As I polished off beer number two in less than five minutes, I giggled to myself. *Oops! Lookout! Lightweight coming through!* I filled up a third cup of beer and decided to head back into the other room where I'd seen the group of boys on my way in. One of them would surely be up for some fun. I giggled again.

A few minutes later, I found myself sitting on one of the couches, obviously I was buzzed since I didn't remember making the conscious choice to sit. Unfazed, I looked around in hopes of—*oh*—*but wait it looks like what I'm jonesing for might be seeking me out.*

"Hey, pretty girl. How are you doing tonight?" A guy with longish sandy blond hair, and bright crystal blue eyes sat down next to me. He was one of the guys who had been eyeing me when I'd gone in to get beer just a few minutes ago.

He was kind of cute, and I could sense some power coming off of him. It was very faint though. When I reached for it mentally, it brushed against mine, feeling like thousands of tiny fingers running up and down my exposed skin, causing goose bumps to erupt along my flesh. I tilted my head to study him for a moment. Like called to like, and I just knew. *Seer.* I mean, he wasn't—obviously—but I was picking up on the dormant power in his blood. *Maybe he's exactly what I've been searching for.*

"Hey yourself." I grinned. "What does it look like I'm doing?"

"Well," His eyes slid over me blatantly. "It looks like you're wasting that dress sitting all alone on the couch."

I fought the urge to roll my eyes because obviously he needed his checked if he thought my dress was anything beyond frumpy.

"Mmm … What do you suggest I do instead then?" I asked, giggling.

"Come with me." He pulled me up from the couch and I stumbled into him.

Oh yeah, now things were starting to get good, at least I hoped. I smiled back at him, allowing him to lead me out the back door, and into a small patch of woods at the edge of Ryan's property. He pulled a slim flask out of his pocket, taking a swig, before offering it to me. "It's Southern Comfort mixed with some lime."

I took it from his hand, the metal warming in my palm. I eyed the thing suspiciously like it would jump up and bite me. "Yeah, I don't know, I'm already kinda buzzed. I don't wanna get sick, it could get in the way of *other things*," I purred suggestively.

He responded with an easy grin. "It's just Southern Comfort, it's not that strong. Give it a go."

Well, I don't want the happy buzz I have going to wear off. What will one little taste do to me? I brought the flask up to my nose for a quick sniff. I tried to ignore the almost sickly sweet aroma that tickled my nostrils. Taking a shot's worth into my mouth, I forced myself to swallow. "Blak. That stuff is horrible." I winced at the slight burn it left in its wake.

He grabbed the flask from my hand, taking another swig. He then screwed the top on, stuffing it back into his pocket. I was still processing the horrible taste of the Southern Comfort, when I found myself abruptly pushed up against a tree, a slug-like tongue shoved down my throat.

My world spun on its axis. "Hey," my protest came out in a slur. Slobber from his sloppy kisses ran down my neck. "Hey, wait a second. Stop." I pushed at his chest, but my strength was no match or his. Rough hands roamed over my body as I continued to fight. When he reached down to hike up my dress, anger took hold. "Stop," I grated.

"Awe, come on baby, it'll be good. Just relax."

"No, it most certainly isn't gonna be good if you don't slow the hell down!" The hands that were currently fumbling with the zipper on my dress stilled, but only for a moment.

"Don't worry, it'll be good baby." The guy's roaming hands slid up, skimming over my underwear, and I sighed in resignation. Maybe he would be better than I thought he was going to be. *A girl can dream, can't she?*

Throwing myself into the moment, and hoping for the best, I wrapped my legs around his waist, grinding myself against him. I needed relief, in fact lately, I always needed relief. I knew I was a hormonal teenager but sometimes I couldn't help but feel that my needs were far vaster than some of my friends. But sex was sex, no one ever said feelings had to be involved. There was plenty of time to find that when I was older, if I was lucky.

I must have spaced out a little, being buzzed more than I thought maybe, because I suddenly felt my current partner pushing into me. I, of course, was ready for him— I was always ready lately. And as he searched for his rhythm I again tried to just go with it. But before I could really begin to enjoy myself…it was all over.

"I told you it would be good, baby," Mr. Two Pump Chump said, smiling as he righted himself and re-zipped his pants.

"For who?" I grumbled as I too attempted to right my clothes.

Either not hearing me, choosing to ignore me, or just not caring Mr. Two Pump Chump leaned over to give me a peck on the cheek. "Maybe we can do that again sometime? Can I maybe get your number?"

I guffawed. "Yeah, no, I don't think so. That was a one-time ride for you. Not happening again."

Before he had a chance to respond I strode off back to the party, still a tad woozy. In the end it didn't really matter. None of my partners ever seemed to make me crave a repeat visit, whether they satisfied me or not. I always felt like I was searching for something...something *more*.

"Time to come back now," a female voice assaulted my ears, simultaneously coming from everywhere and nowhere. And then a bright white light ripped through my skull, followed by blinding pain.

I WAS HURTLED into awareness mid-scream, minus the pain, thank God. Acute awareness of what the night of Ryan's party would have been like for me if I hadn't known Bryn sped through my mind. That had been a pivotal time in my life, a night where all things had changed. I'd realized my love for Bryn and had my very first premonition. "Are you telling me I would have been —worse than Jenna without Bryn?" My face heated as an image of me having sex with some strange guy like it was no big deal passed before my mind's eye. *I never even asked him his name.*

"A young female dragon just coming into her powers is a force to be reckoned with sexually," Morag said with a knowing smile, which I chose to ignore.

"But it's not like Bryn and me were doing the nasty the entire time. It seemed like I'd been sleeping around for a while, it seemed like—"

"You had feelings for Bryn before you recognized them. You were already bonded with him on some level emotionally, and just because you didn't know you were a dragon—your hormones most certainly did. They knew what you were craving and didn't bother with searching for anything else when Bryn was the only one that could satiate your needs. Without him there you and your dragon hormones were searching blindly for some unknown quantity."

"Okaaay...but as much as it weirds me out that I would have been a mega slut, why did my mother care so much about that? Please don't tell me that she sacrificed Bryn, made both of us miserable, all to keep my reputation in tack. And what about Khol? He would have still come for me soon, right? And then I probably would have just taken him as my *Anam Cara*. End of story, right?"

"Wrong. You would have been so focused on searching for what you didn't understand that you would have been … weak. Khol was first awakened and drawn in not just by the strength of your powers but the strength of your character. He would not have come for you. Holding yourself in control with all the hormones beneath the surface of such a young dragon shows more strength than you know. None of it has anything to do with how many partners you may have had, dragons don't care about such things, but they do care about control—control equals power. Khol wouldn't have sensed yours the way that he did, and he wouldn't have been awakened. You would have been forced to face everything else on your own as well. Not to mention Jeremy."

My stomach dropped. "What about Jeremy?"

"Without Bryn or Khol in the picture you would have had no reason to deny Jeremy's advances."

"But him and Jenna—"

"Never would have happened." Morag came to crouch in front of me, and I, for the first time, noticed that I was sitting on the floor of a cave. "Bryn's presence made you stronger. He made you who you are today. Without him, all would have been lost."

"But how could Khol not come for me?" My heart squeezed with betrayal. "He said my birth mother let him know that we were meant to be together so that would mean we're meant to be in any timeline regardless—he said—"

My throat closed up as I remembered the kiss I'd witnessed between him and Zen. "He doesn't love me at all, it really has been all about my power from the beginning. And just when I was beginning to think that maybe we could make it work as *Anam Caras*."

Morag stood, throwing her hands in the air. "The young—so utterly clueless." She cocked her hip, glaring down at me. "That male is so in love with you he acts like a moron sometimes. He gave you to Bryn, something that caused him immeasurable pain, just so you could be happy. If he simply desired you for your powers or any other such nonsense you're considering, things would have been very different." How the hell did she know all that? Probably more dragon powers that I wasn't aware of... *Of course.*

I crossed my arms over my chest and studied the ground. "He was kissing Zen."

"Or was she kissing him? Maybe he didn't have a chance to react, a chance to push her away. Did you give him an opportunity to explain? No, you didn't. You ran. You ran away because you were afraid of being hurt again."

Irrational anguish swirled in my gut. "He wouldn't have come for me if I was like that. He was what I needed most and he wouldn't have come." I thought Khol would always come for me, and the fact that he wouldn't have burned through my veins like poison.

"You weren't the same. You were her—in her head— you know I'm speaking the truth."

"She was still mostly me. I still felt like me...but not."

Morag sighed heavily. "Child you are utterly exasperating. Listen—I showed that to you to help you. And you're completely missing the point. Which would be why your birth mother placed Bryn in your path. He was there to help you become who you are today. A stronger, better version of anything else you could have become. And Khol loves you—the you that stands before me now."

"I'm sitting," I grumbled, but she ignored me, continuing on.

"The powers your mother carried, and now you carry, are both a gift and a burden—something that you will discover with time. Your mother saw a way to make you what this world needed in its direst time, and for you to also have the chance at being with Khol, someone who is your perfect match in every way. Bryn was not, despite what you believe. Star-crossed, not star-aligned lovers." She sighed again. "Your mother did everything she could. The rest is up to you."

Tears began to slide down my cheeks. I was overwhelmed and frankly more confused than I had been before. "I just don't know," I mumbled around a sob.

"You don't know what, child?"

"Everything, I just don't know about everything."

"Come, you need rest. You have a lot to think about. We will continue this after you wake."

"What about Khol? He'll be worried—"

"Let me deal with him for the time being, for now you must rest." Suddenly my fatigue pushed more heavily upon me and I was no longer able to resist it.

Chapter 15

Morag appeared just behind the clearing so she could silently observe the small party of three before approaching them. Khol was slumped over on the ground, his legs splayed haphazardly, his face in his hands as his muscled shoulders shook. His brother Lorik was crouched so close to him that they were practically touching. Lorik, in fact, appeared completely baffled, his face scrunched with uncertainty and concern. And Zen, who wore an expression of horror created from equal parts guilt and sorrow, paced the area in front of Khol, every so often glancing at him with grief. The clearing the trio was in was completely destroyed, Morag observed. It looked as if a small bomb had exploded, decimating around it.

Morag's curiosity was piqued. Was the destruction caused by Khol's unparalleled anguish? And then did his grief cause him to do something almost unthinkable for someone such as him? Was the great and mighty Lord of the *Rua Arach* actually crying?

As she crept closer, she realized he indeed was. This pleased her immensely, and yet she felt compassion in herself to extinguish the cause of his pain. A dragon such as Khol would only shed tears over the perceived death of his future mate, his one true love. To exhibit that kind of vulnerability meant Khol was well and truly in love with P.J. and that was very good news.

"She is not lost to you."

Khol rose quicker than it should have been possible without his powers, and he stalked towards Morag with menace. "Where is she? What have you done to her to break our connection, if not kill her?"

Morag raised her hand to silence Khol. "I would not hurt my niece." She paused a moment to let her words fully register with her rapt audience. "I am in fact helping her." She speared Khol with a disdainful expression. "She was quite...distraught over what happened between the two of you." Morag then motioned between Khol and Zen. "Her emotions are very fragile—I dare say she is completely human in that respect. And there lies the problem, she carries more power inside of her than any dragon in existence, more than even me, and it's all run by the emotions of a human girl." Khol grimaced in reaction.

Morag continued on, "She is as strong as circumstances have allowed her to be, but it's not good enough. She must learn to embrace who she truly is before it's too late. You can't help her Khol. You can't do this for her. She must realize who she is on her own."

"I-I—" Khol stammered, completely at a loss.

"I will guide her on this journey, and you will wait. She will seek you out in the end, you can find comfort in that truth."

"But in what way?" Khol pushed for what he really wanted to hear.

"You'll just have to wait and find out. What's a few more months in the long life of one such as yourself?" And with that Morag shifted back to her cave, and to where her slumbering niece was waiting for her.

"An eternity," Khol mumbled after Morag was already gone. "An eternity wrapped in an eternity." He then reared around to face Zen with an unreadable expression on his face. "I want you gone. I never want to lay my eyes on you again. What you have done—" Khol's words choked off in his throat. "You are dead to me."

A strangled cry erupted from Zen's chest, her face crumpling with panic. "No, you can't mean that you—"

"Take her out of my sight before I do something I regret!" Khol roared, and Lorik stepped forward to pull Zen protectively behind him.

"I'll take care of her, brother. What will you do?" Lorik asked.

"I will wait. I will wait as long as it takes for her."

Lorik nodded once before turning to wrap an arm

around the now sobbing Zen. He began walking due south, back in the direction they had come. It was obvious that Khol would be on his own, but Lorik had a feeling that's just the way he wanted it. Until his queen returned to him.

Chapter 16

I watched myself speaking to Morag. The other me, the me in the vision, had a more pronounced baby bump, so I guessed that the vision was one from the future. That, and the fact that I'd only had one conversation with Morag and it was nothing like the one I was witnessing.

"Why didn't you tell me you had that kind of power? Why would you hide it from me?" I screeched at Morag, fire sprouting out of my fingertips and running up my arms.

"I wasn't hiding it from you, child. I was merely waiting for the right time to inform you. You weren't ready for that kind of information yet." Morag's eyes blazed a bright dragon gold with her reciprocated anger. "And I have to wonder why you never asked me about the meaning behind my hair color."

Frustration washed over the other me's features. "I

don't know," I huffed. "I thought the white hair was synonymous with power, and maybe you dyed the rest. Like dragons can't do that?" I ground my teeth together. "Other dragons besides me that is."

"If you want the answers you need to ask the right questions," Morag said, expelling a long breath.

"Well I'm asking you now."

But instead of answering the me that was in the vision, Morag turned towards the other me, the me that was currently watching the vision—like she could see me. A chill ran up my spine as she met my eyes. "You won't need to ask them now, because you will have already asked them because you didn't before, and you will now already have the answers you seek."

"What?" Both versions of me said in unison.

"Ah, niece. You have so much to learn about the fluidity of time. Your lessons begin now."

With her words I sat straight up in bed, fully awake. My eyes immediately sought out the source of the presence that was watching me. "Morag," I whispered, narrowing my eyes. "What the hell was that?"

She waved her hand at me as if to brush off my question as something silly. "You already know. Let's get to the point of it all, shall we?"

"Okay. Yeah. How about answering the questions raised by the vision I just had? Let's start with that. What exactly are your powers? And what does your hair color have to do with any of it?"

Morag's eyes twinkled with delight, despite the anger I

was directing at her. "I am the oldest and last of the brown dragons."

My eyebrows shot up. "Brown dragon? But I thought there were only four dragon factions…the red, the black, the silver, and the gold."

"Aaah, there are only four factions *now*. In times long gone, there used to be many more: brown, green, purple, blue—there was a faction for practically every color in the rainbow."

"What happened?"

"Some factions were too weak to survive, there was always fighting and biases between factions. Dragons aren't so different than humans in their emotions, they just pretend they're superior." Her lips tipped up. "But you've already figured that out for yourself. Matter of fact, dragons have more intense emotions than humans. They burn through us like the magic that pulses in our blood. That's why dragons as a whole have always strived for more control. But the young are impetuous, and the best-made plans… " Her voice trailed off as if lost in thought.

A few moments passed and then she blinked rapidly as if realizing where she was again. "Like I was saying, some factions were too weak to survive, and others killed each other off in the continuous battles they waged against each other. The factions of the other colors are forever gone"—I wasn't completely sure, but I swear I saw tears glistening in Morag's eyes— "but a few of us live on, without the comfort of what we once had."

"I thought my mother was a red dragon, *rua arach*." I

knew my mother's hair was white, but I assumed before the power had changed it like mine, that it had been red.

"The father in a dragon pairing is dominant in the offspring. Your mother was a brown dragon like me."

"So what kind of dragon is a brown dragon then? I mean, a red dragon is a fire dragon and a black a water dragon so…" I looked at her expectantly.

"The brown dragons hold dominion over time. We are time dragons."

My first thoughts reflexively went to one of Bryn's favorite Sci-fi shows that he used to force me to watch with him…*Doctor Who.* Laughter bubbled up within my chest, escaping in a weird sputtering sound. "So the lord of the brown dragon faction would have been what…a time lord?" I fanned myself as tears of amusement ran down my cheeks. "Wait—can brown dragons travel through time? Can *you* travel through time?"

Morag frowned at me. "It's not that simple. I said we hold dominion over time, but our gifts vary differently for each of us. For instance, your mother had the ability to see through time…all time…but not physically travel through it."

"So none of the brown dragons could travel through time?" *Damn.* That would have solved everything to have a time traveler in the family.

"I didn't say that either, child. There were some that could, but as some magics strengthen over time, others weaken still." She tilted her head, staring at me expectantly as if she was waiting for me to connect the dots.

"So you could travel through time? Oh my God—" I bounced up and down with excitement. "Can you still, at all?"

"No, the days of me shifting through the fabric of time are long gone, child, and I'm sorry for that. There is much I could have done to help you and the humans you care for if I still had that gift."

Disappointment washed through me. "Yeah, okay." I had nothing else to say. I now held the gift of being able to see into any moment of time, the past or the future, and even if I could control my gift fully, it wouldn't solve my problems.

Disappointment quickly morphed into hopelessness. "How will I stop the Riders? What good is all the power I have if I can't even do that?" I slumped over, rubbing my belly in an attempt to comfort myself.

"Why the *rua artaire* necklace you wear, of course. Is that not why you sought me out to begin with, to learn how to wield its magic?" Morag's voice had taken on a motherly tone again, one that she seemed to fall into rather easily. It made me wonder if she was the older sister to my birth mother, after all, my mother had been the queen and she never held the title of "the Ancient". Or maybe Morag had children of her own? I would ask her soon, but now didn't seem like the right moment.

"Yes, but even if I learn how to control this necklace" —I reached up to play with the warm metal resting against my throat— "there are so many of them. How will I be able to remove them all? And how will I manage to not kill Jenna when I remove hers like in my other vision?" So many different questions and battling emotions were swimming through my brain. But one pushed to the forefront. "Why didn't you come to me, why did you wait for me to seek you out?"

Morag threw her head back and laughed. "I'm surprised you haven't guessed, my sister and your mother of course. She told me to wait, she said it was the only way, and I've learned to trust her powers over the years. She also told me exactly what I would need to do when you finally did arrive. Although like I mentioned before… somehow you weren't what I expected when she told me about you."

I nodded my head. "I guess I kind of suspected. She's had her hand in every part of my life so far, hasn't she?" It was all beyond creepy if you asked me, but I didn't say that out loud. And I wasn't really sure how to take Morag's repeated comment of me not being what she expected. My birth mother had informed her of what to expect so that didn't even make sense. Was I living up to the expectations or being a huge disappointment? And she made the necklace I was wearing for me, and yet she didn't know me at all. The precursors of an eminent headache throbbed in the back of my skull.

"Her gift was a burden, one that you now bear, like I've said." She stood, reaching her hand out to me. "It's time for me to journey off of my land for the first time in a very long time."

I clasped my hands in my lap tightly, eyeing her warily. "Where are we going, and why?" *God, she hasn't been off her lands in who knows how long? How did she not go completely insane?* Then again, maybe she was completely bonkers, and I was placing my fate in the hands of a deranged psychopath. A twisted knot formed in my stomach at the thought.

A fierce expression settled over Morag's face. "I want to see these Riders for myself. I want you to show me what's become of my beloved world while I was forced to hide here all of these years."

"Oookay," I said shakily.

It was kind of hard to believe that anyone would hide themselves away like she had just because her sister said that it was necessary, but then again so many things in my life were hard to believe. *Can I trust her?* I steeled myself with the knowledge that my birth mother hadn't led me astray so far. Although the key words could end up being *so far.* Faith was taking a leap and trusting something or someone would be there to catch me. *Time to take that leap, what other choice do I really have?* I either risked trusting Morag, and maybe she could help me to eventually defeat the Riders or I didn't trust her and the Riders would definitely win. I had nothing left to lose. I reached my hand out to let her take mine and the familiar weightlessness of shifting rushed through my system.

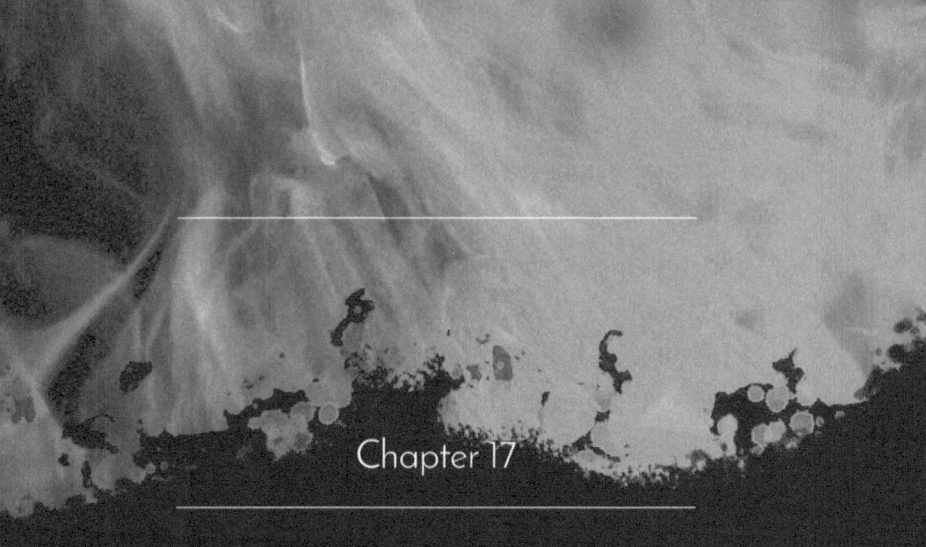

Chapter 17

A deep base reverberated through my body, beating against my senses and causing my heart to thump out the same rhythm. Strobe lights pulsed in my direction, making it difficult for me to focus on my surroundings at first. As my eyes and ears adjusted, I realized that Morag had shifted us to some kind of dance club.

I glanced over at Morag who was bouncing with the beat and seeming a little too comfortable with the club for someone who hadn't been out in the real world for as long as she claimed. She leaned over and yelled in my ear, "This is amazing! Is this the kind of thing I've been missing?"

"This is *not* amazing!" I yelled back, rolling my eyes at her. *Who is the ancient dragon out of the two of us anyways? Seriously ... not only does she look young, but she seems so modern in both her attitude and language. How is that even possible?*

"Point one of them out to me!" she yelled in response, ignoring my obvious disdain for the club.

Okay. So she brought me to this club so I could point one of the Riders out to her. Do Riders like to dance? Not really sure what her plan was, I decided to just go with it. "Yeah, hold on," I mumbled, sure she wouldn't be able to hear me over the music. I scanned the clubbers who were writhing around on the dance floor and hissed in a breath. *Yep... apparently Riders do like to dance...a lot.* Almost every single human on the dance floor had one of them inside of their bodies.

Morag's hand touched my arm. "Well?" she yelled.

"Take your pick!" I said, motioning to the throng of enthusiastic dancers in front of us.

She quirked an eyebrow at me in surprise, then nodded in understanding. "We need to isolate one of them. Get him or her away from the crowd." I scrunched my face at her and widened my eyes. What did she expect me to do? She was the dragon lady with a plan. Obviously noting my snarky facial expression Morag decided to take matters into her own hands. She moved forward on the dance floor, bouncing to the music again. Before I had time to blink she was sandwiched in between too hot guys.

"Hey," a male voice shouted too close to my ear. "What are you doing?"

I turned towards the source of the voice, a tall, thin goth looking guy, and raised my eyebrows. What did he think I was doing?

"You're pregnant."

I delivered the guy and his sanctimonious Rider a look of "duh".

"So why are you here, in a club?"

I snorted. "Like I can't go anywhere once I'm pregnant or something?"

"I hope you're not drinking. How old are you? Where's the father, or do you even know who he is?" The guy began peppering me with questions, which in order for me to hear, he had moved a little too close for comfort.

I shoved at him. "Look. What I do or not do is none of your business."

"Is this a wig?" The guy grabbed a handful of my hair and tugged.

"Ow!" I hissed.

His grip tightened in my hair and the Rider inside of him began to shine brighter. "You're her, aren't you?"

Panic clawed its way through my chest. *Where is Morag?* My eyes flicked around to search for her. I should have known better than to come somewhere out in the open without a disguise. "Who? I don't know you," I ground out. Sure, I could burn him, but then I'd probably have to burn him and all of his Rider friends, which was practically the entirety of the club. It would be a massacre.

The goth guy was joined by a friend, who looked at us with curiosity. "What are you doing, man?"

The goth guy smiled down at me, making my skin crawl. "This is her. The queen."

The second guy, who was tall and blond, and not at all goth, stared at me with disbelief. "No shit?"

"I'm just as surprised as—" Morag appeared beside our little group and both the goth guy and blond guy stopped short.

Morag looked at me and smiled. "Good choice!" She touched my arm, shifting the three of us out of the club.

We reappeared back in Morag's cave, the goth guy still clutching at my hair. Surprise working on my side, I managed to slip out of goth guy's grip, but I swore he took a clump of my hair with him. What was with Riders pulling on my hair anyways? A brief memory flashed in my mind of a party in Spring Hill, Tennessee with some gropey Riders that ended with me losing some hair then too.

"So this...boy...has one of the Riders in him?" Morag was circling him like a shark that just found her next meal.

"Yes," I said, rubbing my scalp to check for a bald spot. Luckily, I found none. *Phew.*

Goth guy cringed away from Morag as she poked at him with her index finger. "Strange how he feels like a regular human to me. But if you say so..." She then turned to look at me expectantly. "Well, I've brought you your first test subject, go ahead and try to use the *rua artaire* necklace to remove the abomination from him."

Goth guy's eyes widened, the Rider within him panicking, and he turned, attempting to run. Fortunately for us, the only thing he succeeded in doing was getting himself knocked out when he ran into the corner of the wall...literally. "Do they lack depth perception or something?" Morag mused, poking at him with her leather clad foot.

"Maybe he's drunk?" Since the Rider was in a human host then it seemed possible that they could still get drunk. It was the only feasible explanation I had to offer.

Morag shrugged her shoulders, no longer concerned with the current topic at hand. "Maybe it's better if he's unconscious so his screaming doesn't ruin your concentration."

"Why would he be screaming?" I asked nervously.

"Oh child, they always scream." She motioned for me to come closer to her and the passed-out goth on the floor. When I hesitated, she grabbed my wrist, tugging me forward. "Go ahead, try to use the power in the necklace to remove the Rider from its host body."

"But I don't know how!" I yelled, completely flabbergasted.

Just like that, she expected me to know how to do something that was the entire reason we had sought her out? Maybe she had gone a little batty being separated from society and other dragons for as long as she had. Which brought up a very good question—

"Exactly how long have you been here? By yourself?" I tried to keep my tone light, simply curious in nature, and not filled with assumed implications of her lack of sanity.

Regardless, Morag seemed to pick up exactly what I

didn't want her to. "I'm not insane. And I haven't been here all by myself. I've had…visitors." The way a small smile played across her lips, I could guess precisely what kind of visitors she'd had.

My face heated. "Yeah, ummm, I don't wanna hear anymore, you're my aunt." *Ewww*, I silently tacked on.

"You asked," Morag responded with annoyance. "Now quit stalling and use the necklace."

I ground my teeth together. Just because she hadn't been in solitary confinement didn't guarantee her sanity. "I don't know how," I repeated, glaring at her.

"All right, maybe you need a little direction first."

"You think?" I huffed. "And I thought you weren't gonna help me with this until I went through your little emotional building maze or whatever you were talking about before."

"I changed my mind. It's been known to happen. I have other plans now."

I rolled my eyes. "Oh, okay." She had answered absolutely nothing, not really anyways.

"Pay attention, I'm only going to explain this once." I fought the urge to roll my eyes again and instead decided to play the good little student. "Just focus all of your fire energy into the stone on the necklace, then focus that power onto the Rider and use it to draw him out of his host. Last but not least, imprison him in the stone." She paused, or at least I thought she had as I waited for her to continue with her explanation. Instead, she waved her hand at me to begin.

I blinked at her in shock. "That's it? That's all of your explanation?"

"Yes, well maybe I'm not the best teacher."

"Understatement of the year," I grumbled under my breath. "A few questions first then."

"Fine," she snapped, as if it was going to be such a pain in the ass to her.

"Why couldn't you or my birth mother have used the necklace to remove the Riders? Why me?" It seemed like everything was coming down to me, and I still didn't quite understand why.

"It's your fate."

"Seriously?" I shook my head in disbelief. "That's what you're gonna give me—it's my fate? What kind of crap is that?"

Morag's eyes slid shut and she inhaled deeply before her glowing eyes reemerged from their hiding place. "I learned to trust my sister's powers. Sometimes the combination of being the right person, at the right time, and in your case also with the right powers makes all the difference in the world. My sister always looked at every possible angle, and so clearly, it became your fate because she made it so, and she made it so because you were the best outcome."

I was starting to get a headache. "My powers?"

"Fire magic is needed to control the *rua artaire* necklace. Fire—"

"All dragons have fire magic. Any—"

"She saw something, I trust her gift. End of story.

There isn't any point in trying to figure it all out, I learned that many—many years ago."

"Fine. Whatever." I obviously wasn't going to get the kinds of answers I wanted out of her so why not give the necklace a go? What else did I possibly have to lose?

I reached inside of myself mentally, and roused my dormant, and yet always ready fire magic. It instantaneously appeared at my fingertips, running up the length of my arms. But when I tried to imagine it going into the necklace…it didn't.

"Well, what are you waiting for?" Morag asked.

"My powers don't always cooperate with me," I growled, baring my teeth at her.

"You must have more control than that, and I know you have more magic in you than you're showing as well. Come on, I want to see it." For a brief second, angered by Morag's almost condescending words, my fire flared out towards her. Her eyes widened briefly and then a look of complete understanding washed over her. "I forgot how much young red dragons' powers are ruled by their emotions. I had a lover once I thought had hardly any magic at all but"—she sucked in an appreciative breath—"get his emotions involved and things turned scorching fast."

I had a feeling she didn't mean scorching in the way I wished she did. "No more talk about that kind of stuff. You're my aunt. Do I have to say it out loud to shut you up? But—eeewww."

Ignoring me, Morag gave me another pointer. "Think

of something that makes you angry—beyond angry—enraged. Think of that thing and let your instincts take over. The rest should be easy after that."

I was willing to give it a shot. And finding a subject to enrage me definitely wouldn't be difficult either. I immediately pictured Bryn's father's face in my mind's eye, and how he had looked at me just before he stole Bryn from me forever.

He grinned down at me.

"Like I said, he wasn't really my son anyways."

Silence engulfed me, fueled by my rage. *It's not fair! None of it!* That Bryn had been taken from me. That Bryn's father's body had been used as the instrument of my torment. That even after I watched his father burn to death on the ground, becoming nothing more than ash—it would never be enough to calm my inner rage. Never.

A scream pierced the silence—a scream of complete and utter agony—and my vision focused in on the goth guy as he writhed on the floor of Morag's cave, surrounded by a red glow emanating from my necklace. I watched, as if I was seeing someone else in my place, as I poured all my rage into creating the fire magic that was ripping the Rider out of the goth guy's body.

Suddenly, the Rider was free of his host and for a split second it hovered in midair before clawing at nothing and disappearing. But I was still connected with my rage, and unfortunately for goth guy he was my unlucky target. My fire magic sprung free of the necklace I'd been pouring it into, and as the red glow faded, my fire rapidly moved towards its desired victim.

"P.J.—no. It's gone. The abomination is no longer inside the boy, otherwise the light wouldn't have faded." I heard Morag's voice, but I felt disconnected from my own body.

Goth guy screamed for a completely different reason as he began to burn. It was only then that I came back to myself and I let my magic recede—but it was too late. Goth guy was dead, his body charred beyond recognition. I knew I should have been horrified, but I was too numb to care.

Morag touched my arm, and I turned towards her, not really seeing her. What I wanted more than anything in that moment was Khol. I wished he was there to take me into his arms where I would find the comfort I needed. "Khol," I mumbled, as if his name alone could conjure him. And in the past, it would have.

"You need to learn to cope with these things on your own, without Khol. It's natural to feel guilt, but you need to know that as a young dragon—"

"I don't feel guilt." I gazed at what used to be a human being's body. "There are causalities in war, and collateral damages. That's what he is—was—collateral damage in our war against the Riders." I swallowed around the lump in my throat. "Maybe once I would have cared, but not now. I'll do whatever it takes to learn how to use this necklace. I have to. I won't let anyone else I care about get hurt." Images of Khol, Jenna, and Jeremy swam through my mind. "I won't lose anyone else."

Morag didn't respond and just stood there studying me. "What?" I snapped. "Nothing to say about any of this?"

She tilted her head at me much like a dog does when he's trying to understand something. "Maybe your emotions are more dragon than I originally thought." She squinted at me. "Or maybe they're becoming that way." She was then moving about in a flurry of motions. "No matter. I guess the first one was a failure, but not to worry, we'll keep trying until you get it right. Next time we won't do it here. Seriously, it's going to take forever for the burnt flesh smell to go away." She crinkled her nose at me as if her observation conjured the fowl aroma itself. I didn't realize how bad it was until the rank odor suddenly overwhelmed my senses and I gagged.

"I need Khol," I muttered, focusing in on him. Maybe, just maybe I could find the control to shift to him.

"Oh, no you don't. Don't make me take your powers away again. The whole back and forth thing will start to be a drain on both of us," Morag snapped, digging her fingers into my forearm. "You need to learn to cope without him, like I already said. Only then—when you don't need him will you be able to find solace in his arms."

Dizziness swam through my head. "But if I don't need him then why would I seek out his comfort?"

Morag laughed darkly. "Because child, nothing is sweeter than knowing you can make it on your own, that you don't need anyone, and to have them only because you want them."

"I wanna be—"

"No, right now you still need. And—"

I hunched over and ejected what little food was in my stomach at Morag's feet. When I was done, I curled into as tight a ball that I could, being that I was pregnant, and I lost consciousness, yet again.

Chapter 18

"**M**y little queen," Khol rumbled, his deep voice lulling over me as he smoothed my hair from my face.

I opened my eyes, peering up at him with confusion. "What are you doing here—wait—" I realized I was in Khol's large bed. "How did I get here?"

"You're not actually here, and neither am I," he responded, his illuminated green eyes met mine, growing brighter. "But I had to check on you—I had to—I had to see you."

"So we're—"

"Communicating like we did when I first came to you." A soft smile tipped up the corners of his full succulent lips. "It seems like such a long time ago, doesn't it?"

I thought back to the time in the woods when I'd lost consciousness and believed I had woken up at his feet. It turned out we were communicating in my mind only. "So much has changed."

I'd lost so much since then: my family, Bryn, basically everything I thought I knew about myself. But I'd also gained a lot: Khol, my powers, knowledge of who and what I really am. What I'd gained clearly didn't offset all I'd lost but at least it was something.

"You've been right by my side since that first night, haven't you?" It wasn't a question I needed him to answer.

He ran his thumb over my bottom lip, and I nipped at it. "Right where I belong."

"What happened with Zen?" I was happy to see Khol, I had missed him more than I wanted to admit, but I couldn't let what I'd witnessed between him and Zen go, at least not yet. Not without a satisfactory explanation—if one existed.

Khol's fist tightened around the lock of hair he'd idly been toying with. "She kissed me. It meant nothing."

"Why did it take you so long to pull away? Just because it didn't mean anything—" I swallowed a few times trying to open up my suddenly constricted throat. "Did you feel something when she was kissing you? Even when I was in love with Bryn, when you and Jeremy kissed me, I felt something, physical at least." My heart sped up as I anticipated his answer, and also because I hadn't missed the slip of my tongue...*was* in love with Bryn? *Past tense?*

"I won't lie to you." Khol's gaze flicked away. "Zen's always been a very good kisser."

My eyes burned. "Okay."

Khol's hands captured my face as his gaze burned into mine. "I love you. Her kiss took me by surprise, and for a moment I enjoyed it. Nothing more and nothing less."

"I get it. I won't be a hypocrite. I understand." Oh, but I wanted to be—a hypocrite that is. Khol loved me. I had no reason to pay any credence to the gut-wrenching jealousy that was currently eating at me. And for a male dragon I knew what loving someone meant. Khol would never love anyone but me. Then again, I heard what Zen said, and maybe she was right. Maybe Khol wasn't really *in* love with me.

"I can feel your emotions—see the doubt in your eyes —*damn her*," Khol growled.

"Don't blame Zen. I can't really blame her for trying." I nibbled on my bottom lip, attempting to prevent the tears that were swelling in my eyes from spilling over.

Khol tried to force me to meet his gaze, but I couldn't —I just couldn't. "She caused me to hurt you"—Khol's voice cracked with heavy emotion— "I never thought I would hurt you—not like this."

"It's nothing," I lied. "Not really. I'm just being hormonal. I'll get over it." *Hopefully.* Because there was no way I could deal with this gut-wrenching agony every time I was around him.

"I love you," Khol whispered, his voice pleading. "I can't bear the thought that I hurt you. Please forgive me."

I shook my head slowly, still attempting to deny the truth. "Khol, no, I told you it's just me being hor—"

He stole the rest of my words with his mouth, his

tongue diving in to entangle with mine. Heat immediately rushed through my body, and I let him take control of me. I was desperate, driven...and something else I couldn't quite identify. I knew I wanted Khol—all of Khol in that moment.

"Please, "I said brokenly. "I need you."

Khol's muscles tensed under my wandering hands, his mouth pausing where it was at the base of my jaw line. "We won't bond if we have sex in this state, I can't claim you this way."

"I know." I could have Khol completely without the consequences of becoming his *Anam Cara* in this mental plane.

"No," Khol thundered, pulling away from me. "Even after everything—you still don't want me?"

I reached for him feeling bereft without his touch. "I do want you, just not as—"

"Your *Anam Cara*," he finished for me.

I nodded meekly, still hoping he would return to my embrace and give me what I wanted.

"No. You will have all of me, or none of me. I won't allow you to treat me this way. No longer."

His tone was sharp, like a physical blow to my face. I blinked up at him in shock. "But Khol—"

"I'm tired of you pushing me away. You hold me at arm's length and then give me scraps of attention that give me hope." He grabbed my shoulders and lifted me slightly off the bed. "Should I stop hoping? I thought—just tell me —should I stop?"

It seemed that despite what Khol had previously said to me about being whatever I needed for however long I needed him to be that—those terms had come to an end. *What changed?*

When I didn't answer him, Khol dropped me back on the bed, and stepped away. "I'm not going to so much as put a finger on you until you beg me to." Khol's eyes sparked into flames.

"What?" I definitely hadn't been expecting that.

"I *will* claim you. You will be my *Anam Cara*." Khol's expression hardened. "But not until you're on your hands and knees before me, begging me to, and not one moment sooner."

Anger of my own flared in my system. "I'll never beg you." I notched my chin up with defiance. "I am your queen." I clenched my jaw, not trusting myself to say anything else. I hated when Khol got like this, all Alpha male asshole.

Before I could blink, he was beside me, his mouth millimeters from my left ear, but he held true and didn't touch me. "You will beg for my touch. You will plead on your hands and knees for me to claim you as my *Anam Cara*. And when I finally do—you will know I am your king, not just in name, but because I will have taken possession of your very soul." I shuddered as his warm breath swept over my ear and along the side of my face.

Before I could come up with a coherent response, he was gone.

Jolting awake, I sat up on a small bed in a cave that was

clearly Morag's. *But damn.* I thought I hated when Khol went all mega Alpha male asshole on me, but—but— *Damn.* What he just said to me was beyond hot. If only he was really here, now, then maybe he'd actually have me right where he wanted me.

"P.J.?" Morag's voice rang out in the darkness.

"Yeah," I croaked, my throat raw and scratchy.

The room I was in slowly began to grow brighter until everything was illuminated in a soft glow. Morag entered, dragging a tall thin guy with floppy blond hair behind her. "I brought you a present," she said, grinning.

My eyes widened, my current interaction with Khol still clouding my thoughts. "Ummm...?"

"He has a Rider in him, doesn't he?" Morag scrunched up her face, glancing back at the completely terrified guy that was cringing away from her.

There was no dual imagery shining out from within him. "Actually, no, there isn't."

"Oh, well, that would explain a lot. Just a moment then." Morag and her prisoner disappeared and less than a minute later, barely time for me to process what had just happened, she reappeared with a completely different guy in tow. This one was shorter with dark brown hair. And yes, he most definitely had a Rider inside of him.

"We have a winner," I confirmed before Morag could ask.

"Oh good." Morag smiled sheepishly. "That was kind of embarrassing."

"Uh, okay." *Embarrassing?* What about the poor kid

who probably just wet himself? He'd been terrified, and now he probably thought he was insane. "So why—"

"Try to remove the Rider from him," Morag demanded, cutting me off. My mouth opened and closed a few times but no words came out. She wanted me to try again so soon after I fried the last one? "Come on, I don't have all day. And we both know we don't have all the time in the world for you to learn this."

I reluctantly pulled myself out of bed, facing down the Rider, who was turning paler by the moment. "Just let me go," he mumbled. "I haven't done anything to you."

"You've got to be kidding me, right?" Was he really going to try and play the innocent card?

"Joe needs me. I complete him. And we haven't done anything wrong."

"Unbelievable. Are you actually trying to convince me that your host needs your help? Do continue," I added, sarcasm coating each syllable, although the Rider didn't seem to pick up on that part.

"Joe would have never talked to Marie, his girlfriend, I gave him the nerve, and he never would have gone after the promotion he wanted. I gave him the courage he lacked, and he appreciates me. He—"

"Doesn't know he has a leech inside of him," I growled.

"Please, not all of us are bad," the Rider pleaded. "Some of us help."

"Yeah, okay, this conversation is over." I reached for my fire power using my anger to focus it into my dragon pendant. Just like the first time, a red glow began to emanate from the necklace and the Rider was sucked out of its human host screaming in apparent agony. The Rider turned large pleading eyes at me before it disappeared like the first one. "Where do they go?" I wondered out loud.

"No!" the guy whose name was Joe cried out. "Bring him back! I need him!" He dropped to his knees, clutching at his head. "Just bring him back!"

"You don't mean that. You don't know what you're saying." I attempted to adopt a soothing tone for Joe, but it didn't seem to be working. I was shocked Joe even knew about the Rider inside of him.

"How dare you just take him, how dare you—" Morag grabbed him by the shoulders and they both disappeared. She reappeared a moment later by herself.

"I took him home, he'll be fine."

But I wasn't so sure. "I don't know what to think. I thought—I thought he'd be relieved."

Morag waved her hand in dismissal. "You're missing the most important part—you removed a Rider from its human host and the human is still alive."

"You're right, I did." I chewed on the inside of my cheek. *Maybe I'll actually be able to save Jenna after all.*

"Does that mean I can—?"

"No."

"You didn't even let me finish."

"It doesn't matter. My answer is still no. You removed one Rider from its host successfully. You need to practice more."

"What about Khol then? Can I at least see him now?"

"No."

My face fell, and Morag barked out a laugh. "Just like a red dragon, all emotion. The world could be falling down around you completely, and it almost is, by the way, and you'd more concerned about your love life."

I crossed my arms over my chest, glaring at her. "That's not true, it's just that I need Khol."

She raised her eyebrows in challenge. "For what exactly?"

"Well for—for—well I need him for—"

"That's what I thought. You don't need him. You want him." She rolled her eyes. "Like I said, typical red dragon. And Khol, despite his age, is no better."

"That's not true!" I protested.

Morag snorted. "Are you going to look me in the eyes, child, and try to deny that you aren't completely driven by your emotions?"

"Everyone's driven by their emotions. People are emotional creatures."

"For one, you aren't a people, at least not a human people. And for two, no, not all of us are driven by our emotions. The fact you think that to be true only reinforces my point."

"I don't understand. What else would anyone be driven by?" I couldn't wrap my mind around being driven by anything besides my emotions. *What else is there?*

"You won't understand. It's not in your nature to understand being motivated by anything beyond your emotions. Red dragons have a reputation for being crazy for a reason. Even other dragon factions give the lot of you wide berths.

I remembered when I'd first met Nala, she had referred to me as a crazy red dragon. "But black dragons are just as passionate, I would know." Not only because of Bryn, but because Nala had betrayed us to the Riders, all for a chance to have Bryn for herself. Ultimately, her actions ended up getting both of them killed.

"No one, not even other dragons, experience the world quite like the red dragon. You burn more brightly, just like the element of fire you control."

"Okay, whatever, but I don't get why I can't see Khol." I couldn't help the pout that formed on my face.

"Stop. You remind me so much of my sister—your mother when you do that—and I miss her." Sadness swam through her eyes, but only for the briefest of moments. "We have a lot to do. I won't let all the work and planning of my sister go to waste. We will honor her memory by making sure her death wasn't in vain." And with that Morag disappeared again.

She's probably going to get my next Rider victim. I hope she doesn't bring another empty human. That poor kid is probably a mess. Ugh.

I drummed my fingers along my thigh.

How long is she going to take? And what am I supposed to be doing in the meantime? Hmmm ... I wonder what Khol is doing right now? Is he still mad at me? I wonder if—okay, maybe Morag has a point about the whole red dragon thing.

Chapter 19

I spent almost every waking moment, when I wasn't eating or other such trivial things, practicing the removal of Riders from their human hosts. A very surprising thing that I kept coming across though, was that a lot of the humans weren't pleased with me after I ripped their 'friend' out of them. In fact, plenty of them were royally pissed. I just couldn't understand why. Were the humans who hosted the Riders better off than the rest of the un-hosting humans?

The Riders, led by President Bill Wexington had successfully done what they had set out to do: enslave humans. The saddest part was that most humans seemed to welcome the chains that bound them. Under the guise of protection and help, the Riders had used the governments of the world to slip their chokehold on the human population.

The Riders controlled everything, from where and when they could receive medical help, to how much heat they could use. The humans willingly went along with it so that they and their children would be safe. They couldn't see that all of them had never been in more danger.

How was I supposed to help the humans, when they didn't seem to want the kind of help I could give them? I felt hopeless, confused, trapped even. What if I reached my goal of cleansing my world of the Riders and nothing changed for the better? What if it was already too late?

Perhaps some of the dragons like Lorik had a point about not getting involved with humans. Maybe I would be better off letting Khol claim me and turning a blind eye to the humans, because as time passed I thought of myself as less and less human and more dragon. I just couldn't comprehend how the humans let themselves be controlled. Didn't they realize how screwed up the world had become?

Despite my doubts, I still cared deeply about a few humans in particular. "Maybe I'm ready to try it on Jenna?" I mused out loud, trying not focus in on the vision I had of killing her in the extraction process. Would I ever be emotionally ready to try it, was the real question.

"Yes, I think it's time," Morag answered, even though I hadn't really been asking her.

I chewed on my bottom lip, dropping my gaze to the floor. "What if I kill her, like in my vision?"

"What if you don't?" Morag countered.

I heaved a huge sigh, dispelling none of my anxiety. "Maybe I could try removing a few more Riders from other people first."

"I understand your anxiety, Jenna is very important to you, but sooner or later you're just going to have to face your fears. Either that or forget about trying to remove the Rider from her altogether, at least that way you can guarantee she stays alive. Is that what you want?"

"No." I shook my head slowly. "I don't want her to have to live with one of those things in her. She's miserable. The animals won't talk to her anymore and I know what her ability means to her."

"No time like the present then." Morag touched my arm and just like that, I found myself standing outside the familiar room that housed Jenna's makeshift prison.

A moment later my skin prickled with awareness as Khol appeared before me. Anxiety combined with excitement sizzled through my veins, leaving me lightheaded. As I stared up into Khol's illuminated green eyes they turned to flames. Apparently, his emotions were running on high as well. It was the first time I'd seen him in the flesh since I caught him and Zen in a lip lock.

He raised his hand to cup my face, letting it drop before he made contact with my skin. I hid my disappointment. Was he really not going to even lay a single finger on me unless I begged? *Stupid dragon Alpha male asshole.* "Khol," I said evenly.

"Paige," he replied in the same even tone.

Him not using his pet name for me was a twist of the knife in my heart, but I continued to outwardly remain steady. "Morag thinks I'm ready to remove the Rider from Jenna."

Khol nodded, his cool demeanor towards me in stark contrast with the flames in his eyes. "Jeremy is with her."

I snorted. "Jeremy is always with her."

"Do you think it's wise to have him present when you attempt the removal of Jenna's Rider?" he asked.

"Would you leave me if I was in her situation?"

Khol turned away, his muscles tensing. "You've made your point."

I reached up to push the door open, allowing my nerves to stall me for only a moment. Finally, I found the resolve to swing the door open, and I marched in with Khol and Morag tightly at my heels. Jeremy and Jenna whipped their heads around, wearing matching expressions of surprise.

Hope flitted across Jeremy's features as he stared at me. "Does this mean...?"

I attempted to smile but was sure I donned a grimace instead. "Yes, I'm here to remove the Rider."

I glanced over at Jenna, still chained to her large bed, and noticed that her hair was now purple. My heart squeezed at the sight, because it was almost the same shade it had been before all the craziness with the Riders had begun. It seemed like a lifetime ago.

"Jenna, before I try—" My throat closed off. I swallowed and tried again. "I just wanted to tell you—" But again I couldn't bring myself to say what I really wanted her to hear. Because what if telling her that I loved her somehow jinxed me by preparing for her possible death? But what if she died and I didn't let her know one last time?

Understanding donned on her face and she smiled thinly. "I know, P.J., you don't have to say it."

Tears welled in my eyes, and I nodded at her, the two of us in perfect understanding. The Rider inside of her was another story. The visage that shined out from inside of her took on a panicked expression as it pushed for control of Jenna's body. Jenna contorted as the Rider forced her to fight her bindings. It was in that moment, when I could no longer see my Jenna, only the Rider, I pulled forth my fire magic. *It's now or never.* There was no real point in dragging the whole affair out. What would be would be no matter how I wished otherwise.

I pushed the magic into the dragon pendant and then into Jenna's body. Jeremy took a step towards me as if he meant to put a stop to it, and Khol was there in an instant to restrain him.

The Rider inside of Jenna screamed. Sweat trickled down my spine and I gritted my teeth as my pulse pounded in my ears. This particular Rider was proving to be more difficult to remove than I was used to, but finally it was ripped from her. The Rider screamed again as it floated briefly in the open air before vanishing. A flash of bright light preceded the disappearance of the red glow emanating from my pendant. Morag had explained to me that all of them—all the Riders that I pulled out of their hosts were contained inside the stone in my necklace. For my sanity, I tried not to ever think about the part where I carried them around with me around my neck all the time.

Rushing towards Jenna, I leaned over my friend's body, reaching out a trembling hand. *Please don't be dead. Please don't be dead. Please don't—*

Just as I made contact with the skin on her neck to check for a pulse, her eyes snapped open. A startled scream ripped from my chest. *She's alive! I pulled the Rider out of her and—and she's alive! My vision didn't come true!*

Hurling myself at her, I wrapped my arms around her small frame. "I did it! I actually did it!"

The next thing I knew I was being shoved out of the way and Jeremy was pulling Jenna into his arms. I watched as the two of them began to kiss like they hadn't seen each other in years. When Jenna let loose a long moan, I knew it was time to leave the two of them alone, at least for now. I really didn't need to see them get naked. *Now I know how they feel when I do that kind stuff in front of them. Blah! Karma is a bitch!*

But even with my seemingly underappreciated role in saving Jenna from her Rider, I couldn't wipe the smile off my face as I left the room, Khol and Morag close behind me.

"Khol!" I turned, bouncing up towards him with open arms. "I did it, I saved her!"

Khol sidestepped me and I frowned. "I knew you could do it," he said, obvious pride in his voice. But not only had he avoided my touch, but he didn't use his term of endearment for me either.

My frown deepened into a scowl. "Khol, we need to talk."

"No, we don't. You already know what you need to do to fix things between us. There's nothing else left to discuss." The muscles in his jaw ticked as he looked off over my head, not meeting my gaze. "I'm not staying here. I'll be at my brother's, but I will still hear your call if you're in danger or need me for something important."

My stomach roiled. "Zen—" But I wouldn't ask him, that's what he wanted. Would Zen be at his brother's with him? Would he be seeking comfort in her arms? Or did he just want me to think he was so that I got jealous and gave him what he ultimately wanted. "Fine," I finished up with instead.

I turned to Morag who was shaking her head with a bemused smile on her face. "Will you stay here then? Please?"

"I'd be happy to stay here for a bit, niece, maybe see what the local scenery has to offer an old dragon like me." She winked at me before disappearing, clearly not meaning scenery as in landscape. *Again with her...ewww.*

Turning back towards Khol, I realized he was already gone.

Slumping against the wall, I sighed heavily. There I was, in my moment of victory, with no one to celebrate with. *Whatever.*

Trudging to my room, alone, my mood turned slightly sour, despite the happy turn of events. *It's these damn pregnancy hormones and not because of Khol. Definitely not because of him. Not even a little bit.*

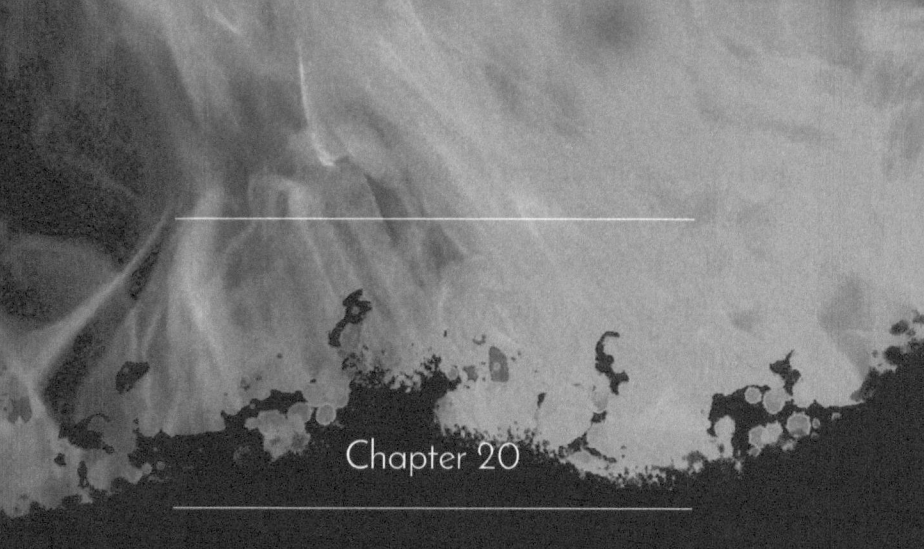

Chapter 20

I was in my room for only about twenty minutes when the door swung open, and in rushed Jenna, her purple hair flying and her face aglow with delight. Behind her trailed five squeaking rats. I should have been surprised but somehow with her, I was only taken off guard when things were normal. The unusual was completely normal for Jenna, with her the unexpected is expected.

"They're talking to me again!"

"I can see that." I laughed despite the fact that five huge rats were now getting acquainted with my room. I scrunched up my face. "Can you please tell your little friends to keep their dirty paws to themselves when they're in my room—like literally?"

"You can't catch anything from them unless they bite you, you know. And they won't." Jenna crossed her arms over her chest. She glared at me a moment before another ear-to-ear grin broke out across her face. "You have no idea what a relief it is to have that thing out of me!"

"I'm glad I can only imagine. So…" I tried to ignore her little friends who were not complying with my hands off policy. "That was a pretty quick reunion with Jeremy," I said distractedly. Why did the filthy rodents have to be so smart? One of them was currently opening my desk drawer to peer in. *They better stay out of my clothes drawers because I'm so not in the mood to rewash everything.*

"Oh, we're gonna catch up more thoroughly later." Jenna winked at me. "I was just too excited about everything else to have anything more than a quickie. Plus, with Jeremy, all that's needed is for him to touch me for him to take care of business. But what about you, have you done the deed with Khol yet? Are you guys like dragon official?" She made a move to look at the back of my neck.

I quickly ducked out of her reach, blushing as I remembered from first-hand experience how Jeremy's Gatekeeper powers could take care of a girl with little more than a kiss. "No, we haven't bonded as *Anam Caras* yet."

Her lips tightened and she frowned. "Well, why the hell not? At least you said *yet*. Although I thought I'd convinced you that you were just torturing yourself by denying yourself the lusciousness of all that is Khol. Please don't tell me you ignored my advice, as usual."

"Everything's just so complicated, Jenna."

"Well duh, life is complicated, and you're always so

angsty and overly dramatic. Watching you and your love life is like getting to see a living version of a soap opera." *Now where have I heard that before?*

"Hey, that's a little uncalled for and over the top. My life does not—" *Well hell, maybe it kind of does. She isn't the only one to think so either.*

"You're thinking about it now, aren't you? Realizing you have a problem is half the battle."

"I'm not overly dramatic." *Is my nose growing?* I had to fight the illogical urge to check. "Sooo... I found out that Bryn being in my life basically kept me from having a sex with a bunch of guys. I would have made you look like a nun."

"Whaaa?" Jenna guffawed. "Ummm...this I need to hear."

I spent the next thirty minutes, give or take, filling Jenna in on everything that I could think of that she missed, and it was the longest in our entire lives that she'd ever remained silent.

"Hooooly shit," she drawled out when I'd finally finished. "That is a lot to take in."

"I know." I sighed, relieved from finally getting to spill everything to her. I'd missed her so much.

"Your life would make the best made for T.V. drama ever. I had to fight the urge to tell you to hold on while I went and popped some popcorn." She laughed.

"Jenna, you're kind of missing my point." I waved my arms around. "My life could be a made for T.V. drama." I stared at her expectantly.

She twirled a purple piece of hair around her finger. "Yeah, things are a bit more complicated than I originally thought. Except for one part."

"What?"

"Just sleep with Khol and get it over with already."

I groaned as I dropped my face into my hands. "Oh my God, I just had a flashback but instead of you saying that about Khol you were saying it about Bryn and we were in the school cafeteria, and you were eyeing up Evan Thompson... hell, your hair was even almost exactly the same shade of purple."

She chortled. "Would you have really left me with Evan sloppy seconds if Bryn hadn't been around?" My face heated with mortification, which was answer enough for her. "Niiiice."

"Eww. I can't believe you just said that."

"It's funny because it didn't really happen. Trust me, if you would have done that to me for real I would have had to smack you around some."

Time to talk about something she probably didn't want to, which also served as the perfect distraction and subject change. "Have you seen Macon yet?"

She grimaced. "No, and why would I want to?"

"Because he still cares about you and was worried. At least let him know you're okay now."

She huffed and began picked at her nails. "I'm sure he's heard by this point."

"Jenna, you have to listen to me, red dragons feel things differently, more deeply. Even if he isn't in love with you, his feelings for you are probably more intense than any normal guy."

"More reason to avoid him. A clean break is better—easier. Besides he seems to think I'm only with Jeremy because of that little trick he can do with his powers. I find that super insulting."

I rubbed at my temples. "Easier for who? And are you?"

Being with with a guy who could get you off from little more than a kiss definitely was an added bonus but not a reason to be with him. Jenna seemed to genuinely be into Jeremy, more than I'd ever seen her be into anyone before, but sometimes it was hard to figure out what was really going on with her.

"Yeah, it's easier for me, of course. And his Gatekeeper mojo certainly doesn't work against him." Her brown eyes glittered. "By the way, it was pretty kickass what you did for me, you know I love you, right? I'm sorry I—well that I tried to kill you."

"It wasn't you," I said gruffly, trying not to spiral down into a sappy moment. *I cry way too much as it is with my pregnancy hormones.*

"That's what I keep telling myself," she grumbled, her head dropping forward as she stared blankly at the floor. A few heartbeats of silence passed before she perked up again. "So now that you've figured out how to remove the Riders, and you saved my ass, now what?"

"Yeah, I hadn't really gotten past the saving you part. That was kind of high up on my list."

"And next on your"—she demonstratively cleared her throat— "*to do* list, most definitely should be Khol."

"Jenna, come on. Seriously… I'm starting to feel déjà vu all over again. Don't you understand about Bryn?"

"Sure I do. But you can't bring him back, P.J." She nibbled on her bottom lip. "I miss him too, you know."

"I know you do, but it's just not the same."

"Well duh," Jenna said.

"The thing is, no matter how I feel about Khol, I chose Bryn. It doesn't matter that he died, he was the one I picked. All this talk of Khol and me being destined to be together, like Bryn was some kind of cannon fodder, well, what if he hadn't died? We would be together. I just can't even begin to fathom that Bryn was destined to die just so I could have Khol."

"He didn't die just so you could have Khol, P.J. Maybe it was his fate to die protecting the woman he loved. Maybe—"

"But the only way for me to have ended up with Khol, no matter what way I look at it, is if Bryn died. I chose him, we were bonded, he was my *Anam Cara* fully and completely. If my birth mother placed Bryn in my path to help me become who I am today, then fine. But if I was meant to be with Khol I should have chosen him at that point, not Bryn."

"You can't torture yourself with the what ifs. You just have to go with what is laid out before you now. Khol is here, and you love him. He may even be the father of your child. Stop over analyzing what could have been with Bryn," Jenna said softly.

"I think it's just the fact that my birth mother told Khol in that letter that we—-Khol and me—would end up together—for him to be patient—I mean—what the hell? Maybe if it wasn't for that all of this wouldn't bother me so much. I feel like Bryn was used, and I was the one who used and discarded him only so I could end up with Khol in the end. It just doesn't seem right."

"P.J. stop. Just stop. I think your hormones are making you act more crazy than normal. Let the guilt go." Jenna sat up, staring at me as if she was trying to figure out a complicated puzzle. "Just let Khol love you, and love him back. It really is that simple."

Our girlie bonding time was interrupted by a knock on my door followed by Jeremy's intrusion. My worries were temporarily forgotten when I saw how happy he seemed. It was like going back in time with him as well. He ran his hand through his already messy brown hair and shifted uncomfortably. "Hey, I just was kind of wondering when Jenna was—well she's been in here talking with you a long time."

Jenna went to him, wrapping her arms around his waist. "Awe...are you being needy?"

He grinned sheepishly at her, avoiding eye contact with me. "Yeah, I guess, it's just I didn't think you'd be gone so long."

"We had lots of best friend stuff to catch up on. But I

think it's time P.J. goes and finds Khol to do more than just talk."

"Jenna...seriously." I let out a long sigh.

Jenna and Jeremy turned and started towards my door, her little rodent friends scurrying after her. A big black one was carrying one of my socks. I figured I'd let him keep it. "I fully expect to see one of those tattoos on the back of your neck the next time I see you, Miss Stone."

I didn't respond. Instead I just glared at Jenna's back. She pulled the door shut behind her and I slumped back on my bed. I was left alone...yet again. It was a pattern I was really starting to resent. Being alone with my thoughts was always hazardous to my health.

Is Jenna right? Should I just go to Khol and turn my brain off and simply let my feelings run the show? But what if he was trying to not think about me while he was in Zen's arms? What if he was testing out her theory of not loving me? What if she was right and he bonded with her? What if I already lost Khol forever?

My chest tightened as I struggled to catch my breath. It was only then, as panic had me in its strangle-hold, that I fully realized how royally stupid I'd been acting. *What if it's already too late?* I tried to tell my lungs to fill with air, but my body wasn't responding. I clutched at my throat, my arms and legs going numb, as the edges of my vision went fuzzy.

It'll be okay. If I pass out, I'll start breathing automatically.

Unless something is really wrong and I'm going to drop dead right here, right now from lack of oxygen. Oh my God! I'm dying, aren't I?

I continued to gasp for air.

Khol's already moved on. He won't even care that I'm dead.

And my son. Will someone save him before it's too late for him too? Is he even developed enough to survive outside of my body yet?

We're both dying, aren't we? Help us! Someone please help us!

If only I—

Crumpling to the floor, my world went dark.

Chapter 21

My lungs burned as they filled with oxygen, and I sighed with relief. *I must have passed out and started to breath, just like the logical part of me knew would happen. You're fine. Your son is fine. Everything is fine.*

Someone cleared their throat, and I rocketed into a sitting position, blinking Lorik's face into focus. "What are you doing here?" I scanned my room to see if he was by himself. "Where's Khol?"

"He wanted me to come check on you. He felt your distress." Lorik reached his hand out and helped me into a better sitting position. Luckily, I'd already been in bed when I passed so I didn't have to worry about my baby being injured from the fall. *I really have to stop passing out, it's absolutely ridiculous. Embarrassing, really. Although not all of them are one hundred percent my fault.*

Wait. What? My heart dropped into my stomach as Lorik's words sank in. Khol felt my distress and he sent Lorik to come check up on me. "Why didn't he come himself?"

Lorik met my eyes with something resembling pity. "I think you already know why."

My throat became constricted again and my breathing labored. "Zen, he's with Zen."

Lorik shook his head. "No, but he should be with her."

Confusion washed over me. "I don't understand. Then why isn't he here?"

"He wants you to pursue him." Lorik tilted his dark head to study me. "But we both know that won't ever happen." He then stood, pacing the confines of my small room. "Look, I just want my brother to be happy. Zen would make him happy. She's been falling all over him since we were kids. She'd treat him the way he deserves. She'd—"

"He doesn't love her," I interrupted. "He loves me. You know what that means for a male dragon."

"I'm not entirely sure he's in love with you. Zen makes a very good point about that. And the only way to test that theory is to get him to try and bond with her. If the bond happens, then he isn't in love with you. If it doesn't, then he is."

"But isn't—aren't you and Zen—I mean—" I sputtered.

"Yeah, Zen and I are lovers, and I care about her, but I can never love her the way she needs. I lost the one I love and will probably never feel that way again. Zen—well, Zen and I have an understanding, a very convenient one, but I'm not the one she really wants. I'm the wrong brother."

"So you came here to talk me into letting Zen have Khol or something? Or at least to let her see if he really is in love with me?" I narrowed my eyes at him. "If Khol wanted her he had plenty of chances before he met me—before he fell in love with me."

"We could go back and forth on this for a while. The only way to really find out is to give the two of them a chance."

"No! Khol is mine!"

"Then you should have let him claim you like I know he wanted." Lorik stepped closer to me, his eyes growing brighter, illuminating the intensity in them. "I'm sorry."

A chill ran up my spine. "For what?"

"For what I'm about to do." He reached over, gripping my arm tightly and shifted me out of my bed.

We reappeared in a small room I didn't recognize and before I had a chance to react, he slapped a huge metal cuff on my left wrist. I flew at him, absolutely furious, but he shifted out of my grasp and outside of the open door, which I realized for the first time had bars blocking the way. In a panic, I tried to shift after him but nothing happened. My head swam and I clutched at the bars. I didn't feel right, it was like when I'd first gone to Morag's land and my powers had been stripped. I glanced down at the cuff, realization dawning. It was spelled, I just wasn't sure to what extent. I had no powers. "What are you doing?"

"Don't worry. I'm not going to hurt you. You are our queen after all, no matter how young you are."

"What are you doing?" I asked again, my voice climbing a few octaves.

"I thought I'd made that part clear. I'm giving Zen and Khol a chance to explore Zen's theory, but for that to happen you need to be out of the way," Lorik stated calmly, as if he wasn't talking about ruining the last chance I had at happiness.

My knuckles whitened as my grip on the bars tightened. "Please—Lorik—don't do this to me. I love him. You have to know I love him. But I just lost Bryn and I'm still grieving. I don't have my head on straight. And what about our child?" I was hoping he still thought my son was one hundred percent Khol's so I could use him as leverage by way of guilt.

"Khol will still be a father to that child no matter what happens. I think you already know that."

"Please—please don't do this to me. Didn't you hear me? I love him. I'm just…it's just—"

"You just don't love him enough. I know all about Bryn. I know about everything. Khol was so distraught he actually confided in me. I just want my brother to be happy." Lorik looked at me and frowned. "I'm really sorry about all of this—it's the only way to know for sure."

"He's gonna know you did something to me—he's gonna come for me—"

"I'm going to tell him you weren't there when I went to check on you. He felt your panic. He'll assume the worst. And when he finds out otherwise, it'll be too late."

"What about the Riders? I have to save this world!" I was grasping at straws, I knew Lorik didn't care all that much for humans, but I had nothing left to try and persuade him with.

"You know I don't care about any of that," he said, echoing what I'd just thought.

I glanced at the cuff on my wrist. "So this thing, it blocks all my powers as well as my connection with Khol?"

Lorik nodded in affirmation. "Yes, after the panic he felt in you right before I put the cuff on, he was probably already searching for you in a panic of his own. But then he would have felt the connection break and he's going to assume you're dead. I better get back to him." Lorik looked at me with pity again. "I really am sorry."

He disappeared.

"Noooo!" I screamed. "Don't do this to me!"

I shook the bars, pulled at them, pushed at them...but they refused to budge. If I had my powers I could shift out or melt them with fire. The real problem was the spelled cuff on my wrist that was blocking all of my escape options.

Okay. I need to think. I just need to think. I scanned the room for possible aids to my plight, but I saw none. I sat down on the floor and studied the bracelet. It was thick and smooth, with no visible seam. I ran my fingertips over it to try and find the opening, but nothing. I gritted my teeth with frustration. *It must be spelled to stay on me too. Great.* I couldn't even fit my pinky finger between the metal and my skin.

How can Lorik do this to me? I'm going to burn him to a crisp. Khol probably thought I was dead. Adrenaline surged through my system as I considered what he must be going through. "Oh, God," I muttered to myself. What if he really did turn to Zen for comfort? With a forced break in our bond, would that be enough even if Khol really was in love with me? Could the forced break fool the—the whatever—that keeps a male dragon faithful once they're in love? Or would he only be able to bond with Zen if he wasn't in love with me like she hoped? Either way—Khol could still find comfort in her arms. How would I feel, even if he didn't bond with her, if he did have sex with her?

My stomach clenched and bile shot into throat. Would I be able to forgive him—welcome him with open arms, if he had sex with Zen? It wasn't like they didn't have a past.

The visceral memory of them kissing raced across my mind, but then it veered off into something else, fueled by my fears. Images of them naked, kissing, their bodies writhing together—

I pulled my knees up as tight as they could go with my baby bump and wrapped my arms around my legs. Tears streamed down my cheeks as my fears continued to provide graphic imagery of Zen and Khol together.

It's my fault, all my fault. If only I'd let Khol claim me as his Anam Cara *when he wanted, I wouldn't be here in this situation. I wouldn't be here, alone, while I wonder how long it'll take before my fears become a reality.*

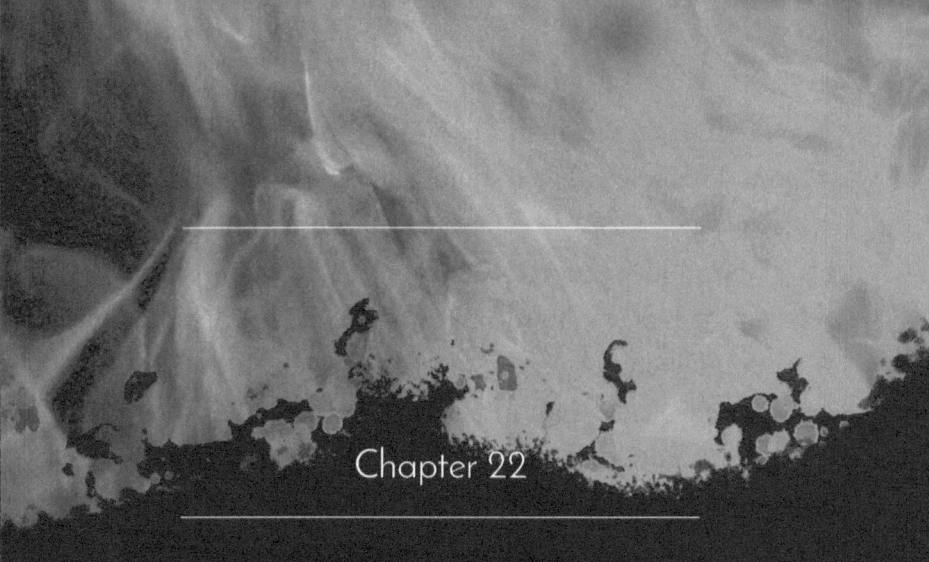

Chapter 22

My life had taken on a very distinct circular pattern, which colored it all in an eerie déjà vu-ish vibe. Because here I was, locked in a room to keep me from the man I loved. Sure, the first time around it was my room in my parent's house, and it was Bryn and not Khol but, I mean come on... I'd have to be deaf, dumb, and blind to spot the parallels. Or maybe it was because I just kept repeating the same mistakes and not learning from them? How did that saying go? If you don't learn from the past, then history is doomed to repeat itself. Well, my history was definitely repeating itself.

I sighed, turning away from the huge flat screen T.V. that was mounted on the wall across from the bed. I guess Lorik thought he'd offer me some kindness in the form of distraction while I was his prisoner. But he apparently didn't get the memo that I was more of a book girl, and I couldn't take much more of the crap running on the limited channels that I could tune in to. *He could at least have gotten me some decent movie channels.*

My mind wandered to a subject I'd been pondering a lot in the last few hours, give or take a day or three since I'd completely lost track of time. My birth mother had informed Khol that him and I were destined to be together. Did that info translate to me not needing to worry? Or was that outcome contingent on me doing something to put my future on that path? *Should I just be sitting here all complacent, twiddling my frickin' metaphorical thumbs, or should I be taking action? Coming up with a plan? But what? I'm out of ideas?*

Rubbing my belly idly, I let my boredom lull me into a semi-conscious state of sleep. I wasn't really dreaming, more of daydreaming, and my mind naturally carried me back in time to my childhood when I'd been similarly bored. Of course, that also meant I'd conjure memories of Bryn.

"Be careful!" Bryn called from the kitchen countertop across from me. There's alligators in that moat. If you fall they'll get you." Bryn gave me a wide-eyed look and pointed at the completely harmless linoleum floor.

I narrowed my eyes at him. "I thought the floor was lava." I hated when Bryn changed the rules of our games mid-play. It really messed with what I was imagining.

He shook his head and grinned at me, his dark hair falling into his mischievous blue eyes. "It was...but we got away from that. Now we're seeking sanctuary in the castle. But first you have to jump over the moat."

I crossed my arms over my chest. "Sanctuary from what?"

"Ummm..." he drawled while scratching his head. "I don't know, something evil, something really, really evil." He grinned, opening his arms to me. "Come on Peej, just jump."

I scrunched my nose at him. "I'll jump when I have a good reason. I—"

"Just jump! Come on—just jump, Peej! Jump!" Bryn exclaimed with excitement. "If you don't it's gonna get you! It's right behind you! Jump!"

Grinning, I let out a squeal as I jumped towards him. I slid across the counter in my socks and nearly knocked Bryn over. He laughed. "You're safe inside the sanctuary of the castle now. Don't worry."

"I wanna meet the lord and lady of the castle. Is there a prince?" I demanded of him.

"Of course there's a prince, and you're looking right at him." Bryn stood up to his full height and puffed out his chest. He turned cool eyes to me. "Prince Bryn at your service." He bowed low.

I stood up and shoved at him. "You're not a prince, at least not mine anyways." I giggled. "I'm gonna marry a prince one day, and then I'll have my very own castle."

"No, I'm not your prince, because you're gonna marry a king, and I'll be your Guardian knight. You'll be my queen." He knelt down in front of me. "And I'll slay all the dragons you want me to for you."

Of course we'd had it all wrong as kids. Instead of

slaying dragons, we'd turned out to be dragons. And I didn't need to marry a king to become queen.

I wiped at the wetness on my cheeks, trying not to dwell on Bryn anymore, or Khol for that matter. But what was I left with? I didn't really want to think about the Riders either, since I was stuck as Lorik's prisoner without the ability to do anything about them.

Ah! I can't take this anymore! I need out of here! Fighting the urge to scream, which would ultimately be pointless, I sprung to my feet and began to pace. *How long will I be trapped here before Lorik is satisfied that Khol and Zen had sufficient time to explore what was really between them?*

After burning off some of my anxious energy, I finally settled back down on the bed, allowing my frustration and boredom to suck me all the way down into sleep.

"Peej! Wake up!" Someone was yelling seemingly right next to my head. "Peej! You need to wake up! Now!"

Jolting up, my heart thrashed against my ribcage as I took in the image of an almost transparent Bryn standing right next to the bed. "Whaa—?" I started, but thick smoke caused me to choke. Confused, I glanced around frantically while attempting to shake off the heaviness in my body.

"There's a fire, you need to—goddamnit it—this can't happen!"

Dropping to the floor, I held a pillow against my nose and mouth. Smoke poured into the small room, thick and black, shooting panic through my system. "Bryn! What do I do?"

His translucent form paced in front of me. "I don't know—I don't—crawl into the bathroom—wait—take the sheet and comforter with you."

Without giving much thought to the fact that Bryn was helping me as some kind of spirit, or that I was in danger of being killed, yet again, I followed his directions. Although I didn't so much as crawl, but scurry on my hands and knees into the bathroom. Crawling with a baby inside of me wasn't something that I felt was feasible, let alone good for my unborn son's health. Once inside the bathroom I pushed the door shut with my foot. "Now what?" I coughed.

"Soak both the sheets and comforter in cold water and then stuff one around the bottom of the door and then you get in the shower and wrap the other around you. Once you're in the shower, turn the cold water on. Hopefully the pipes won't break, and that'll be enough."

"Enough for what?" I asked while hurrying to do what he directed.

"Enough to keep you and your baby alive."

"Oh, well, me fighting for my life, that's nothing new." I couldn't help the bitterness that seeped into my tone. "If it's not one thing, it's another. Maybe it'd be a relief to leave this all behind. What good am I doing anyone anyways?" I didn't mean it, I was just angry, and tired… mostly tired of having to fight so hard for just the ability to keep sucking oxygen into my lungs on a daily basis.

"Don't say that! Don't you ever say that again!" Bryn's voice vibrated with anger.

I crawled into the tub, turned the shower on, and then pulled the already soaked sheet around me. "I'm sorry." I shivered. "I didn't really mean any of that. You know how I can be." I tugged the sheet over my head and closed my eyes. "Bryn?"

"Yeah?" he snapped.

"Come and talk to me so I can pretend you're really here."

"I am really here, Peej. I'm just a useless spirit is all."

"You're not useless Bryn, you woke me up, and that could make all the difference in the world." I paused to cough, my throat raw from the inhaled smoke I'd already inhaled. "How are you here? I mean how can I see you?"

"Honestly, I don't know." There was a long pause before he spoke again. "I'm always kind of...watching over you. Still trying to be your Guardian, I guess. I mean, I try not to but I can't seem to help myself. I'm not supposed to, you know." He chuckled darkly. "But yeah, like I said before, neither one of us has ever been very good at sticking to the rules. So I was watching you when the fire started, and I wanted to be here so badly—to protect you —and then suddenly you could hear me."

I smiled, although I knew he couldn't see it. "So you're stalking me from beyond the grave?"

I could hear the answering smile in his voice. "Yeah, I guess I am."

I sobered when I really thought about what that meant. "But you shouldn't worry about me anymore, Bryn. You should be doing whatever it is you should be doing after you die."

I swallowed past the lump in my throat. I missed being able to just talk to Bryn. Sometimes it felt like things weren't real because I didn't get to tell him. He had always been the first person I ran to with good or bad news. Now I had no one. Maybe Khol could have filled that role eventually, if I hadn't royally screwed up our relationship.

"What is it that you should be doing?" I asked, burning curiosity taking hold.

"Yeah, I'm not too sure about that either. I'm in some kind of limbo—well, not limbo exactly, I mean it's nice and all but I don't get to go anywhere until a few things are decided first."

"Like wha—"

"And before you ask like what, I can't tell you. Sorry," he mumbled.

"Mmmm …" I grunted. "What started the fire?"

"It's electrical, caused by some wiring from the cable hookup."

I ground my teeth together. "Figures. I'm gonna be done in by bad reality T.V. shows."

We sat in silence for a few moments before Bryn spoke again. "I miss you, Peej."

I choked back a sob. "I miss you too—so much Bryn—so much."

"But—"

I snorted. "How did I know there was gonna be a but?"

"But I'm not alive anymore. You can't spend the rest of your life mourning the loss of me."

I threw back the sheet from my head, blinking rapidly as the water from the shower beat down into my face as I focused in on his translucent form. "I know you're dead! Don't you think I know that? But you know it's not that simple. How can you want me to be with Khol?"

Bryn stared at me, his expression grim. "I walked away once when I was alive because I thought it was best for you, and now I'm dead. I just want what's best for you." He flicked his gaze to settle somewhere over my shoulder. "At least I had a brief moment of complete happiness with you before I died."

"It's not good enough, Bryn! It's just not!"

"It's more than some get."

"It's not—" I started but he rose, going to the door. He glanced back at me before passing through it. He was only gone for a moment before he reappeared, his expression panicked.

"Get back under the sheet and turn the water all the way on cold."

I immediately complied, shaking under the freezing water and soaked sheet. "The fire's almost here, isn't it?"

"Yeah," he rasped.

I closed my eyes and shuddered. "Of all the ways I thought I might die, I never imagined this."

"Don't say that. There's still time."

"For what Bryn? The only one who knows I'm here is Lorik. I haven't seen him since he brought me here. He stocked the room with food and water so he wouldn't need to come back often. By the time he comes to check on me it'll be too late."

"Goddamnit!" he bellowed. "This can't be happening!"

"Bryn just come talk to me, it might be the last chance we have." I couldn't stop shaking. I peered out of the opening in the sheet, so I could see Bryn's face.

He crouched down in front of me, reaching out his hand as if he was going to touch me, but dropped it back to his side instead. "I wish I could touch you, Peej. Even just for a second."

"I wish you could too," I managed around chattering teeth.

"Peej, you have to promise me, if you make it through this—*when* you make it through this—you'll take Khol as your *Anam Cara*." His sea storm eyes implored me.

"Why?" I cried out. "Why would you want me to promise that?"

"It's time for you to stop mourning me. I hate seeing you deny yourself happiness. He's better for you than me, and he always has been."

"Name one thing that makes him a better choice over you," I growled.

"He's alive."

"But you tried to walk away even when you were alive. What makes you think he won't too? Why do you—"

"He can give you things I can't, Peej. I knew from the beginning" —he dropped his gaze from mine—"from our first kiss that it wouldn't last." He clenched his jaw, running his hand through his tousled and still dry hair, which served as a reminder that he was in spirit form. "I wanted it to—you have to know I wanted that more than anything. But it became abundantly clear that he's who you're meant to be with—not me. You should have chosen him. I know you love him. Don't try to deny it."

He lifted his dragon blue eyes to meet mine again, and he smiled faintly. "That you love me the way you do, even when you've moved on and you love him more—because you will, Peej. You will love him more, and you'll wonder how you ever stayed away from him for so long. Well—I'm just thankful I got to experience the bliss of loving you and having you love me back, even if it was for a short period of time."

His eyes glazed over like they were filling with tears. *Can ghosts cry?* "I just want you to be happy. Now that I'm dead I can be truly selfless for the first time with you. He'll make you happy."

Bryn knows I love Khol. Guilt and shame engulfed me. "Bryn—"

"Just promise me."

I shook my head. "No. I can't—" *I'm so screwed up. I think even my issues have issues.* I loved Khol. Even Bryn knew it. And yet I still couldn't fully commit to the notion of letting Khol claim me as his *Anam Cara*. Was it all guilt caused from Bryn's death, or fear that if I let Khol in all the way and lost him that I'd be completely destroyed? I almost didn't come back from losing Bryn. If I lost Khol—my life actually would be over.

Bryn stood abruptly and exclaimed, "Jenna! Why didn't I think of it before?" The door exploded as flames consumed the wood hungrily, and I screamed. "I just hope it's not too late." He then wavered and disappeared, leaving me to stare at the advancing fire alone.

Scrambling as far into the corner of the tub as possible, I prayed that whatever idea Bryn had just stumbled upon would give me a last minute reprieve. I didn't want to die, and I really didn't want to burn to death. The irony of someone like me succumbing to a regular fire, just because of the stupid power-dampening bracelet Lorik had placed on me was almost embarrassing. It would be like a Mermaid drowning.

I pulled the sheet over my head completely, not wanting to watch as the flames crackled and popped their way towards me eagerly. Fire was not going to be a fun way to go. I'd seen people burn to death and it looked like it hurt...a lot.

"Where is she?" an achingly familiar voice bellowed.

"In here!" I croaked, my throat raw. "I'm in here!"

A blur of color moved through the flames, and suddenly I was being scooped up into Khol's strong arms. His voice filled with rough emotion, he rumbled something in a language I didn't understand as he clutched me to his chest and shifted me away from danger.

Chapter 23

Khol quickly stripped the wet clothes from my body, turning his shower on, and placing me in it. The temperate water soothed and relaxed, calming my nerves and chasing away the chill from the ice water I'd doused myself in for protection. The cuff that Lorik had placed on me clattered to the tile with just one touch from Khol. I wasn't sure how he'd done it, but I didn't care as long as the stupid thing was off. He then stripped himself, stepping under the spray with me. He pressed his burning body against mine, running his hands slowly over my skin. A tingling sensation sparked through me as he set to work on healing any injuries. My abdomen spasmed, and I gritted my teeth. *Something isn't right.*

Khol tipped my face up towards him, gazing into my eyes with determination. "It will all be fine. Trust me."

Even though I was naked and in the shower with Khol,

any chance of it turning sexual in nature evaporated when the meaning of his words sank in. He was trying to heal my unborn baby. *Something really is wrong.* I glanced down at the shower floor and saw blood. "Oh my God!" I gasped. "Kho—"

"Shh—" He whispered soothingly. "He's going to be just fine."

Lifting my head, I locked my gaze with Khol's, anchoring myself to him. His eyes blazed with raw determination. "Okay," I said. He would save my baby, and make everything better again, just like he always did.

As his healing touch roamed my body, a different kind of heat swept through my system, despite me thinking it would be impossible a few moments before. Clearly my son was now out of danger if my rising desire for Khol was any indication.

Heaving I sigh of relief, I stood on my tiptoes in an attempt to reach Khol's lips with mine, but apparently, I was the only one feeling amorous at the moment.

"Let's get you dried off and into bed. I healed both of you, but your body still had quite a shock, and you need to rest," Khol rumbled, scooping me up. He swaddled me in a large towel and carried me into his bedroom.

I peered around anxiously, half-expecting to see Zen there. Khol would protect me no matter what happened between him and Zen, so what if him not wanting to kiss me was more than him being concerned for my current state? What if the lack of sexual tension in the beginning of our shower encounter was because he didn't want me anymore? What if he was bonded with her? My heart pounding out an erratic rhythm, I squirmed in Khol's arms, trying to nonchalantly get a look at the back of his neck.

"What are you doing?" Khol glanced down at me with curiosity as he deposited me on his bed. He then disappeared one moment and reappeared the next, holding in his hands my favorite pair of pajamas. The pants had little penguins on them, and the top had two penguins snuggling together. Being from Pittsburgh, I always associated any penguins with our hockey team. Most of the stuff I slept in was covered with the cute little guys. Khol handed them to me and subtly turned around so I could put them on. But I had other more pressing matters to concern myself with.

When he turned, I tried to get a look at the back of his neck again, but instead of seeing anything, I ended up slipping out of bed and landing on my ass, completely naked. *Fabulous. Good thing Khol and his healing powers are nearby, just incase.*

"What are you doing? You'll hurt yourself." Khol came to me in a blur of speed and he placed me back on his bed. "Do you need help?" He eyed my pajamas speculatively.

My cheeks burned and nervous energy pinged around in my gut. *Why is he acting so cold towards me? It most definitely isn't a good sign. Fuck, fuck, fuck ...*

"Are you bonded with Zen?" I notched my chin up and gritted my teeth. *Don't break down. If he is bonded with her, you will not break down in front of him. You will be emotionless.*

Khol's lips pursed as he studied me like I'd suddenly sprouted a second and third head. "Why are you asking me that question?"

Fisting the sheets, I forced myself to remain where I was. "Just answer the question," I hissed.

Khol grinned. "No. Why would you think that?"

"Why are you smiling at me like a loon? I hate you!" The relief of his answer caused some emotional dam to break inside of me and I began to sob. "I hate you so much." I had no idea why I was telling him that I hated him, when I meant the exact opposite. "If you're not bonded to her then why didn't you let me kiss you?"

Khol had me cradled against his chest in a flash, cupping the back of my head to him with his large warm hand. He was wearing nothing but a towel around his waist and my hormones took notice.

"I just healed you, and your unborn son." He paused to pull away from me, tilting my face up so he could meet my gaze. "I also just learned the woman I had been mourning, the woman I love was not, in fact, dead like I thought." He toyed with the ends of my still damp hair. "If I would've allowed myself to kiss you, I wouldn't have been able to stop."

I smiled through my tears. "You still want me?"

He dipped his head, his warm breath rushing over my shoulder and along the side of my face. "As if I could ever not want you."

A shiver ran along my spine, leaving fresh desire in its wake. "Oh Khol!" I threw my arms around his waist, burying my face in his chest. "I thought—I thought—"

"After everything, you still doubt my feelings for you?"

I tightened my grip on him and inhaled his fresh scent, letting it sooth my nerves. "Zen and Lorik both seemed pretty convinced that things might not be what I thought they were between us. And Morag showed me another version of reality, that if I hadn't known Bryn, you wouldn't have come for me—"

As I started to explain I realized how much that had been bothering me. I wanted to believe Khol would come for me no matter what, even though, I knew deep down that the me from the other reality wasn't the same me at all. If Khol loved me for who I was—the person that was in his arms right now—then he wouldn't be able to love that other version of me. It was like I was two separate people. I knew that intellectually, but my heart still felt betrayed. Of course, I'd learned that little tid bit of information right on the heels of seeing him in a liplock with Zen. I knew I had no right to doubt his feelings for me because of all of that—but—okay maybe everyone had a point about me being overly dramatic.

"So you allowed yourself to doubt my feelings for you in this reality because the me in another didn't feel for you as strongly as I do for you here?"

"Yes," I said sheepishly. "But you make it sound completely different than how it sounded in my head."

"You mean I make it sound utterly ridiculous? Because that's how it sounds to me," Khol growled.

"Khol—" I wrapped a piece of his hair around my finger. "How did you find me? What happened—with everything?" As usual I was full of questions—always so many questions.

"Not now—I can't talk about" —a low growl emanated from Khol's chest— "about what my own brother did to me—to you. I want to forget any of it happened." The hand that had been holding the back of my head to him slid down my spine and I bowed into his touch, moaning. "Right now, I just want to hold you."

"Just hold?" I was surprised by the raspy quality of my voice.

Khol stilled, and I could feel the tension in his body. "You need your rest—"

"But you healed me—maybe I don't want you to hold me—maybe I want more."

It was time for me to stop living with all the *what ifs* in my life. I needed to take the opportunities I had for happiness when I had them, and to stop repeating the same mistakes over and over again. I had an epiphany in that bathroom when the flames had been racing towards me, my death eminent. What terrified me about Khol—why I felt so damn guilty about Bryn's death, was that I knew I loved Khol just as much as I had loved Bryn.

I missed Bryn but I wanted to move on with Khol. And I hated myself just a little for that desire. Bryn was gone, and I needed to be at peace with it. But I was afraid if I moved on with Khol that I would one day forget Bryn, therefore dishonoring all that we shared.

I thought the kind of love I had with Bryn only came once in a lifetime, but I was beyond lucky—because for me it'd come twice. And it was different, the love I had for Bryn and the love I felt for Khol. Bryn and I had grown together over many, many years, and an understanding of each other had come from that. But with Khol—he understood me now, who I was becoming and who I needed to be in my future. And in that future, he was the man I wanted by my side. Khol had been right all along, what Bryn and I shared was beautiful, but fleeting. The love I could share with Khol was meant to last the rest of my lifetime.

"Khol—" I said, peering up into his iridescent green eyes. "I want...more." Hadn't he said when we'd first met that I'd come to crave more, and that he'd be the one I came to when I wanted whatever that was? Well, I wanted more, from him, and it was time to take it. "I want you to claim me—but more importantly I wanna claim you."

Flames erupted within Khol's eyes, and just before his lips came crashing down on mine, he delivered me a dazzling smile. One that stole the breath from my lungs and made my heart take off at a gallop. And that kiss—it was anything but gentle. All of his pent-up feelings for me were there on his tongue, and in the tension of his lips as he demanded complete control of my mouth. He took what he wanted from me, but this time I gave it with no reservations. His power snapped out of him, and swept into me, causing every sensation that his touch invoked to heighten to the point of almost pain—but not quite. The first time we'd had sex, it felt like my heart had turned to a block of ice in my chest, but that was because I didn't love him then.

Now, everything had changed.

"Khol, don't wait," I hissed in a breath as he nipped at my neck. "I need you—all of you—now."

A savage snarl ripped from Khol as he tore all barriers between our naked flesh to shreds. He slid into me with no resistance, and a raw moan parted my lips even as I struggled to breath properly. Our powers swirled together, intertwining in a unique dance mirroring our connection.

As our gazes collided, I saw the extent of my foolishness in rejecting Khol there within his eyes. His love burned within their fathomless depths, seemingly defining his very existence. I was his world. And I always would be.

"I love you, Khol."

His eyes shut briefly before he dipped his head to kiss me again, careful not to put his weight on my stomach. He pivoted his hips, and I gripped his shoulders for balance, tearing my lips from his as I threw my head back in pleasure.

We moved as one, and as I hung on the precipice of ecstasy, waiting for him to release me, I felt the first semblance of his power marking the back of my neck. He was claiming me for his, but more importantly I was making him mine.

"I love you," Khol growled. The combination of his declaration of love, while he was moving inside of me, as our powers where busy completing our *Anam Cara* bond —worked as a perfect storm to push me over the edge, and I let loose a keening scream of pure joy. Khol grunted at the arrival of his own release only moments later as I was still immersed in mine.

When we were finally spent, Khol tucked me into his side as I nuzzled his chest. His heart thrummed under my ear, and I inhaled his spicy scent that was stronger from his recent exertion. *Seriously, how does his sweat smell good?* Neither one of us said anything. There was no need for words at the moment, what we'd needed to say to each other had been fully expressed with our bodies, each word communicated artfully with the touch of our fingertips and the slide of our skin against one another's—so for the moment—we were all talked out.

SOMETIME DURING MY FITFUL SLEEP, Khol had come to cuddle up behind me, acting as the big spoon to my little one. His large body held me in a cocoon of warmth, with one of his arms draped possessively over my stomach, and one of his legs thrown over mine. His face was pressed up against the back of my neck, and as I stirred, he nipped at the spot where I was sure I wore his *Anam Cara* mark.

"How long have you been awake?" I asked, blinking blurry eyes into the dim lighting.

He moved his hand over my stomach, splaying his fingers out over my ever-growing baby bump. "I want him to be mine," Khol murmured wistfully.

I disentangled my legs from his and rolled onto my back. He settled himself on his elbow so that he was looking down at me, as his other hand came to rest on my belly once more. "You'll be his father regardless of the genetics. So he'll be yours, just like I am." I smiled up at him.

Khol studied me with tenderness in his face, and contentment in his eyes. "I knew you were meant to be mine the moment I awakened from my sleep and saw you. Although you put my patience to the test."

My smile widened. "I had to test you to make absolutely sure before I just gave myself to you."

Khol brushed his lips against mine, murmuring against them, "And to have you be absolutely sure made it almost worth the wait."

All uncertainty about being with Khol had been completely washed away. It felt like my heart had been healed, and although I missed Bryn, just like I was sure that I always would, I no longer felt the agony of his loss deep inside my soul. Maybe Khol had been right about the *Anam Cara* bond's magic helping me to move on. Or perhaps when I'd made my choice something inside of me had finally accepted Khol into my heart completely, and his love for me served as the glue to put it back together.

I intertwined my fingers in Khol's loose auburn hair. "Spend the day with me—in bed—naked—so that I can start making up to you for all the time I wasted making you wait for me."

A low growl rumbled within Khol's chest, and his hands slid down my body with intent. "You are well and truly *my* little queen now, and I intend to make sure that you and everyone else is well aware of that fact," he rasped, his voice barely human.

"And how are you gonna do that?" I purred as I arched up to give him better access to my exposed skin.

He licked and nibbled in an extremely sensitive area causing me to moan his name. "Just like that, although I intend to make you scream my name so loud that no one will ever doubt again who you belong to."

"Aren't you being a little full of yourself? I mean... *scream*...really?" I bit my lower lip to keep from smiling. I couldn't seem to help myself. I was burning with the heightened lust of being a newly bonded *Anam Cara*, and I was goading him on.

Khol chuckled as he set to work, and I arched up with a scream already building in my throat. Soon everyone within a five mile radius, if not farther, would know exactly who owned me in and out of the bedroom: Lord Kholkikos, ruler of the *rua arach*, and *mo Anam Cara*."

"NO, I'M NOT READY YET," I grumbled as Khol tugged the sheet off me. I reached blindly for him, the fatigue of our day in bed together still weighing heavily on me.

Khol's heated chest pressed up against my back and I shivered as he whispered in my ear, "We can at least shower together, my little queen." He danced his fingertips down my spine as he pulled away. "Because as much as I wish I could stay in bed with you indefinitely, we still have a world to save—Riders to banish."

Blinking my eyes open, I stared up into Khol's burning ones. I smiled at him. "Well, why didn't you say we'd be taking a shower together?" I bit my lower lip, letting my eyes slide down his magnificently naked body, picturing it slick from the shower as he—

Khol laughed, scooping me up in his arms. "Female dragons, completely insatiable."

"Like I hear you complaining." I nuzzled my face into his neck, inhaling deeply. His scent had changed slightly to me somehow, it was stronger, fresher, and it was *home*. Bryn used to be that place for me, but since bonding with Khol as his *Anam Cara* I was beginning to think that my dragon senses combined with Bryn and my fledgling bond was what was responsible for me feeling that way. There was so much about being a dragon that I still didn't understand, but I was sure Khol would be a very willing teacher.

Khol and I took a longer shower than necessary, for obvious reasons, and when we were finally dried off I was extremely pruney, but I couldn't be bothered to care. I wanted more Khol—more of his kisses, more of his touches, more of his scent intermingled with mine...just *more*. He'd been right from the beginning. When I came to crave more, he would be the only one who could give me what I truly needed.

As he got dressed, I stood behind him, running my hands wantonly over the expanse of his rock hard chest and abs. I idly wondered what he would say if I asked to eat ice cream off his perfectly sculpted six-pack. My mind conjured up an image of me doing just that— *But uh-oh the ice cream is melting, and some of it is dripping...down, down, down his body, and I wouldn't want him to get all sticky. It's probably a good idea if I lick up every last drop, even if it takes me hours.*

"My little queen," Khol hissed as if in pain. "Our bond is even deeper now that we're *Anam Caras*—I can almost pick the images out of you mind." He whirled around, pushing me up against the wall, capturing my wrists with his hands and stretching them over my head. "Please—" he choked out as I stared up into his eyes and kept on imagining what I had been thinking of doing to him.

I quirked an eyebrow at him playfully. "Please what? Stop? Or do it for real?"

"We must—"

"We must what?" I asked, cutting him off. "I'm just thinking about how delicious you'd be with a side of ice cream." I licked my lips provocatively. "Or without."

I slipped out of Khol's hold, and he groaned. Somehow, I managed to Uno Reverse our positions, not that he put up much of a fight, and he ended up being the one leaning against the wall. Dropping down to my knees, I undid the pants he just put on. I gazed up the line of his body, meeting his blazing eyes as I began to kiss him intimately.

I felt so confident and powerful as his fingers delved into my hair with abandon. Even though I was on my knees before him, there was no doubt in my mind that I was the one in control as I demanded pleasure from him with my mouth.

Yep...Khol has most definitely created a monster. Lucky for him I'm his monster.

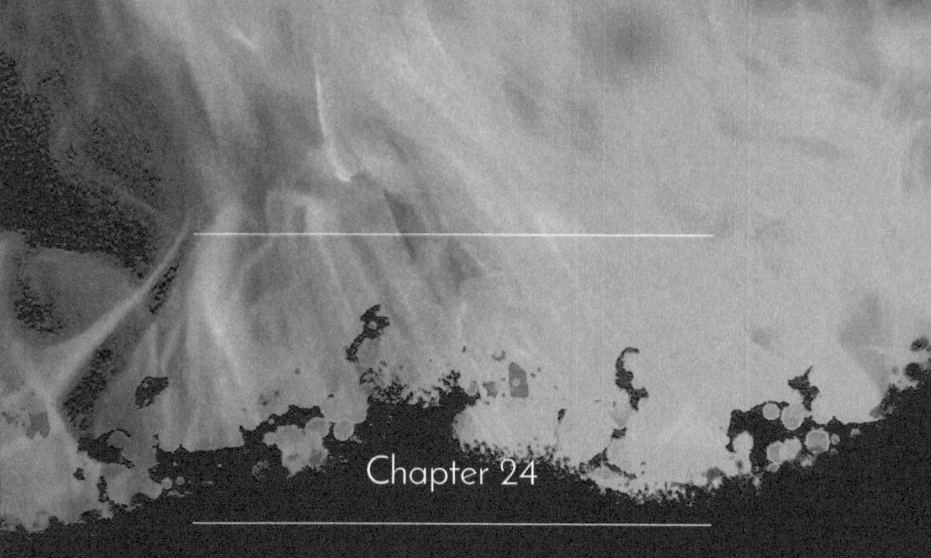

Chapter 24

Khol finally managed to get me dressed and out of his room, although I was currently pouting like a thirteen-year-old boy being denied his gaming system. "I only wanted like five more minutes alone with you," I grumbled as Khol led me by my hand to one of the common rooms.

I could hear the smile in his voice even though I couldn't see his face since he was in front of me, which was fine with me because the man had one fine behind. Which I was ogling shamelessly. "You've been saying that for the past five hours."

But Khol wasn't really complaining. I'd never seen him so happy. He was exuding an aura of contentment that was practically tangible. I was also quite satisfied, not just physically, but emotionally. I liked feeling so close to Khol, so…intimate.

He tugged me forward and into his side, so that as we

entered the room I was held snuggly against him. I wrapped my arms around his middle and leaned into him, happy to let him hold me any way he wanted, just as long as he held me. My skin felt bereft and incomplete when not in contact with his, and it positively crackled with energy when I touched him.

As Khol took a seat and situated me in his lap, I noticed we were the last ones to arrive to our tiny group meeting. Jenna sat with Jeremy, the two of them smiling and whispering to each other. Morag sat with Macon, although Macon was ignoring her and glaring at Jenna and Jeremy. *In this tiny room are all the faces in the entire world that I totally trust.* There was no one else left. They were my inner sanctum, or my closest advisors, whatever you wanted to call them, but above all they were my friends, and I knew they had my back.

"Ahem." Khol cleared his throat to get everyone's attention.

"I see you guys finally came up for some air." Jenna winked at Khol and then smirked at me. She then got up, rushed over to me, and somehow I ended up bent forward with my hair flung in my face, with her studying the back of my neck. "Niiice."

How the hell did she do that? "Hey," I grated as I sat up, waving my hands behind me to get her to give me some space. "You could have just asked to see it. No need to get all shovey."

"Sorry," Jenna said, sounding anything but sorry. "I just wanted to see what it looked like. I mean it's red like I knew it would be, but I wanted to see what shape it would be in. Yours and Bryn's were different, but I didn't know if that was a black and red dragon thing or if—"

"Okay, I get." I settled myself back into Khol's lap comfortably, who was now running his fingers over the back of my neck. Of course, when he touched my *Anam Cara* mark I shivered with delight. "Now you've seen it. Back off."

Jenna rolled her eyes as I leaned more into Khol's touch. *If I was a cat I'd be purring.* "Am I gonna have to separate you two with a crowbar or something? Seriously..." She grinned. "You know, Khol's mark almost looks like a *K*. A very loose interpretation of a *K*, but—"

I groaned, peering up into Khol's amused dragon green eyes. "I told you that I wouldn't be the only one to think that. It looks like you branded me or something." I pouted, although at the same time what was really bothering me was that my mark on Khol wasn't a big P. In fact, I wouldn't have minded if it said *P.J.'s Property* right across the back of his neck in glowing letters.

"I rather like it." Khol leaned forward, nipping at the mark, causing goose bumps to erupt all over my skin.

"Of course you do," I complained. "How would you feel if you had a big old *P* on your neck?"

"I'd wear it with pride because no matter the shape of your *Anam Cara* mark on me it doesn't matter as long as it's there." Khol's tongue snaked out, tracing the shape of the design, and my gut suddenly clenched with need.

"Khol," I rasped. "I'm not the one who insisted we come here. You need to stop."

He gave me one last lick before he placed my hair back in place. "Right you are, my little queen." And I knew I was because, well, after all, I could tell how much he wanted me since I was sitting in his lap. I rubbed my bottom against him and his hands came to rest on my hips to keep me from moving. "None of that," he murmured so that only I could hear.

Khol turned to address everyone. "As you all know, P.J. has been working with the dragon pendant to remove the Riders from their human hosts. She has now successfully done so, numerous times. The next step is to plan the best form of attack to take full advantage of this new power."

Macon stood. "My lord, can she remove more than one at a time?"

"First question out of the box and you ask exactly what we still need to find out," Morag said, an amorous smile on her face directed at Macon. Clearly my dear Auntie really did have a thing for younger dragons. *Can you still call a dragon a cougar?*

"Then we need to find that part out before we make any more plans," Jenna chimed in. "We should get a bunch of test subjects."

"What I was thinking precisely." Morag nodded her head in agreement at Jenna. "P.J. I'm going to need you to come with me to show me which humans have Riders in them."

I groaned, but luckily Jenna came to my aid. "You

know, I could have one of my friends go with you to show you. They can see the Riders in people too, and then P.J. can...rest a little while longer before we see if she can remove more than one at a time." Jenna not so subtly winked at me.

Of course having some more alone time with Khol before we went after the Riders sounded like a brilliant idea. Jenna bent to scoop up a large white and black rat. She extended her arms towards Morag. "Here you go, he'll help you out."

Morag smiled with delight, much to my surprise. "Why, this is wonderful." She stroked the rat like he was a cat, and he leapt from her hand to her shoulder, obviously expressing his mutual adoration for her. "I will be back with some test subjects shortly then." She glanced over at Macon with longing before disappearing.

"When Morag has the—" Khol began, stopping short when Zen strode into the room.

I immediately jumped from Khol's lap, my fire magic shooting up my arms. "What the hell are you doing here?" I hissed.

Zen dropped to her knees in front of me, bowing her head, much to my complete and utter shock. "Please, have pity, your majesty, although I won't deny that I wanted Khol for myself, I know that he is now completely out of my reach. Even when he thought you were dead, he wouldn't take the comfort I offered him with my body. What Lorik did"—she gulped loudly— "what Lorik did, he did on his own. I had no knowledge of it."

When she finished speaking, Zen remained before me with her head bowed. I looked to Khol for help, but he was glaring at her with anger of his own simmering in his gaze. "What do you want? My forgiveness?" If what she said was true, no matter how much I wanted to hate her, I knew it wouldn't be right. A person can't help who they fall in love with. *I, of all people, know that first hand.*

"For starters, yes I would like your forgiveness," she replied.

"Don't push it," Khol grated through clenched teeth. "She has every right to kill you, and I wouldn't stop her."

Zen's head jerked to the side as if Khol had slapped her. "I want to help," she said, her voice thick with emotion. And because of what Khol had just said I almost felt sorry for her.

"Help with what?" I asked softly, my flames going out.

"Don't trust her!" Jenna exclaimed. "She's gonna try and do you like Nala did! She'll try and kill you in your sleep or something just so she can have your man!"

"I would never!" Zen protested indignantly.

"Whatever, you can save it for someone who believes you!" Jenna retorted.

Seeing Zen's shoulders slump inward and knowing how I felt when I thought I had lost Khol forever did kind of pull at my sympathy strings. Zen had loved Khol almost all of her life. What if Bryn had wanted someone else the way Khol desired me? I would at least have tried to entice him away.

"I forgive you," I said.

"No! Are you out of your mind!" Jenna protested. "P.J., I thought you were smarter than this!"

I glared at Jenna. "I said I would forgive her, but not forget. It's not like I'm gonna trust you anytime soon, Zen. You're gonna have to prove yourself." Zen lifted her face towards me, hope filling her eyes. "But don't think I'm gonna let you near Khol anytime soon either."

I scowled, remembering their kiss in the clearing. "Okay—ever. If you really wanna help then you can help. But there's a five foot rule with Khol if I'm not in the same room." I paused, biting my lower lip as the same image of them kissing insisted on popping up, yet again. "Make that a twenty foot rule. And if you try anything, say anything— so much as breath in his direction—I'll burn you to a crisp."

I slid my hand into Khol's large one, pulling him after me as I stalked from the common room. "Now nobody bother us until Morag comes back with the Riders. I need some alone time with *my Anam Cara*." I not so subtly flipped my hair over to the side so Khol's mark was exposed.

Jenna burst into laughter as we left the room, and I smiled to myself. I would forgive Zen, but there was no way in hell I would keep from flaunting my relationship with Khol in her face. Maybe I would have been more considerate if she hadn't tried to steal him away, making sure I was well aware of their past together. For that reason alone, I was going to make damn sure she was well aware of my and Khol's future together.

"What you did back there with Zen," Khol said softly. "It showed the kind of compassion of a true dragon queen. I'm proud to call you *mo Anam Cara*."

While I hadn't done it to make Khol proud, his words colored my cheeks with delight anyways. "I love you, Khol." My chest bloomed with warmth as I confessed my feeling for him again. "I wanna show you how much again." *God, I'm like a friggin' cat in heat.* I couldn't decide if I was worse with Khol than I had been with Bryn, or maybe my pregnancy hormones were factoring in.

"Another decision based in compassion, my little queen," Khol responded, his voice rough with arousal.

"Compassion?"

"Yes, what you were doing to me when you were grinding against my lap, when I was powerless to do anything about it, bordered on cruelty. Now you've decided to show your compassion by easing my pain." Khol grinned mischievously at me.

I slapped at his shoulder playfully. "Just hurry up and take us to—" Khol shifted us to his room where I showed him exactly how compassionate I could be with him.

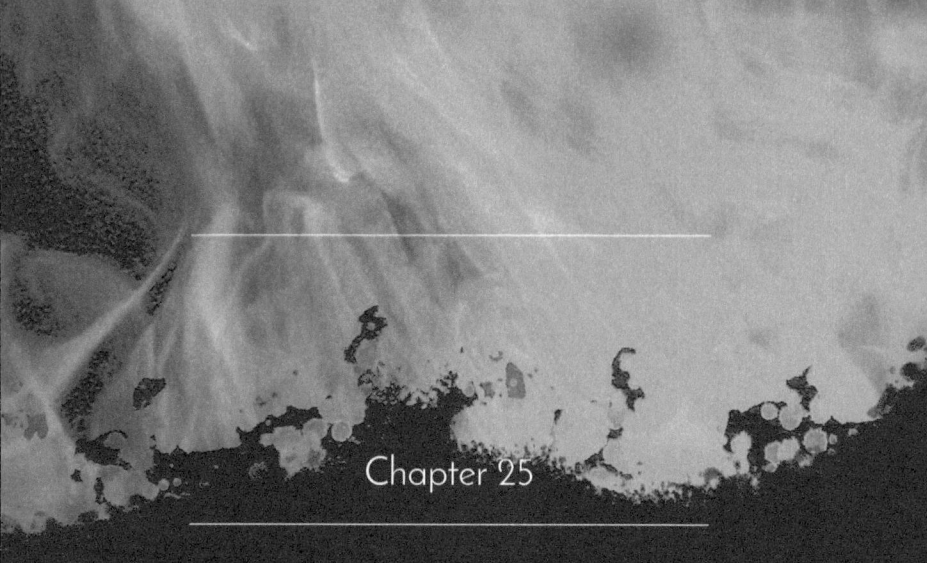

Chapter 25

"**A** young Seers' mind will never show her something she's not ready to handle." The words echoed in my head as a fog-like scene took shape before my eyes.

I strode forward knowing what I'd just heard was a bad omen pertaining to the vision I was about to be shown. tried to push through the fog, but it was like a solid wall. I reached up to touch it, and it felt smooth, soft, and slimy, with a definite solid mass not typical of normal fog. I began to circle the fog like wall, searching for an opening. I found none.

An abrupt scream rent the air.

"Khol! No!" I stopped short when I realized that the voice was mine. An inhuman roar then met my ears causing a chill to run up the length of my spine. With a renewed urgency I began circling the wall of fog again, looking for a way in.

Then I heard the words again. "A young Seers' mind will never show her something she's not ready to handle."

I turned to find the source of the familiar voice, but then the entire scene suddenly turned black.

My eyes shot open, my heart pounding in my ears, as I tried to make sense of what I'd just seen. It was a vision, of sorts. But the fact that I hadn't been shown what was inside the fog, and couple that with the words—well, it felt more like a portent of doom than a vision.

Great. Like I need another one of those.

My mind raced. Was that why I hadn't received any new visions lately? Was there too much I wouldn't be able to handle seeing? But if everything in the future is changeable depending on the choices made in the present, then what could it all possibly mean?

Khol pulled me to him, and I snuggled into his embrace, inhaling his comforting scent. I wanted nothing more in that moment than to lose myself in him. "My little queen," he murmured. "I'm here if you wish to talk."

I heaved out a huge overly dramatic sigh. I didn't really want to talk, but I knew it was probably healthier for my psyche. "You saw my vision?" I knew he had, but I was stalling.

Khol ran his hand down my naked back, settling it in the curve just above my butt. It was both comforting and yet provocative. *Damn hormones.* "You know I did."

"It scares me. What could it mean?" I ran the fingertips of my left hand in small circles on his smooth muscular chest.

"It could mean many, many things." His voice dropped

an octave letting me know that he too would rather be doing something other than talking.

An idle thought skittered across my mind as I continued to run my fingertips over the expanse of his chest. "What's your skin like, when you're in dragon form?"

Knowing that Khol had another form, and that apparently I did too, freaked me out, so I tried not to think about it most of the time. Although, lately, it was less and less anxiety provoking and instead curiosity piquing.

Khol caught me by the wrist, pulling me up on his chest so we were face to face. "I could show you." There was an excitement in his eyes that was hard to miss. *Is this a part of himself that he has been wanting to share with me? Have I been denying him of it?*

I wasn't sure if I was ready for the dragon quite yet, so I decided to ask him some more questions first. "Can you fly?"

"We could fly together." Khol smiled, his excitement crackling in the air. "I used to see my parents flying together as a child, and many other *Anam Cara* pairs since then. I've long since desired to share the experience with my own mate.

"Do only *Anam Caras* fly together? Don't you fly around with, I don't know, friends and family?"

"It's different, I am told, with your *Anam Cara*. Everything is different with them." He tugged me to him, closing the last little bit of distance between us, and kissed me softly, yet passionately.

A knock sounded at his door and in strode Morag. "Hey!" I exclaimed, trying to cover Khol's naughty bits from her sight. Strange how I was more worried about covering him up than myself. *She may be my aunt but only I get to see Khol naked.*

"It's nothing I haven't seen before, child," she said flippantly. "If I left the two of you—two newly mated *Anam Caras* to your own devices—then we'd be lucky to see you within the next few months—no matter your good intentions."

"You have secured the Riders to start testing?" Khol asked, his voice becoming all business.

"Yes," Morag replied in the same tone.

"We will find you shortly then." Looking satisfied with Khol's response, Morag turned and left, yanking the door shut behind her.

Khol shuffled the two of us from bed, faint disappointment scrolling across his features. "We will continue our conversation about our other forms later."

"Yeah okay," I said, relief washing over me.

I wanted to make Khol happy, and although I was less nervous about the topic, I wasn't sure if I was ready to do anything but talk yet. *Baby steps people, baby steps.*

A FEW MONTHS AGO, I might have felt a slight twinge of guilt towards the small group of people who were going to be my guinea pigs. Of course, now all I saw were the Riders inside of them, and not their host bodies. It had been different with Jenna because I'd known her practically as long as I'd known Bryn. But the group of random people Morag had gathered for me, despite the fact that they quivered and shook with fear, invoked nothing but hatred from me. I hated the Riders and what they'd done to my world. I blamed them for the fear that shimmered in the eyes of the people who served as their puppets. It wasn't my fault if they suffered, it was the Riders'.

"What are you going to do to us?" a girl somewhere in her mid-twenties with long brown hair and pale skin asked, her eyes as big as saucers.

I ignored her and spoke to Morag, "The rat did good. Every one of them has a Rider inside of them."

Morag smiled, nodding. "Yes, the cute little creature was quite helpful."

"All right. I guess I'll just—do this then."

I slipped my hand reluctantly out of Khol's, who had been standing silently beside me the entire time. Both Morag and Khol took a few steps away from me as I began to gather my fire magic. I let my thoughts turn as usual to Bryn's murder and how he was ripped away from me—despite my new bond with Khol, my anger wasn't diminished at all. My fire tore through my body, and into the dragon pendant, causing the room to glow bright red. The magic then ripped a swath towards the group of Riders. Screams of raw, agonizing pain echoed through the room in chorus, all ten of the Riders joining in to create the macabre music. A few moments later the Riders hovered in the air before disappearing into their new home inside the stone of my pendant.

I turned to leave the room, not wanting to hear the incriminations of the human hosts who were left behind. I knew they wouldn't be grateful like Jenna had been, no. Instead, they would cry out with indignation and resentment, cry for their shackles to be returned to them in the form of their individual Riders. Why couldn't the humans see that the Riders weren't something they should want, but something they should run screaming from?

"I did it," I said to no one in particular even though I knew Khol was right behind me.

His hand slid around my waist from the behind, pulling me against his chest. "So you did," he murmured as he kissed the top of my head.

I turned within his embrace, wrapping my arms around him, and buried my face against his chest. "So why does it feel so empty?"

"Because in the beginning, you weren't expecting them to resent you. You expected for them to offer thanks for saving them." He kissed the top of my head again as he ran his hands over my shoulders. "Things are rarely that simple, my little queen."

"Then what am I even doing? If all of the humans want those stupid Riders inside of them because they're under the misguided impression that they're helping, then what am I even doing? Why not let the humans fend for themselves and stop risking my own life, and those of who I care about? Those left anyways."

Did Bryn and my family die for nothing? Were the humans beyond redemption? Just because I'd been raised human didn't make me any more human than Khol. And humans like Jenna and Jeremy weren't Regs, so that would explain them being different as well.

"Don't allow yourself to become disillusioned. We aren't working to remove the Riders for the thanks of the human race, but to save them and all of our world, whether they realize it or not."

"Yeah, I guess. But some thanks would be nice," I huffed.

"I think it's time to take our show on the road," Morag added in cheerily as she strode out of the room after us. "It's time to rid ourselves of a nasty little Rider infestation."

I pulled myself away from Khol, meeting my aunt's gaze. "What's your plan?"

She grinned at me in a very Jenna-like way. "Well, I thought you'd never ask. We're all going to have so much fun!" Morag's eyes glinted with eagerness.

I clutched Khol's hand, listening intently to Morag's plan. Sure, it was ballsy, but it might just work. Of course, only time would truly tell.

Chapter 26

Khol, Morag, Macon, me, and yes, even Zen, stood outside The White House. Our little crew was made up of dragons only. We'd decided it was too dangerous to expose Jenna and Jeremy to the Riders unless necessary. After all, I'd just removed one from Jenna. I wasn't in the mood for a repeat performance. Morag's plan was basically to march right in, or shift in rather, find President Wexington, and remove his Rider. She thought once we cut off the head of the metaphorical monster, the rest would be easy. I wasn't sure any of it would be as simple as she hoped though, especially because most monsters had the ability to regenerate, and it wouldn't be long before a new head was grown.

"Is everyone ready?" Khol asked the group, but I knew his question was really directed at me. He was just trying not to hurt my feelings, apparently.

"Yes," I whispered, although there really wasn't a reason to keep my voice low at the moment. I was positive that our enemies inside the White House had already taken notice of our little group.

"Then let's go." And with that, Khol shifted the two of us straight into the Oval Office. I guess it really didn't matter whether or not anyone else was ready since I was going to be doing the heavy lifting in our plan. I briefly scanned my new surroundings, the Oval Office looked just like it did on T.V. but less impressive. I internally shrugged. My real focus wasn't the room, but the man, or Rider rather, in it. President Bill Wexington.

I curled my lips up at him in what I'm sure was a sneer. "Good to see you again, President."

He smiled his most charming smile back at me, only the slightest bit of anxiety showing in his eyes. "I've been expecting you." He unfolded himself from his chair, standing to his full height. The Rider within him blended more fully with its host than any other Rider I'd seen before. They moved as one—they were one.

"You know why we're here then?" I asked casually.

"Yes," he replied, his eyes shifting briefly over my shoulder as I sensed the rest of our dragon crew appear in the room. I wasn't sure what delayed them, but it didn't really matter, they were here now. "But you will fail."

I tilted my head to study him. He seemed so sure, and it honestly was making me nervous. I hadn't believed him before, and it had cost Bryn's life in the end. "I think this time you're wrong."

President Wexington grunted. "So young, I almost feel sorry for you. If only you would have listened to me and minded your own business, the young black dragon would still be alive."

A low inhuman growl erupted from my throat. "Bryn's death isn't my doing."

Wexington raised his eyebrows at me. "Isn't it?"

"Just do what we've come to do," Khol interjected. "Don't let him get to you, my little queen."

Khol was right. Wexington was trying to goad and distract me. He was playing the part of the stereotypical movie villain at the moment. So I would choose action instead of words. In fact, Wexington had given me more fuel for my fire, quite literally. I pulled on my fire magic, funneling it into the dragon pendant I wore around my neck. The room filled with the red glow—

"Wait!" Wexington shouted. "Don't you want to know why the humans want us inside of them? Don't you want all the answers? I'm the only one who can give them to you."

Shit. Somehow Wexington had hit the nail right on the head. I did want to know why the humans weren't overjoyed when I removed the Riders from them. I did want the answer to that question and a host of others. My flames flickered and the red light went out.

"This better be good," I hissed.

"No!" Morag exclaimed. "Don't stop to listen to him. That's exactly what he wants."

"I need to know," I snapped, my gaze not wavering from Wexington. "Tell me."

"I'll show you." A red light emanating from a stone in his hand, much like the one around my neck, lit up the room.

I felt so strange, like I was being ripped away from my own body. I whirled around reaching for Khol but he seemed so far away. I heard myself call out to him as if it was someone else screaming.

"Khol! No!" I scrambled towards him, or at least I tried, but he seemed even farther away than before. Everything narrowed down until my vision was filled with nothing but red light. An inhuman roar filled my ears before everything went dark.

I SAT up in a field of pristine green grass. It looked like a painting, fake somehow, rather than real grass. As for the rest of the scenery, it too had a perfect and somehow artificial feel to it. *Maybe I'm dreaming?*

"I've been waiting for you." I turned as fast as I could to face the direction the voice had come from. A young dragon that looked to be about my age, with light brown hair, gazed at me expectantly. He appeared young, innocent, and vulnerable—I'd long ago learned that appearances are almost always deceiving.

"You're a brown dragon. Like my aunt."

He smiled and nodded. "Yes, and therefore you already know we control time and space then. I'm already dead... and yet not." He shook his head at me. "It all can get very confusing if you're not used to it. You may call me, Tye."

"Okay, Tye," I drawled. "Why am I here? I'm guessing what just happened was the part of my vision that my mind didn't wanna show me, but why?"

Tye nodded approvingly. "Very perceptive. And I like that you get straight to the point, and therefore so will I. Things are not what they appear. A mistake was made a long time ago—a very, very long time ago, and your mother, Mori has been trying to set it straight ever since. The problem is, the only way to fix it, is to not have let it happen at all to begin with. Unfortunately, that would change too much, so the only other solution is controlled chaos, so to speak."

"I don't understand." I didn't have the faintest clue what he was talking about. "And how am I here... wherever I am...sent by President Bill Wexington...a Rider...and you a dragon, are the one waiting for me?" A chill ran up my spine. "Are you working with the Riders too?" I immediately thought of the dragons that had stood with the Riders and not against them on the day Bryn had been killed.

Tye shook his head. "No, I'm working for the good of all, and sometimes that means I work in the grey areas. There is no black and white here. There is no good versus evil. Everything that you've been taught is a lie. I have been waiting here for you for a mere moment and yet all of my life."

I fought the urge to roll my eyes. "Oh come on. I swear all you ancient dragons talk in code just to confuse me."

Tye gave me a bemused smile. "I suppose to one such as yourself it would seem that way. But to another brown dragon, or once you gain full control of your powers, our explanations will no longer seem encoded to your ears."

I grunted my disdain. He still wasn't giving me any answers. "Why am I here?" I grated.

"Watch." Tye waved his arm in a circular motion, and the air began to wave much in the same manner as when heat rises off the pavement in the summertime. Slowly a picture formed where the waves were. "A long time ago—" He began as a woman with white hair came to stand in the center of the image.

"In a galaxy far, far away?" I sniggered to myself, before meeting Tye's less than amused eyes. "Sorry, do continue. I just couldn't resist." *There is really no appropriate time for my snark.*

"As I was saying," Tye began again. "A long time—" He paused to glance at me, his lips pressed together in a thin line. "Many years ago—" he amended, which caused me to have to suppress a giggle. "When humans were still so new, at least to us dragons, the original dragon queen viewed the world as her domain, all of it and every creature within the planet belonged to her."

"Wait," I interrupted. "I thought my birth mother was

the first dragon queen. That"—I pointed at the white-haired woman in the image— "is not my mother."

"No, it isn't your mother. It's your grandmother."

I gasped in surprise. I mean, I guess I knew I had to have one, but since my birth mother was the first dragon queen, or at least I'd thought she'd been, I hadn't really considered the matter. It made me begin to wonder how dragons were created, how humans were for that matter, and how the worlds came into being. It brought up a whole bunch of existential questions that were making my head hurt.

"Not many know of her," Tye said. "She was older than time itself." Again, my mind began to spin around with too many questions. How could anything exist before time? How could—"Careful. You don't want to hurt yourself." Tye chuckled as he eyed me speculatively. "Only with age does a dragon come to fully understand such things."

"Yeah, okay, good to know," I muttered, gnawing on my bottom lip.

"Your grandmother saw much potential for destruction within humans." Tye motioned to the image again and I saw my grandmother standing on a bluff studying two human men who were apparently fighting. "But since they'd come to amuse her, much like a beloved pet, she didn't want to eradicate them from this world. She sought to improve them instead."

The image then shimmered and changed. I saw my grandmother standing over what looked like a cauldron, reminding me of a witch from a movie or TV show. She was dropping bits of things into the cauldron while chanting low. The image shifted again to show a man, a human man on his knees, his head thrown back as a bright light encased him. A moment later the light separated from his body, and there stood what I'd come to think of as one of the Riders.

Shock vibrated through me as I turned towards Tye. "That can't be. The Riders are from another world. They can't be from humans." Turning back towards the image, I watched in horror as it flickered quickly from one random human to another, each of them producing a Rider. The image shimmered and changed once again. This time it showed my grandmother with a stone, a red stone much like what President Bill Wexington had, and the one in my pendant. I watched as my grandmother pulled all of the Riders into the stone and cast them into what looked like a gate.

Tye waved his arm again and the image disappeared completely. "Your grandmother meddled where she should not have." I stared at him unable to find any words. My mind was still trying to take in what it was just shown and hadn't even begun to process what it all meant. "The reason why no other Seer saw the Riders breach the gates, is because they were originally of this world. Only you, with your blood, can see the Riders for what they truly are. The animals can see them as different, but not the way you do. The Riders are unnatural, and yet not. They are the worst parts of a human's nature, and they have been destroying other worlds for centuries, until finally they found their way home."

"But humans still fight, they aren't all good and perfect. They aren't—"

"Correct." Tye smiled sadly. "No creature is perfect. But they were worse before, much worse, or at least their potential to be worse existed. Although, when your grandmother meddled with her magic she created an imbalance. All magic users come to learn that once there is an imbalance, things will find a way to right themselves in the end." He shook his head. "She was young and egotistical, but her heart was in the right place."

"So why didn't she have one of the brown dragons go back in time and fix it? Have her stop the whole thing before it started? Have her—"

"Then she never would have met her *Anam Cara*—me." I gulped, realizing what his words revealed. *Tye is my grandfather.* "I am the only one besides her who knows what she did, and now you of course."

"Why are you telling me all of this?"

"There will come a time soon, when you will be faced with a choice, not the choice your mother saw, but one completely different. You mother thought the way to solve things was to have you entrap the Riders and send them away again, but too many things will go wrong with that path. Your grandmother was stronger with her gift, more in tune with it. She was still young when she created the Riders, unfocused—things changed as she matured. There is only one option left, and it is your destiny to find it. All of this will end with you. Your actions and your decisions alone will fix what was broken.

"Ummm...but that's not true at all. If everyone is meddling with my life and everything around it then it's not my decision alone that will decide the outcome." *Why did it always have to come down to me? Well, I guess it's just bad genetics.*

"You *will* decide the outcome." He reached behind his back, producing a thin metal bracelet with a purple stone charm on it. He offered it to me in his palm. "This is for you."

I shook my head vigorously. "Oh—huh-uh—no way! I've had enough with spelled or charmed or whatever kind of jewelry that is. Things never seem to go well for me."

"When you place this on your wrist, you will forget what I have just shown you, you will forget me." I wasn't liking the choice of the word *when* instead of *if*.

"Why would I wanna do that?" I asked incredulously.

"So you can continue on the path you were on...until it's time to have this knowledge. Now isn't the time for the knowledge, now was simply the time I could give it to you."

"Yeah, okay, now it all makes total sense." I hoped he was picking up on my sarcasm.

"When it is time for you to remember, simply break the stone, and all that you have just learned will return to you." He took a step closer to me, offering the bracelet again.

"I'm so confused. How will I know when it's time to remember—if I don't remember any of this? It seems like you, my birth mother, and my grandmother are making things way more complicated than they need to be. Why would not creating the Riders result in you and my grandmother not being *Anam Caras*? I mean if that's the case I guess I understand—" I thought of Khol and frowned. "Okay, I can totally understand, but if my grandmother could see that then couldn't she simply—"

"One day you will understand, but not now." He came to stand by me and pinched the ends of the bracelet in his fingertips. "I'm going to secure the bracelet to your wrist but before I do, I wanted to tell you that I'm proud of you, granddaughter, very proud."

He smiled at me warmly as he reached down to put the bracelet on my wrist. As soon as it touched my skin, I was surrounded by purple light that quickly turned to red. I blinked rapidly, a fog settling around me—and realization hit. The fog in my vision that was preventing me from seeing these events was *this* fog. It meant I had already accepted the bracelet.

This time controlling thing is beyond confusing. I wasn't sure I'd ever understand it like everyone kept telling me I one day would. As the fog settled more thickly around me, everything faded to black... yet again.

This is seriously getting old.

~

AS SOON AS I opened my eyes, my gaze landed on Khol, but instead of taking the time to question what exactly happened, I pulled myself out of his arms and stood to face President Bill Wexington, who for some reason was blinking at me with confusion of his own. He glanced down at the red stone in his hand and frowned.

"What happened?" he muttered to himself, but loud enough that I could hear.

The last thing I remembered was Wexington saying that he was going to show me something and being engulfed by red and purple lights. What happened was a very good question, but not one that I was going to wait to receive an answer to at the moment.

"Nice try," I grated. "But your stall tactics aren't gonna work anymore."

Without waiting for him to react I began funneling my fire magic into my pendant, the red light encompassing the entire room. My fury fueled my powers, growing and pushing, reaching and stretching and until I sensed that the whole White House was saturated with my red light, and therefore every Rider within the perimeter was about to be ripped from his or her host.

With great satisfaction, I watched as the Rider, the head Rider, the Rider indirectly responsible for Bryn's death, was torn from Wexington's body. A bloodcurdling scream echoed in the room before it disappeared. A moment later the red light blinked out, signaling that all the Riders in the vicinity were now being held inside the red stone in my dragon pendant.

I sagged into Khol's waiting arms as I let go of my magic. "I can't believe it," I said, my lips numb. "I did it."

Khol pulled me into a tight embrace, burying his face in my hair. "I knew you could."

"But—but—that can't be it. I mean—it was all so—anticlimactic."

I was having a hard time wrapping my head around the fact that within minutes it was all over. And without even a battle of any kind. Perhaps I'd watched too many movies and I'd been expecting some kind of epic last stand while the music swelled to heighten the dramatics —I wasn't quite sure, but it didn't feel like a satisfying end.

"It's not quite over yet, my little queen. We still have an entire world to rid of Riders, although it should be easy now if we move swiftly." Khol's hot breath fanned along my neck causing me to shiver.

"But I don't know—it feels—wrong somehow," I persisted.

"Who are you and what are you doing here?" I heard President Bill Wexington demand with alarm. I idly wondered why he seemed to have no recollection of his Rider.

Before I could give it any more thought, the door to the Oval Office burst inward and Secret Service men swarmed us. There was no need to worry though because we all merely just shifted away—back to what I'd come to think of as headquarters.

Jenna rushed me with excitement as soon as we

appeared. "Well? What happened? Did the plan work? Did you get the head Rider?"

"Yeah, we did. We got him." I responded flatly.

Jenna jumped up and down before turning to launch herself at me. As she wrapped her arms around me, I hugged her back. *Why aren't I more excited?* I felt nothing except numbness.

Jenna pulled away, clearly noting my lack of enthusiasm. "What's wrong? Why aren't you—I don't know—jumping for joy like me? Is it because you're pregnant? Maybe Khol could lift you?"

I stared at her while I tried to find an answer. "It hasn't sunk in yet," Khol supplied for me. "She's in shock."

"Oh," Jenna said, and instead of pushing it like she normally would, she turned and launched herself at Jeremy who was grinning from ear to ear. "P.J. did it!" she shrieked. "P.J. saved the world, and she's my best friend!"

Jeremy grinned at her indulgently. "Yeah, she did. Wanna go celebrate?"

Jenna took his hand in hers, tugging him from the room. "Like you need to ask. Later everyone! P.J. we'll talk in a bit—after—well you know." And with that Jenna and Jeremy left to go 'celebrate'.

"Time to get started on finishing them all off," Morag said, grinning. "I'm so proud of you P.J. I'm proud to call you my niece."

When I didn't say react Khol tipped my chin up towards him so he could look into my eyes. "Are you okay, my little queen? Are you ready to take on the rest of the Riders?"

I pursed my lips and stared into Khol's beautifully chiseled face. "Yeah, I'm ready. I guess I'm just still surprised how easy that was." After all this time the power struggle between us and the Riders was essentially over. *I really should be jumping for joy, celebrating...something. So why does it feel like one big lie?*

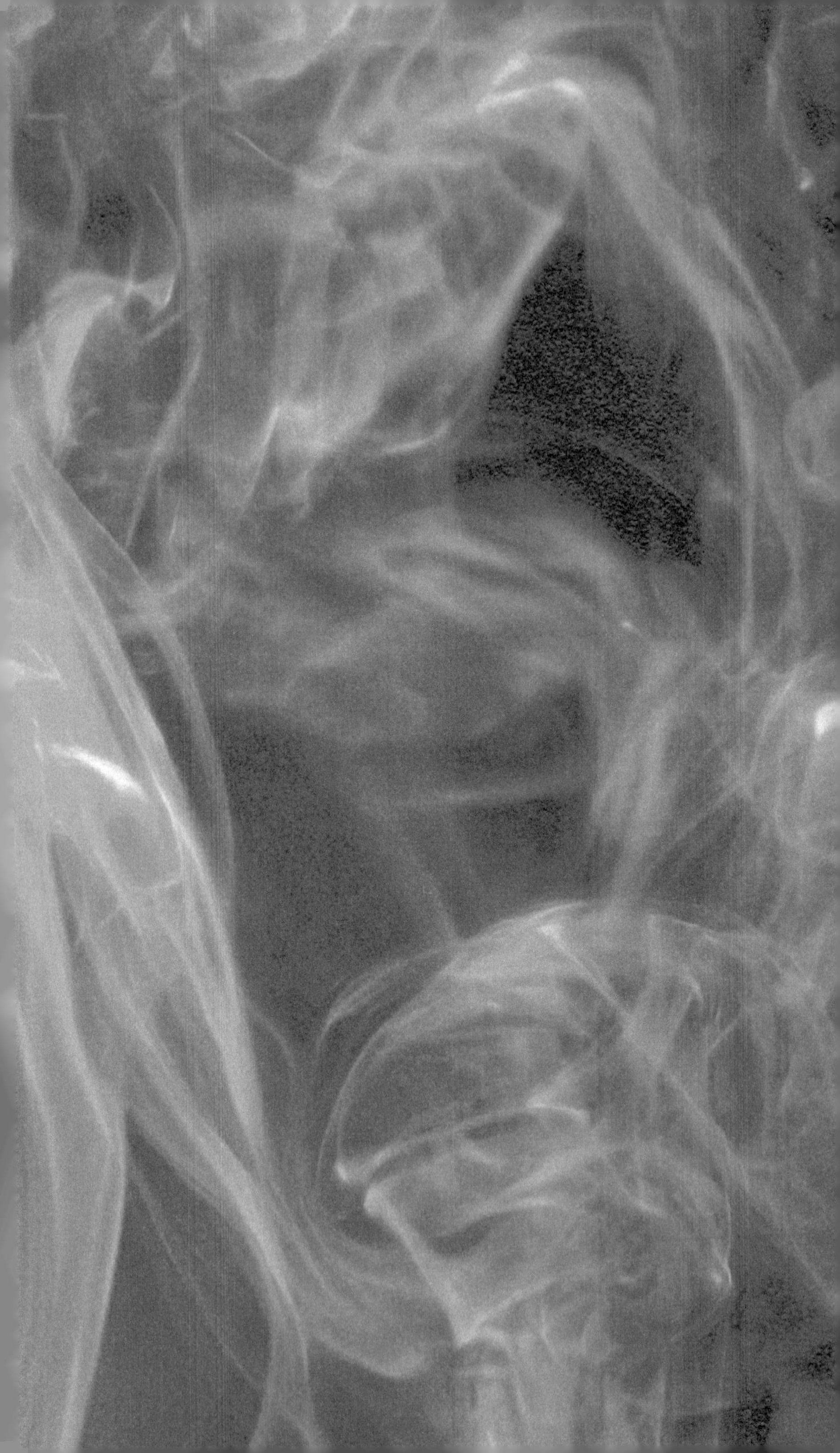

Chapter 27

Months passed, equaling hundreds of thousands of Riders coming to find their new home inside of the red stone, or *rua artaire*, in my dragon pendant. There had been many, many … more Riders than I had even begun to perceive. And with the removal of them, we again had Gatekeepers, and Guardians in the world. Unfortunately, there were still no other Seers, or Speakers. The joy of having defeated the Riders was overshadowed slightly by what that could mean for future generations. Jenna and myself wouldn't live forever, and when we did die—then what? Even if Jenna had a child one day, there was no guarantee that it would be a Speaker. In fact, if she conceived it with Jeremy then it most definitely wouldn't be.

Who will watch the gates and our world in the generations to come?

And there was one other little problem that no one but

me seemed willing to acknowledge: nothing had really changed. Sure, with the Riders being gone, their human hosts had lost all knowledge of us, and we were no longer hunted, but that was the extent of things. President Bill Wexington was moving ahead with all of his agendas, and well...the rest of the world hadn't suddenly gone back to the way it was before the Riders either. Perhaps it was more evidence that I'd watched too many movies and read too many books since I obviously expected everything to be magically reset once the big-bad was defeated.

Khol and I had settled comfortably on his land, setting up house in his castle, which I guess was now technically our castle, since I was the queen and we were *Anam Caras*. Jenna and Jeremy had taken up residence in their own wing of the castle after Jeremy proposed. But even though we were technically all roomies, I hardly saw them. Of course, I was a tad cranky because of my beached whale status, and Khol was the only one brave enough to engage with me when my temper flared ... literally.

Morag had gone back to her realm, but she stopped by to check up on her favorite and only niece regularly. Although I wasn't deluded into thinking I was the only reason she visited so often. I knew she had a thing going with Macon. I tried not to think about it because it kind of skeeved me out. I was relieved that Macon had turned out to not be in love with Jenna, saving him from a life of misery since she'd abandoned him for Jeremy.

Even Zen had started a relationship with some young gold dragon. She sometimes still cast furtive yearning glances in Khol's direction, but she seemed content at least with the knowledge that he would never be hers. Everyone seemed happy…except me.

"My little queen," Khol murmured, running his hand tenderly over my swollen abdomen. "It should be any time now."

I huffed out a breath. "How do you even know? Because I resemble a beached whale? How can you even look at me when I'm like this?" For some inexplicable reason Khol's ardor towards me hadn't dwindled in the slightest, even though I couldn't see my toes anymore. *How can he possibly find me attractive when I look like I belong at Sea World?*

"You're beautiful like this." He splayed his large hand over the top of my baby bulge. "Even if he isn't mine, my thoughts are consumed with either giving you my child to carry, or our second."

I scowled. "You've got to be kidding me. There is no way I'm going through this ever again."

"You'll change your mind." Khol kissed me tenderly. As his tongue leisurely explored my mouth, his hands slid down to massage my back. "I love you," he breathed.

And yeah, okay, with how loved and cherished Khol made me feel, and with how happy the idea of a second future child seemed to make him—fine. I'd probably give him whatever he wanted, if not a bit begrudgingly.

Khol shifted over me, careful not to put any of his weight on my stomach, and as he deepened his kiss, I reached up to run my hands through his shorter hair. He'd recently cut it, wanting to appear more modern, and although I sometimes missed his longer locks, his hair was still long enough for me to get a good grip on it. I loved pulling his hair when he—

"P.J.!" Our bedroom door slammed open. "I need to talk to you!" Jenna screeched.

Khol stiffened above me and pulled away. "Do no locks keep you out?" he growled.

Jenna narrowed her eyes at him. "I wouldn't know because the door wasn't actually locked."

Khol shifted away, returning fully dressed with a robe for me in his hands, to which he helped me into. I hadn't been naked, yet, but my nightgown wasn't exactly the type for public consumption.

Jenna rolled her eyes. "I've seen both of you in less, and it's not like you guys were doing anything."

I growled under my breath. I wasn't in the mood to argue with her. "Okay, so what's so important all of a sudden?"

"My wedding of course!" It was then I noticed that Jenna had a plethora of magazines in her arms. I didn't need to guess what kind they were.

"You can't be serious? After everything that's happened you wanna plan a big wedding?"

"Duh. Because of everything that's happened I wanna plan a big wedding. Well, maybe it won't be big because of guests in attendance but I want a wedding with all the frills." She speared me with an intense look. "And it's your duty as my best friend to help me."

"Look at me." I motioned to my ginormous belly. "I'm about to pop. Can't this wait until after the baby comes?"

"Khol, you need to vamoose. Like now," Jenna demanded, as if he wasn't an ancient powerful dragon who could squash her like a bug. "We need some girl time."

I didn't miss the relief that smoothed out the lines in Khol's forehead. Did all males hate this kind of stuff... even dragon males? "Call for me if you need me," he said before disappearing.

Jenna wasted no time fanning the magazines along the end of the bed. "There's so much I need to decide! But the most important is what color should I dye my hair?" She turned her wide dark eyes towards me, and I bit back a laugh.

"Well, what colors did you pick for the wedding?" I asked.

"You mean like the overall color scheme?"

"Yeah. What other color scheme would I be talking about?"

Jenna grimaced. "Green and gold."

I quirked an eyebrow at her. "Why do I feel like Jeremy had something to do with that?"

Jenna heaved a long exasperated sigh. "He just won't bend on any pretty colors like pink or purple...or pink. And I don't want blue or yellow or orange—so we settled on green. But because green is kind of boring and reminds me of grass, I decided to add gold as the accent color to pizzazz things up."

"Green and gold? That's gonna be—" Her puppy dog eyes got to me as she hung on my every word. "Interesting?" I more of asked than stated. "Ummm... well..." What could I say about her atrocious color combo? And then a light bulb went off. "You can still change the accent color, right? Just as long as you stick with green?"

"Yeah." Jenna eyed me speculatively.

"Lime green!" I exclaimed in triumph.

A huge grin broke across Jenna's face. She immediately understood me in only a way she could. "Brilliant! He never said what shade of green! Lime green and—"

"Black!"

"Yes!" Jenna pumped her fist in the air. "It's perfect!"

I shook my head, laughing. "Jeremy is about to learn a very important lesson through all of this."

"Yeah, don't mess with me and a color scheme!" Jenna donned a smug smile and picked up one of the magazines. "Lime green hair then?"

I imagined Jenna in a wedding dress with perfectly coiffed lime green hair. It was so perfectly her. "Of course. So when is this extravaganza gonna take place, and where?"

Jenna tossed the magazine she had been looking at over her shoulder and started flipping through another one. "It's gonna be here, of course, because, duh, it's beautiful and I kind of have an in with the queen that resides over this land."

"You did, until you burst in on her and her *Anam Cara* when they were about to—"

"You and Khol are always about to." She mock glared at me. "When did you become more of a sex fiend than me anyways?"

"When I bonded with Khol, apparently." In the past I would have blushed and tried to avoid the conversation, but I no longer was embarrassed by my sexual appetites. I loved Khol, and he loved me, so I had nothing to be embarrassed about.

"I always knew you had it in you." Jenna threw another magazine over her shoulder.

"I hope you plan on cleaning all of those up because I won't be able to bend over to pick them up," I groused. *This baby needs to hurry up and decide to be born already.*

"What about you?" Jenna shot me a questioning glance.

"What about me?"

She motioned to one of the magazines in her hand. "Are you and Khol gonna lock it down and make it official?"

"I don't know how much more official I can make it with him. We're *Anam Caras*." I shifted uncomfortably, fighting the urge to lay down again to relieve the pressure on my lower back.

"You know what I mean, you were raised human. You always thought you'd get married." Jenna tossed two more magazines onto her ever growing pile on the floor.

"Unlike you—" I gave up and eased myself back on the bed. "I never put much thought into what my arranged marriage would be like, or have you forgotten about all of that?"

"Yeah, whatever," Jenna said distractedly. She then appeared in my line of vision from my vantage point of lying flat on my back. "Are you really that tired that you can't even stay sitting up for like five minutes?"

"Look at me!" I raised my arms and let them flop right back down beside me. "I'm like a beached whale! I'm lucky I can move at all!"

"He's due soon though, right? Because I wanna have my wedding soon and I don't want my Maid of Honor to be as big as a house."

"Because my pregnancy is all about you! Seriously... you need to leave now." Not wanting to deal with potentially releasing my temper, she scurried out of the room, without taking the bridal magazines with her. *Of course.*

Suddenly, as if conjured by her words, pain tore across my abdomen. I clutched at my stomach with alarm as it cramped. "Khol!" I cried out. "Khol! I think—" I gritted my teeth as another spasm took hold of me. "I think it's time!"

Khol had explained to me that the delivery of a dragon baby was a lot quicker than a human's. Pretty much as soon as my contractions started, my baby was coming.

Khol appeared before me, his face dancing with delight. Seeing that he wasn't worried in the least helped to calm me down a bit. "Shhh... my little queen. I'm here and all will be fine."

As another contraction stole through my system, Khol

reached out to run his hand over my arm. My entire body relaxed, and my eyes began to flutter shut. Khol and I had discussed this. With his power he could essentially give me a pain free delivery...every woman's dream. The only catch was that I would be completely knocked out during the entirety of the process. And yeah, I was completely okay with that part too, even if it was a bit weird.

Khol pressed his lips to my forehead. "Trust in me, my little queen, and when you awake, you'll be able to hold your newborn son in your arms."

My heart skittered within my chest like a caged rabbit, but I did trust Khol— completely. So I sucked in a ragged breath and stopped fighting his magic, letting it carry me into a deep sleep.

Chapter 28

"**C**hoose. But quickly, my magic will only hold you here for so long," a strange voice said.

"You would still choose him over me?" Khol growled.

"No—you don't understand!" I heard myself croak with desperation. "I still love him but—"

The baleful wale of a baby stole my attention from the sightless vision. But none of that mattered as I blinked my eyes open to Khol, who was beaming down at the screaming baby in his arms. He met my gaze, his eyes illuminated far brighter than I'd ever seen them, brighter than I thought possible. And with two words he answered the question we'd all been waiting for.

"My son," he croaked.

Equal parts grief and elation swept through me. To give Khol a son made my heart feel ready to burst with joy, and yet a part of me, the part that would always be grieving, wanted something of Bryn's to hold onto, despite me being bonded with Khol.

"Let me hold him." I reached my arms up in demand and Khol placed my son gently within them. I stared down into his seemingly perfect face. "He's healthy?" I asked without looking away from the tiny, wrinkly face that held the most vivid green eyes I'd ever seen. He returned my stare blindly but when I touched his nose with my fingertip he smiled a toothless grin that instantly stole all of my heart.

"You're both perfect." Khol hovered above me, gazing down at us in quiet awe.

"I didn't feel any pain. None at all. And I feel fine now." Maybe giving birth wasn't that bad after all.

"One of the many perks of having me around," Khol murmured, running his hand over the thick head of red hair on our child.

"Can I come in yet?" Jenna asked from her position of already being inside our room. Without waiting for an answer, she rushed towards my little family. "Wow, look at all that hair. No doubt he's yours, huh Khol?"

"None," Khol said, lifting his chin with pride.

Jenna reached out a finger and our son's little fist grabbed it. She giggled. "He's so friggin' adorable. Seriously, I'm not just saying that. I would tell you he was cute even if he wasn't, but I'm telling you he actually is." She stared down at him for another moment and I let my gaze linger on him as well. *He really is perfect, absolutely perfect.*

"What's his name?" Jenna asked.

I glanced up at Khol. "Well—I don't know. We haven't really talked about it."

"You definitely should name him something short and not some long complicated dragon name, to which he'd get a nickname anyways. Why not just shorten the process?" Jenna started making funny faces at our child and his cute little mug scrunched up like he was going to cry. I didn't think babies could see that clearly so soon.

"He's dragon," Khol answered my question without missing a beat. "Our senses develop faster. And I'll repeat he's dragon therefore he should bear a traditional dragon name."

I shook my head. "No. You're my *Anam Cara* and I don't even have a clue how to pronounce your full dragon name. Please don't do that to me...or him." I smiled down at our child. "What's your name, little guy? Is it—"

"Lestat?" Jenna offered, excitedly.

"Jenna! What? No." Fortunately my little guy frowned. "See he doesn't like it. He gets to decide."

"What? I like the name Lestat, it's—"

"A vampire's name. You really want me to name my dragon son after a fictional vampire?" I quirked my eyebrow at Jenna. "Hey, where's Jeremy by the way?"

"Oh, he didn't wanna interrupt you guys. He said he'd visit and meet your little guy later." Jenna started cooing. "Whatz wrong wit Lestat?" She asked in baby talk.

"No Lestat," I stated more firmly.

"Fine," Jenna huffed. "So what then?"

I gazed down at the little round smiling face of my son, his green eyes staring up at me intently, as if he too was waiting for what I'd say. I ran my fingertips over his red hair and smiled. "Liam. His name is Liam."

Khol placed a hand on my shoulder and squeezed. "I like it."

"Yeah, I guess it's not that bad," Jenna chimed in, and I knew that was the best I was going to get out of her since I wasn't going with her suggestion.

I leaned down, bringing my face closer to my son's. "What do you think? Is your name Liam?" He smiled up at me to which I took as a yes. Either that or the name Liam gave him gas. I was hoping it was the former.

"Well Liam," Jenna cooed. "Thank you for being born now so your mom doesn't have to look like a stuffed pig in her Maid of Honor dress."

Oh my God—I'm a mom. I'm actually a mom. What if I suck at being one? What if I ruin this perfect little guy's life? Who am I to be a mom? I haven't even figured my own life out yet.

"Khol?" I swiveled my head up so he could see the panicked look in my eyes.

He bent down and kissed my forehead. "You're going to be an amazing mother to our son. And I'll be right here with you the entire time. We'll raise him together."

Just like usual, Khol knew the perfect thing to say to me to calm me down. He was right, he'd be there for me— for us. And even if I was the worst mom ever, I had complete confidence in Khol's parenting skills. After all, he somehow managed to deal with both Jenna and me. "I love you," I said, continuing to gaze into Khol's eyes.

"Okay. So...is now a good time to talk about your Maid of Honor dress?" Jenna asked, interrupting the moment Khol and me were having. "Because I have the perfect idea for what we can dress wittle Liam in." She baby talked the last part of her sentence.

"Seriously...Jenna...I just had my baby. It hasn't even been like an hour yet. Can you please just back off for a little bit?"

Jenna pouted. "Yeah, I guess. I'm just excited, is all."

"I know and I'm excited for you, too," I said trying to placate her. "But you need to give me a few hours at least. Why don't you come back later with Jeremy? He can visit with Khol and Liam while we talk wedding stuff."

Jenna perked up again, grinning. "I'm gonna go check out lime green hair dye online in the meantime." She leapt up and hurried towards the door. "See you all in a bit!"

"Hurricane Jenna has left the building," I murmured in a singsong voice to Liam.

"You already are an amazing mother...to Jenna." Khol chuckled. "See how wonderfully you handled her?"

Huh. Maybe Khol is right. "I'd never thought of it that way." Just then my bracelet snagged on little Liam's blanket, and I reached over to pull it off.

Khol beat me to it. "You still don't remember where you got this bracelet?" He frowned, studying it for the umpteenth time.

"No, so stop asking. Just leave it alone." I had a sudden

compulsion to cup my hand over the bracelet so Khol wouldn't touch it. *Weird.* "Let's go take little Liam around the castle—you know—give him a tour since I feel perfectly fine thanks to you." I got up carefully from bed and handed Liam to Khol. "Let me just put some more clothes on."

Khol accepted Liam with a smile. He gazed down at him with continued awe. "My son," he whispered with reverence, and I couldn't help the fresh smile that his reaction brought to my face.

Every little boy should be so lucky to have a father who loved him as much as Khol. I stood there for a moment admiring the picture Khol and Liam painted together. Khol, a huge, muscular dragon in human form, his one hand alone almost big enough to hold Liam's whole body. His tousled auburn hair framed his ruggedly carved features, as his dragon green eyes cast a soft glow onto the tiny face of our son Liam, whose fire engine red hair and pale face appeared angelic in Khol's arms. There was no doubt whose genetics combined with mine to make Liam. I briefly wondered if he had gotten any part of my physical traits at all? *My ears maybe? Oh well, I do love the way Khol looks so it isn't a bad thing for Liam to take after him.*

Khol lifted his gaze to me, a smug smile turning up the corners of his full succulent lips. He had to know what I was thinking. "I thought you were getting dressed?"

"I am—or I'm about to be." I turned on my heel and practically bounced over to the closet. I glanced down at my toes. "So that's what you look like, I almost forgot." I chuckled to myself. I felt light, buoyant...happy.

And then I remembered the vision from just before I regained full consciousness and I frowned.

"Choose. But quickly, my magic will only hold you here for so long," a strange voice said.

"You would still choose him over me?" Khol growled.

"No—you don't understand!" I heard myself croak with desperation. "I still love him but—"

"What's wrong, my little queen. What has upset you?" Khol asked from directly behind me. He had Liam tucked inside one arm and he reached out to caress my face with his empty hand.

"I'm suddenly tired is all." *Lie! Just tell him!* But why hadn't he seen or heard my vision like he usually did? Although he had been a little preoccupied...delivering Liam and using his magic to keep everything painless and perfect for me. I could tell he'd healed me too. I wasn't even the tiniest bit sore, and I'd just given birth.

"You should rest," Khol suggested. "The tour can wait. You may be physically fine, but you've been through a lot emotionally. And Jenna—"

"Yeah, she won't be put off about her wedding for long." I sighed. I loved Jenna, really I did, but she was a force of nature to be reckoned with sometimes. Okay most of the time—all of the time.

"Come," Khol said, carrying Liam towards our bed. "We'll take a nap together." He settled himself in the middle of our massive bed, Liam in his arms but slightly more to the side so that there was room for me to lie against him as well.

I crawled back into bed and pressed my cheek into Khol's chest while gazing at the wonder he held in his arms. "We made him." I'd always thought new parents said the most ridiculous things, but I had a new appreciation for why now.

Khol's arm wrapped around me, holding me snug against him as he kissed the top of my head. "I never thought I could be this happy." He sighed with contentment. "I have the two most important things in this entire world right here in my arms."

As Khol's breathing evened out letting me know that he was sleeping, my own eyes stayed wide open from a niggling feeling of unease. I wished I could go back to being happy. I'd felt whole and complete for about all of five minutes. But I knew I wasn't being paranoid or suffering from some kind of postpartum depression. No... there was something wrong in our world—or soon to be wrong—and I needed to figure out exactly what it was before it was too late. *If it's not already. No, stop, why would I think that?*

Chapter 29

"Awe...you guys look so friggin' adorable!" Jenna's voice pierced into my subconscious.

"Jenna—I'm sleeping," I mumbled with my eyes still closed. I snuggled closer to Khol whose arm tightened around me as I inhaled his intoxicating scent. What I really wanted was for Jenna to watch little Liam for a while so that Khol could get reacquainted with my post pregnancy body.

Khol stirred beneath me. "I'll take care of Liam while you visit with Jenna," his voice rumbled under my ear. "I'll bathe and change him."

I opened my eyes, rolling to the side so Khol could get out of bed with Liam. I watched with longing as the two most important men in my life made their way towards the bathroom. "But I don't wanna miss his first bath!" I whined.

Khol glanced over his shoulder at me without breaking

stride. "There'll be plenty more." With that he closed the door softly behind them.

"Liam doesn't cry much," Jenna observed. "And you're so lucky to have a guy or dragon or whatever like Khol who wants to help take care of his child. Where can I get me one of those?"

I sat up, rubbing my sleep ladened eyes. "First of all—you had one of those—Macon. You were the one who threw him away. And secondly, aren't you here to plan your wedding to Jeremy?"

Jenna grinned. "I was just sayin'."

It was then I noticed that she was carrying a bag stuffed to the brim. Magazine corners and other unidentifiable things poked out of the top and pushed against the sides. "Sooo…what cha got in the bag?" I won't lie, I was a tad worried.

Jenna walked over to the bed and unceremoniously dumped the bag's contents out. Magazines, bottles of hair dye, color swatches, and other various things to help plan her wedding spewed onto the comforter.

I groaned. "How long is this gonna take?"

Jenna's face pinched with intensity, and she narrowed her brown eyes at me. "As long as it needs to."

A LITTLE WHILE later Khol shifted into the room with little Liam happily warbling in his arms. I was utterly exhausted from doing the whole wedding planning thing with Jenna, but at least she seemed satisfied with everything we'd picked out.

I reached out my arms so that Khol would give me Liam. Khol placed him within my embrace, pulling me into his as I leaned into him. "Where'd my guys go?" I peered down at Liam whose eyes had fluttered shut. He snuggled against me, making a little baby noise, a coo or a garble. Whatever it was, it was adorable.

"I was showing him our lands," Khol said with pride. "I was showing him what one day will be his."

"Hey!" I frowned. "The tour was my idea, and you didn't wait for me?"

Khol stroked his hand through my hair and down my back. "I was merely trying to help."

I exhaled, letting my agitation drift away. "Yeah, I know. I guess I'm really just annoyed that I had to spend the last couple of hours doing wedding stuff when all I really wanted was to be with you guys."

"Knock, knock!" Morag appeared out of thin air with a crib, which she placed right in the center of our room. A gold encrusted totally ostentatious crib. *Damn dragons and their thing for bling.* "I'm here to visit with the newest and definitely cutest little red dragon to have been born in a very long time."

"I asked Morag to watch him for a bit while we have some alone time," Khol whispered against my ear. I shivered.

"But I've hardly gotten to spend any time with him myself," I complained.

"I need some alone time with you," Khol murmured, his hot breath causing tingles to run through my body. *Okay maybe some alone time with Khol isn't such a bad idea.* Having sensed my change in attitude, thanks to him, Khol got up, taking sleeping Liam from my arms and handed him to Morag. She was beaming like the Cheshire cat at my son.

"Don't worry, I've had plenty experience taking care of baby dragons."

"I wasn't really worried until you told me not to be worried," I grumbled. Khol swept me up in his arms and I laughed. "Okay, eager much?"

"There's something I want to do with you," Khol said as he shifted us out of our room.

When Khol had said that there was something he wanted to do with me, my first thoughts had obviously been sex related. I mean the man without fail made my blood boil with desire, but when I noticed that our new scenery was a large open field, confusion took hold. *Unless Khol wants to get busy outside or something? I'm game if he is.* Khol had opened me up to a world of sexual exploration that I never could have imagined myself. Of course, we had been somewhat limited while I was pregnant but now—

"My little queen," Khol growled against my temple. "I didn't bring you here for that, but I can be persuaded to change my mind with ease." He set me on my feet, and I leaned into him, my hands curling into his shirt.

I raised an eyebrow at him. "Then why are we here?"

"You asked me some time ago about my other form—my dragon form. It's time you saw it."

My heart quadrupled in time, and my muscles locked. *Am I really ready for this?* "Khol—" I started.

He brought his index finger up to press against my lips. "It's who I am—who you are—who our son is. You need to embrace this part of you. Why are you so afraid?"

I hung my head. "I don't know—I guess it kind of feels like if I embrace that part of me then I'll truly lose all of my humanity. I mean, I know I'm a dragon, but I still mostly think of myself as human. I'm afraid of what it will mean if I don't have that anymore."

Khol rubbed small reassuring circles on my back. "You'll never fully gain control of your powers until you accept who you are entirely. You are who you are—nothing can change that."

I knew he was right on an intellectual level, but my emotions just didn't want to play ball. "What if your other form repulses me?" *There I said it.* That was another fear. What if seeing Khol in his other form made me not want him anymore in his human form? What if I couldn't get past that? It's one thing to read about shifters like werewolves and to think it's cool and sexy, but what if your man could actually turn into a wolf? *Hello weird.* The only difference was mine couldn't turn into a wolf, mine turned into a dragon. Hell, I didn't even know what a real dragon looked like. Would he have horns? Scales? A forked tongue? Would I?

Without a word Khol shifted a few feet away from me, the air around him beginning to shimmer.

Khol shifted a few feet away from me, the air shimmering around him, and in an instant a huge, red dragon, about the size of a two-story house was in his place. I gasped with equal parts surprise and delight. He was absolutely stunning. His skin was the same dark auburn shade of his human form's hair, and it was just as luminescent. He had a square shaped snout, very masculine in size and form, along with thick curving horns that protruded from his forehead. His wings matched the rest of his body, but appeared leathery, much like a bat's. He was absolutely terrifying, and yet shockingly beautiful at the same time.

I lifted my gaze to meet his green illuminated eyes, and I realized he was still my Khol, just in a very different package. All worries of being afraid or repulsed leached from my system. I went to him, wanting to know more. I ran my hand over his nose, and he snorted. The skin there felt like silk over steal, much softer than I expected. I continued my exploration of Khol, walking around him, all the while running my hands over his magnificent dragon form. The skin on his body was tougher, like armor, and I surmised it was just as hard to damage.

"You're magnificent," I whispered.

The air around him shimmered and he stood before me in his human form again, fully clothed. "Hey!" I protested. "I wasn't done yet."

Khol pulled me to him, slanting his mouth over mine,

his tongue pushing in to claim me fully. A slave to my body's demands, all protests were forgotten when he lowered us to the ground, his large body covering mine.

Khol broke our passionate embrace, balancing himself on straight arms as he gazed down at me with adoration. "You have no idea how it makes me feel that I was finally able to show you my other form...and you liked it."

I ran my fingertips over his human face in the same manner I'd just done to his dragon snout. "I loved it because I love you."

He mimicked my motions as he spoke. "I can't wait to see what your dragon looks like."

I frowned. "One step at a time. I'm definitely not ready for that yet."

Ignoring my comment, Khol's fingertips moved lower on my body as he spoke, "And then we will fly together as *Anam Caras* are meant to." An almost dreamy expression settled onto his features.

A series of completely inappropriate questions— questions that Jenna would probably ask popped into my mind. Although I had to know. I just had to. "Do—um— Do dragons have sex while in dragon form?" I mean, I did Khol's form was beautiful. I hadn't been attracted to it though, but who knew what would happen if I was in dragon form at the same time he was.

Khol chuckled. "No, dragons don't engage in anything sexual while in their dragon form. The armor gets in the way."

I blinked up at him, his words sinking in. Well, I hadn't

explored that part of his dragon form yet. Apparently, a dragon's sensitive bits were protected with armor like skin as well. *Good to know.*

"Yeah, okay." Honestly, I was kind of relieved. Having sex in dragon form would put a whole new definition to the word *freaky.*

"You have so much to learn still, my little queen, and I can't wait to teach it all to you." Khol dipped his head to deliver some scorching kisses to the side of my neck. His power slid into me like second nature, mine rising to meet his.

"I'm your willing student." *Did I just say that? Corny much?* But I guess loving someone had a way of doing that —making all the corny lines and sappy talk seem perfect instead of lame.

"Khol," I said, maneuvering myself so that I was on top of him, my thighs astride his. As I looked down at him and he gazed up at me, all coherent thought fled my mind and all I cared about was getting him naked and inside of me.

AS I LAY happy and satiated in Khol's protective embrace, I began to wonder if I was in fact being paranoid about something ominous looming in the future. After the Riders were removed from the humans not much had changed in the world, but so what? We weren't being hunted any more, and maybe the humans just needed some time to figure stuff out for themselves. Rome wasn't built in a day...time heals all wounds...and all the rest of those cliques.

I did all I could do by removing the Riders. My job was technically done. It was time for me to let go like Khol, Jenna, Jeremy and everyone else already had. I'd lost Bryn, and my family, but I'd just given birth to a perfect little baby dragon, and I was bonded with the most amazing dragon in the whole world. I still had so much to learn about my powers, my heritage, and myself, but I now had the time to learn it.

I deserve to be happy.

I can be happy.

I am happy.

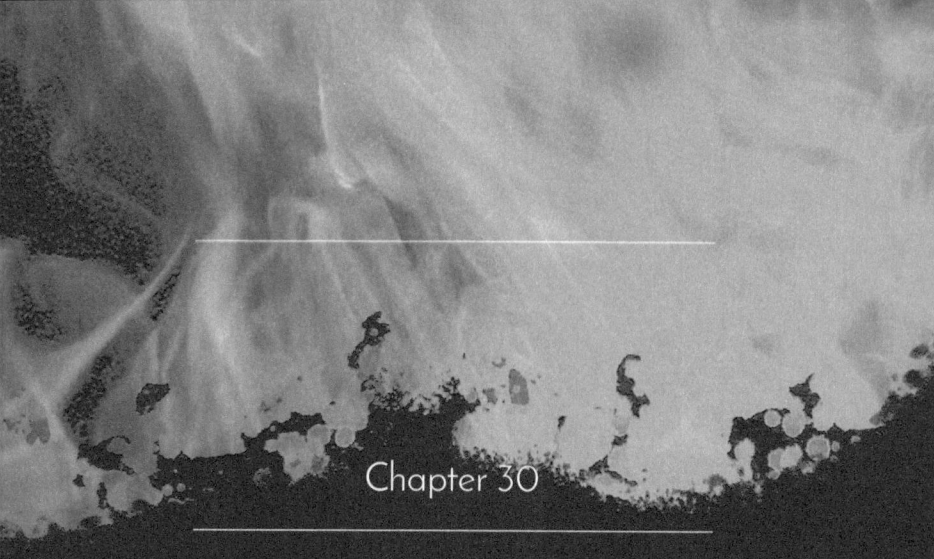

Chapter 30

It was the night before Jenna's wedding and all through the house, not a creature was stirring… except Jenna's mice…and rats and squirrels. I mean, seriously, why did her little 'friends' always seem to single me out to pester? Or maybe Jenna was the one telling them to bother me, but she didn't want to admit it because she thought it was funny.

"Khol," I whispered into the dark, grinding my teeth together. "Khol, wake up."

"Just ignore them," Khol mumbled.

"How can I? I can feel them watching me."

"They're not watching you, they're exploring. Besides if you didn't stash candy everywhere they'd probably be exploring the kitchen instead of our room." Khol's arm snaked out to pull me into his front, his large body curling around mine.

I stared into the dark another few minutes but with

Khol's steady heartbeat at my back lulling me into a sleepy trance, it wasn't long before my eyelids grew heavy. "Fine," I muttered, dozing.

"A YOUNG SEERS' *mind will never show her something she's not ready to handle." The words echoed in my head as a fog-like scene took shape before my eyes.*

I strode forward, hoping this time I would be able to see into the fog—that this time my vision would give me some answers instead of more questions. I tried to push through the fog, yet again, I discovered it was a solid wall. The fog felt smooth, soft and slimy, with a definite solid mass not typical of normal fog— just like before. I circled the fog like wall, searching for an opening, but I found none.

"Khol! No!" I stopped short already knowing the voice was mine. A roar met my ears causing a chill to run up my spine. With a renewed urgency I began circling the fog wall again, searching for a way in. That's when I heard the words again... again...always again. "A young Seers' mind will never show her something she's not ready to handle." I turned to find the source of the familiar voice, but the entire scene suddenly went to black.

Words reverberated within my skull, the same sightless vision repeating itself as well.

"Choose. But quickly, my magic will only hold you here for so long," a strange voice said.

"You would still choose him over me?" Khol growled.

"No—you don't understand!" I heard myself croak with desperation. *"I still love him but—"*

Jolting upright, I clutched at a sweat drenched sheet. I found myself alone in bed, Khol and Liam both gone. My little nocturnal friends seemed to be gone as well. *Thank God.* I glanced at the clock on my nightstand and realized it was still early enough that my alarm hadn't even gone off. Khol must have taken Liam so that I could sleep a little longer before prepping with Jenna for her big day.

My eyes locked on the bracelet around my wrist, and I played with the small purple stone for a moment before forcing myself out of bed. I wasn't going to let my ridiculous unclear visions ruin Jenna's big day, especially since I couldn't do anything about them. I was her best friend and Maid of Honor and therefore it was my job to make sure she didn't lose her shit, not the other way around.

After a quick shower I made my way to Jenna and Jeremy's room. Before I could even raise my hand to knock, the door flew open, and Jenna yanked me inside by my arm.

"Well, what do you think?" she asked, tugging on her still damp but very lime green hair.

I had to admit, I hadn't thought it would, but it complimented her complexion quite nicely. "I actually like it."

"You sound surprised."

"I am," I blurted out before I could think better of it.

Jenna's eyes widened. "And you were just gonna let me

dye it this color when you thought it was gonna look awful?"

I let out an exasperated sigh. "You know I'm not a fan of hair colors that can't be found in nature. In nature on people's heads, you know what I mean."

"True," Jenna huffed, although she seemed somewhat mollified.

"It's time to—"

"What the hell?" I squeaked, jumping back from a squirrel that scurried too close to my leg. That's when I really took in the state of her room. There were squirrels, mice, rats and all manner of small animals in almost every nook and cranny. I shuddered when what looked like a mole scuttled under a pillow on her bed. "Is that a mole—in your bed?"

Jenna waved her hand flippantly in the air. "Ever since you got the Rider out of me, and I could talk to animals again, I just keep more around is all."

"There's something seriously wrong with you." I shook my head. "What does Jeremy have to say about all of them?"

"He understands. He knows what I went through."

"Yeah, okay…whatever. What do you need me to do?" I clearly just needed to focus on the task at hand and let Jeremy worry about the rodents nesting in his and Jenna's room.

"Well get gorgeous dah-ling." Jenna giggled. "Morag said she's sending some people to do our hair and makeup

—" She glanced at the clock on the wall. "And whoever they are should be here soon."

I felt a prickling of power run over me before two silver haired dragons appeared. They both dropped to their knees and bowed. "My queen," the elder of the two said to me in deference.

My cheeks heated. "Today Jenna's the queen. Bow to her, not me." And they actually did. *Wow. Okay.*

A huge grin spread across Jenna's face. "Now that's what I'm talking about."

"You can get up. Seriously, please get up." Maybe one day I'd get used to being dragon queen, but today was obviously not that day.

The two silver haired dragons pulled themselves to their full height, which was almost a full foot shorter than me. They were both kind of plain looking, but cute, with short geometrical hairdos. "Morag sent us," the elder of the two said.

"Yes, we know. What are your names?" I asked.

"Lulu," the elder said, motioning to herself. She then pointed to the other silver dragon. "And Trish."

"Okay, Lulu and Trish, do whatever Jenna wants. Like I said, she's the queen today and therefore the one in charge." I groaned internally. *Did I really just give Jenna free reign over my appearance? I am going to regret this, for sure.*

Jenna squealed, jumping up and down with excitement. "Today is gonna be so amazing!"

I rolled my eyes when she wasn't looking and bit my

tongue to keep my snark in. But what I really wanted to say was: *"Probably just for you."*

I PEERED at my reflection tentatively, while Jenna did the same. She stood front and center in the mirror, staring at herself with wide eyes.

"What's wrong?" I asked her without meeting her dark gaze. I was currently fussing with the curls of white hair that cascaded down my back. The style was beautiful, if only I didn't have white hair.

"Do you think I'm making a mistake?" Jenna's voice came out small and uncertain with a slight waver to it.

I immediately let my eyes drop to take in her appearance. Her lime green hair was pinned up loosely with curls framing her heart shaped face. Black butterfly accents were artfully scattered throughout her tresses. Her makeup was neutral and yet accented her deep brown eyes and features masterfully. Lulu and Trish had out done themselves without question.

"Jenna, you look absolutely beautiful. You didn't make a mistake about your hair. I told you that already. And your dress is amazing too." I smiled reassuringly at her. I meant it. She was stunning. Her dress was a strapless cream-colored mermaid gown. It hugged her ample curves to perfection. Just the right amount of sequins adorned the custom creation, and black and lime green butterflies were woven into the fabric around the skirt. Everything was so perfectly... Jenna.

"No, not all of this." She waved her arms in a slightly panicked motion as she turned to face me. "I'm talking about marrying Jeremy."

It seemed I had discovered more butterflies, and they were currently doing the samba in my stomach. But then I realized it was my chance to be there for Jenna like she always had been for me and my screwed-up love life. "You love him." It wasn't a question. I saw the way Jenna looked at Jeremy. I wasn't clear on all the internal mechanisms of their relationship, but that much I knew.

Jenna nodded slowly. "Yeah, I do."

"So you're just having normal wedding day anxieties."

Jenna smoothed her hands over her dress. "How do I know that's all it is?"

"Well, ummm ... why don't you tell me what you're worried about?"

Jenna paused for a moment before her concerns came flying out of her mouth like verbal diarrhea. "What if he gets bored with me? What if I get bored with him? What if he just changes his mind? Or what if I do? What if he realizes I'm not worth it—what if—"

I waved my hands in front of her. "Whoa—whoa—whoa—whoa—whooooaaaa. Those are a lot of worries." I bit the inside of my cheek, trying not to smile. "But you've come to the right place, over-thinking such things happens to be my specialty."

Jenna rolled her eyes. "You're telling me."

"Hey." I scowled. "Don't mock the person who's about to help you." Jenna just grunted in response. "What do you love about Jeremy? And this is serious—no stupid sex jokes."

Jenna moved over to the love seat, sitting very carefully on the edge. She studied her hands as she spoke. "I love how he makes me feel." She glanced up at me briefly and I nodded with encouragement. "He knows all about my past—all the guys—all the mistakes—and he still thinks I'm special. And I know it sounds really selfish— like it's all about me—but he makes me wanna be a better person—for him. I mean I don't think that's selfish—to wanna do everything for him. I wanna make him proud. And I never thought I'd meet someone who seems to know me better than I know myself. It's like we're connected even when we're not together. And the sex—"

"Jenna," I grumbled. "I said no sex jokes.

She snorted softly. "I'm not gonna make a joke about it. I was just gonna say how amazing we are together. It's like it's more than sex. It's like we have this emotional connection. And maybe you don't know the difference because you haven't slept around like I have—but I'm afraid to lose it. What if I lose it? I can't lose him... " She dabbed at the corners of her eyes to keep her makeup intact.

"Oh, Jenna." I bent to hug her. "You won't. That kind of love just doesn't go away."

"But it did for you—with Bryn," Jenna whispered.

I pulled away from her carefully so I wouldn't mess up

her hair or makeup. "It's not the same for you and Jeremy. And besides Khol—"

"What if I'm Jeremy's Bryn?"

Oh. Now I fully understood what Jenna was trying to say. What if Jeremy had a Khol—someone he was meant to be with over her? What could I say to reassure her? "Jenna, I can't promise you a happily ever after, but I can promise you that there's no point in worrying about any of this. What's meant to be will be. I'm proof of that. Don't be stupid and walk away from Jeremy like Bryn did from me. If you love Jeremy, fight for him, and hold on with everything you have. Life is too short not to."

"For us humans anyways," Jenna mumbled. But I took it as a good sign since she was attempting to joke a little.

She then stood abruptly, meeting my gaze head on with confidence. "You're right. Let's do this. I'm getting married!" She grinned, all traces of trepidation completely gone.

I grinned back at her. "Yay! You're getting married to the love of your life!"

I allowed myself one last look in the mirror, straightening the lime green, long flowing dress that Jenna had picked out for me. I guess I didn't look that bad. And besides, even if I did, it wasn't my day.

THE MUSIC SWELLED and humans and dragons alike stood to watch Jenna march down the aisle to marry the love of her very young life. Shirking tradition, Jenna had asked me to give her away. She claimed it was the only fitting option with both of her parents being gone. I happily accepted. Jenna and I had been through so much together, with her often being the one supporting me. But no more, I would spend the rest of her life doing whatever I could to make up for all that she'd done for me.

Jenna clutched at my arm with the hand not holding her cream, lime green and black accented bouquet. I had to resist the urge to tell her to loosen her grip before she cut off all circulation in my forearm. Instead, I smiled tightly through the pain, walking slowly, taking in the details of everything around us. The beauty of the wedding relied mostly on the setting, but of course that's why Jenna had wanted to get married on Khol's land. White wooden chairs sat perfectly lined on what could have passed for green carpet. The trees and flowers were in full blossom, and Jeremy stood waiting, with Khol by his side, under a trellis, which was decorated with some kind of white gossamer material.

Things were perfect, or just the way Jenna had imagined, if the return of the blood flow in my arm was any indication. I grinned when I spotted Jeremy in his black tux with lime green accents, eating up Jenna with a hungry gaze. But my eyes were for Khol only. A small part of me imagined it was me walking down the aisle to meet Khol for our own "I dos". It was something, until that very moment, I hadn't thought I'd needed or wanted. Would Khol want to marry me in the traditional sense? I mean, we were already *Anam Caras*, what more did I need for everyone to know we belonged to each other?

My inner musings were interrupted when Jenna and I came to our destination. I dutifully handed her over to Jeremy, taking my place to the left of Jenna. As the gold dragon priestess began the ceremony, my attention wandered to Liam, who was sleeping peacefully in Morag's arms in his tiny color coordinated suit, which 'Aunty Jenna' had insisted he wear. I had to admit the lime green accents looked striking with his shock of red hair and pale skin. My eyes then were drawn back to Khol, who was staring at me with a small smile on his face. I shook my head ruefully at him, turning my focus back on Jenna and Jeremy just as they kissed. I clapped with everyone else and silently thanked the heavens that it hadn't been one of those long, boring ceremonies.

Jenna and Jeremy practically ran down the aisle towards the castle. Their poor photographer, who was a black dragon, was frantically trying to get some good shots. But Jeremy and Jenna seemed to have other plans, and I had a feeling that they were going to try and get some alone time in before the reception. Okay, it was more than a feeling since they headed in the opposite direction of the massive tent set up for the reception. I couldn't help but laugh. Jenna would always be Jenna, and I loved her for that.

Khol laced his fingers with mine, leaning down to whisper in my ear as the photographer turned to take pictures of us, since he'd apparently given up on Jeremy and Jenna for the moment. "I wouldn't mind a few minutes alone with you before the festivities begin."

I smiled up at him, liking where his mind was. "I guess Morag can watch Liam for a little while longer."

"My thoughts exactly." Khol nipped at my ear and shifted us back to our room.

I SAT at the reception table next to Khol, holding a sleeping Liam. Weren't babies supposed to cause more drama? Liam hardly ever cried and was so sweet. If he kept this up Khol just might be able to talk me into more children.

I let my gaze wander over to Jenna and Jeremy on the dance floor. They were slow dancing to a fast song and Jenna was practically draped on Jeremy, but he never looked happier. Jenna's wedding had actually gone smoothly, and the decorations were beautiful and yet oh-so-Jenna at the same time. Their five-layer cake was even adorned with lime green, the base decorated in a black pattern with lime green accents. Jeremy and Jenna had dutifully smashed pieces of said cake into each other's faces.

Overall, the day had been amazing and even I had shed a little sappy tear when Jeremy and Jenna were announced as husband and wife upon entering the reception. But I was exhausted and waiting for what seemed like an appropriate time to leave. If the wedding was bigger, I maybe would have been able to sneak off without Jenna noticing, but I knew it was important that I stay since most of the guests where technically strangers to her. The majority of the crowd was made up of dragons invited to join in the celebration and they basically came because I had invited them, and I was their queen. Everyone did seem to be having a good time though.

The next morning Jeremy and Jenna would be leaving for their honeymoon in the newly Rider free world, and I thought that was a wonderful wedding gift.

Everything seemed so settled, so perfect...so why couldn't I shake the foreboding feeling that kept snaking its way into the forefront of my mind? I tried to forget it, to push it aside, to just be happy, but I finally realized as I watched Jeremy lean down to whisper something in Jenna's ear that made her giggle, that I couldn't.

Chapter 31

"**P**resident Bill Wexington has just announced an end to the government cancer research that many had hoped—" The young news anchor droned lackadaisically.

"What's bothering you, my little queen?" Khol asked softly ad he slid onto the couch in our sitting area next to little Liam and me.

I looked up at him and realized I had been scowling while watching the news. I reached for the remote, fumbling with it. "I don't even know why I'm watching this crap."

Khol steadied my hand while studying my face. "Talk to me."

I huffed an exasperated sigh. "Nothing has changed. Doesn't that bother anyone else? Doesn't that bother you? I mean, we removed the Riders and yet this world is still

315

falling apart—why? If anything, things seem like they're getting worse."

"Give it time." Khol tugged the remote from my hand and muted the T.V.

"Something's still wrong, I can feel it." *There I finally said it out loud.*

"You worry too much." Khol ran his index finger over the crinkle in my forehead.

"Well duh! How can I not? This world is falling apart! The humans are still destroying everything even though the Riders are gone!"

"We're safe, your friends are safe. Things will work themselves out eventually."

"You're not listening to me! Something's wrong!" Little Liam started to cry. "Oh, I'm sorry little Li-Li," I murmured, rocking him in my arms. "I didn't mean to upset you. No, I didn't," I cooed in my best baby friendly voice.

"We've done all we can do." Khol's large, warm hand cupped the side of my face, forcing me to look up at him.

I gnawed on my bottom lip as I met his illuminated green gaze. "I'm missing something. I just don't know what it is yet."

Khol glanced over my shoulder at the T.V., tensing. "What—" He cleared his throat and dropped his hand from me. "I'll be back." He disappeared before I had a chance to question him.

I set Liam down on the baby swing by the couch, and picked up the remote again. I unmuted and rewound the latest news story for a clue as to what had made Khol suddenly tense up and pull a disappearing act. I listened to the news anchor's voice as a picture of plane wreckage appeared in the top left hand of the screen. "The hijackers seemed to have picked the planes at random. DL Flight 632 from Paris to Pittsburgh being one of—"

White noise stole the rest of what the anchor was saying. Jenna and Jeremy were scheduled to return today from their Paris honeymoon. They had booked a non-stop flight from Paris to Pittsburgh, and they were going to have Khol bring them back to his lair from PIT. Jenna said the flight was half the fun because she wanted to try and become a member of the Mile High Club with Jeremy. Surely there was more than one non-stop flight from Paris to Pittsburgh. Right?

"Khol!" I cried out, my hands trembling. "Khol!"

He appeared in front of me and before I said a word, his face told me everything I needed to know.

It was if someone had reached into my chest and fisted my heart. It hurt to breath. "Nooo!" I wailed, dropping to my knees. "Not Jenna! I can't lose her too!"

I clawed at the carpet. *This has to be nightmare, or a premonition that is completely preventable. Jenna can't be dead. Not now. Not after everything.* She was like my sister—the last family I had left besides Khol and Liam. I couldn't lose her. I would miss Jeremy, too, if something happened to him, but Jenna—losing Jenna—*no, no, no, no, not Jenna!*

"Khol, please! There has to be…something…just something." My mind had gone into hyper-drive running in circles, trying to find a solution. "I just—nooo!" I screeched. "Tell me how to save her!" I gasped for air, my lungs burning. My vision danced with specks of light as I struggled to come up with a plan.

"I'm sorry. So sorry. But it's too late—"

I didn't hear the rest of what Khol said, my queenly powers had obviously heard my plea and were trying to find a solution to my problem. Thousands of different choices, different paths, different endings began playing across my mind. I was seeing the past, the present, and the future all at once—and somehow, I was understanding all of it. If there was a way to save Jenna, I would *see* it.

But in the end, no matter how it played out, all roads led to Jenna's death. "Nooo!" I heard myself scream as if I was disconnected from my body. "No! I don't accept it! There has to be a way!"

Bryn's voice whispered against my ear, "Break the stone in your bracelet. Now is the time, Peej."

I didn't stop to question that I was hearing Bryn or what he was asking of me, I simply reacted. I crushed the tiny purple stone attached to my bracelet. Instantly, the knowledge of the Rider's origins flooded my consciousness, along with the memory of my meeting with my grandfather. I barely had time to process any of it, when power like I'd never experienced burned through my system, ripping an agonized scream from my chest.

The air around my body shimmered and a door appeared, hovering in the middle of the room. It swung open to reveal Bryn, his large frame illuminated by a bright white light shining from beyond him. My first instinct was to run to him, and my feet hastened to obey.

My grandfather, at least an older version of him, shifted into existence in front of Bryn.

"Choose," he said. "But quickly, my magic will only hold us here for so long."

"You would still choose him over me?" Khol growled.

"No—you don't understand!" I croaked, my heart threatening to crack my ribs. "I still love him but—"

Khol grabbed my arm, and swiveled me around, his expression twisted with a mixture of torment and anger. "If you go through that door, I won't be waiting for you when you come back this time."

"What?" I gasped. "You're my *Anam Cara*—you can't— you can't abandon me—us."

"Clearly even the most sacred bond between our kind, can't keep you from *him*," Khol spat.

I have to go through that door. Inside, I instinctively knew, were the answers, and the solutions I'd been seeking. With how connected Khol was to my emotions, how could he be so blinded? Just because of Bryn? Even after everything that existed between us now?

I shook my head slowly, trying to put all I needed to say into my eyes. "It's not like that. Try to understand. I'm not choosing him over you. But I have to go."

"You need to hurry." My grandfather waved me toward the door.

Khol dropped to his knees, his anger cracking to reveal despair. "Don't leave me again. Please."

I glanced at my grandfather and Bryn, and then at Khol again. "I need to go. But I'll be back. I'm not abandoning you. You're my *Anam Cara* and I love you."

Khol stared at me, his gaze hardening as he pulled himself to his feet.

Taking a step towards him, I tried to get through to him again. "I love you, Khol. I'm not choosing him over—"

"We don't have time for this," my grandfather growled. "If you're coming then we need to go."

I realized in that moment that Khol was going to have to learn how to trust me if we had any hope at real future together, *Anam Caras* or not. I'd hurt him in the past, but things were different now.

"I'm coming back to you. Trust me."

I pivoted and dashed for the door, not sparing him another glance.

"WHERE ARE WE?" I asked, taking in my surroundings. I stood in the center of a room with doors everywhere. It reminded me of something I saw once in an *Alice in Wonderland* movie. They were of all shapes, sizes, and colors, and went on for as far as the eye could see.

"This is how brown dragons travel," my grandfather explained with a bemused smile. "I'm not really sure why it looks this way, but I have a feeling that the first brown dragon had a hand in it and obviously had an odd sense of humor."

"Peej," Bryn rumbled, hugging me tight enough to steal my breath. "I never thought I'd get hold you in my arms again."

"Bryn," I murmured into his massive chest. "I missed you so much." *And what about Khol?* my mind whispered, causing me to pull away from Bryn.

Bryn stared at me, his dragon blue eyes glowing brighter. "You truly have chosen him, haven't you?"

I bit my lower lip. "Yes. And he's the father of my son. What we had—you and me—it was so different than what I have with Khol. He doesn't just make me wanna be a better person like you did, but he—" I paused while I tried to collect my thoughts. "He understands who I've become, the darkness inside of me, and he helps me embrace myself so it's not crippling. He balances me and —and he's exactly what I've always needed and wanted but was afraid to accept. I love him beyond reason— beyond—"

"Me," Bryn interjected. "You love him beyond me."

"Yes," I breathed. "And I'm sorry."

Not wanting to talk about it any further I turned to face my grandfather who had been standing silently while observing. "Where am I and what's happening? How is Bryn here?"

"We are beyond time here. Bryn is both alive and dead in this moment. His spirit is…more here. But only here."

I fought the urge to roll my eyes. "Here we go again," I muttered to myself.

"Your powers helped to open the doors here in

combination with mine. The key to all of this lies in your blood."

"How do I bring Jenna back? I mean that's what triggered all of this—her death, right?" I choked back a sob. Jenna was dead. Bryn was dead. My two best friends were both dead, and I didn't know where I stood with Khol at the moment.

Bryn's voice all the sadness I was trying to suppress. "She can't be brought back. It's against the rules."

I kept my focus on my grandfather. "Then why am I here? Why?" I beseeched.

"Time isn't a straight line like most would like to think. It bends and curves and sometimes even forms a circle."

"I don't care!" Burning tears spilled from my eyes, racing down my face. "I just want my friends back! My world back!"

"I'll give you your choice then. A choice only you can make, and one that only can be carried out by you—only you because of your combined genetics and therefore it's your destiny to make. Everything—absolutely everything that has happened since the first moment when the first white dragon queen created the Riders has been moving towards bringing you here—to this moment."

"Just tell me what I need to do!" I croaked. "This all needs to end—now."

My grandfather waved his hand in the air, and it shimmered like heat rising off of pavement. "This will be your world if you do nothing." Images of war-ravaged lands assaulted my eyes. My world destroyed. "The Riders have done their damage, and it cannot be undone." I stood perfectly still in utter silence waiting for what he would say next. "Or you can change everything."

"How? Tell me what I have to do!"

"You must make a choice. You—"

"You keep saying that! Just tell me what choice so I can make it!"

"I have enough power, that combined with your blood, can send you, and only you, back into your consciousness to the time when you first saw the aliens emerging through the gates—back to your first vision. But your memories will be wiped clean. You won't remember any of this. It would be like a do-over—as you might call it."

I shook my head. "But things still might turn out the same—in fact they most likely will. I've looked at everything with my powers, nothing will work out the way I want—at least not for Jenna, and Bryn, and Jeremy, and all of our families."

"That leaves you with choice number two, your only other option." I inhaled, waiting, every nerve ending in my body humming with anticipation. "I can send you, and only you, back to when the Riders first breeched the gates. You can stop them from ever re-entering this world."

"Yes! That's what I'll do! There really isn't a choice there."

"Oh, but there is." My grandfather stared at me intently. "There will be consequences."

I swallowed around the sudden lump in my throat. "Such as?"

"It will change everything. If the Riders never enter our world, then your mother will never send Drago to impregnate the mother that raised you. You will be the one who is murdered in your crib."

"But why wouldn't my birth mother see that and stop it? It doesn't make sense."

"Because magic always tries to balance things out. Only one of you can exist at a time. If you—if the you, you are now, travels to that version of time then the other you must die."

"But then won't I—" I clutched at my chest. "The me I am now will cease to exist? Like in *Back to the Future* or something?"

My grandfather smiled faintly. "I know of which human film you refer, it was quite entertaining, but completely fictional when it comes to how time works." I nodded for him to continue. "The present you will live, but you will be stuck in that time as you are now. Not a huge change."

"That doesn't seem so bad. All things considered." I bit my lower lip as I considered it.

"There's more." *Of course there is.* "Jenna will live. Bryn will live. Jeremy will live, along with all of your families, but none of them will ever know you." My heart sped up with his words. "It will be as if you never existed—you and the Riders both. You are connected to them through your blood—and without them—there will be no you in a sense. You will exist outside of that bubble of time, distinctly separate and yet within it."

Bryn's fingers slipped into mine and squeezed. "So I would go back to that time and save the world, but then I'd be completely alone? What about Khol—would he—and my son—what about my son?" A panic swept through me. *What if I lose my son?*

"No—no one will know you. You will begin anew as you are now."

I took in a deep shuddering breath. "But everyone would be safe, and the future of the world would be safe as well?"

My grandfather nodded gravely. "Yes."

"So there really isn't a choice, is there?"

Bryn tugged me into his arms, and I listened to him speak with my ear against his chest. "Peej, there is a third choice. You could go back, live your life with Khol and your son. You know the human world can't harm you—not really."

"But you'd all be dead," I choked back a sob. "And how could I live with that knowing I could save you? All of you?"

"Be selfish, Peej. I'm already dead. We're all already dead. Take the life you deserve. No one could blame you."

"I would blame me. I would!" My chest heaved as I sucked in ragged breathes, the weight of the world's future weighing on me. "Maybe in the past—maybe before all of this began, I could have been selfish. I was that selfish—but now—now I'm different. I'm a queen."

And wasn't it a queen's duty to ensure the safety of her people? I could not only do that but more. As Stan Lee's

Spiderman comic books taught me, thanks to Bryn...with great power comes great responsibility. I had to do what was right for the good of many and not just myself. Khol would understand—but Liam—my son—how could I give him up when I'd just gotten him? My stomach twisted and bile shot up my esophagus.

Bryn tightened his arms around me. "Choose him, Peej. Choose Khol and everything he brings with him. I need to know that you'll be happy."

I choked back another sob. "So that's what you meant. That's what you couldn't tell me." Bryn didn't say anything, which was answer enough. "What if I need you to be happy?" I asked softly.

"I won't be happy without you. I won't—"

"You'll never have known me! You can be happy then!"

And ultimately that's what made up my mind. I had chosen Khol, and I wished with more than anything in me that I could remain with him—but I loved Bryn, and Jenna, and even Jeremy. And when you love someone, no matter what kind of love, you'll do everything in your power to ensure their chance at happiness. It was in my power to give another chance to all of those I held dear to me.

Except Khol. But that was my ultimate sacrifice. I would sacrifice my happiness for those who I knew truly deserved a second chance. My grandmother had started this—it was my duty to end it. How ironic, that after everything, duty would cost me my heart's greatest desires after all.

Pulling myself away from Bryn, I whirled around to face the rows of doors. "Which one? Which door do I need to go through?"

"Only you know," my grandfather stated with no emotion.

I slid my gaze over the many doors in front of me, closed my eyes, and spun in a circle. When I stopped, I just started walking with my hands stretched out in front of me. Only when my fingertips brushed over the cool wood of one of the doors, did I open my eyes again. "It's purple." I barked out a humorless laugh. "Of course."

Purple had always been my favorite color but beyond that, I'd always felt drawn to it somehow and now I knew why. With only the slightest bit of hesitation, I twisted the knob, and stood on the precipice of the most important thing I'd ever done in my life.

"Peej, just think about what you're really doing!" Bryn rushed towards me, but he wasn't fast enough.

"I already have."

His hands snatched empty air as I stepped through the door and free fell into nothing.

Chapter 32

I immediately knew where I was—the scene of my very first vision.

Things were different live and in the flesh, because at the time my vision had showed me the past—now I was really here. In front of me, it appeared as if a piece of sky had been ripped into the side of the forest, the jagged edges swaying in time with pulsating shades of purple and blue. The shape of it was irregular, moving as I imagine pure energy does, with a kind of pattern that no naked eye could pick up on. It was more beautiful than I realized the first time I'd seen it in my vision. Perhaps it was because I was seeing it with my heightened powers. After all, a lot had changed since my first vision.

But I also knew what to expect this time.

As I stood there, shapes began to emerge from the gate —Riders. I was feeling a little bit loopy, still in shock, or maybe something more. Hysterical laughter erupted from my chest, because my mind conjured an image of Gandalf from *Lord of the Rings*. I wasn't the white wizard, but I was the white queen, and I was going to kick just as much ass.

My fire magic ripped through me, the flames crackling from my palms and up my arms. I marched towards the gate, and just for good measure I said, "You shall not pass!" *Too bad I don't have a huge staff to bang on the ground for dramatic effect.* A fresh wave of laughter bubbled up within me.

The Riders continued in their attempt to breach the gate, their too large eyes and pinched features focusing in on me with anger. *But why?* Why wasn't I stopping them? This was my friggin' destiny. I'd given up everything for this chance. Failure was not an option. Or maybe I'd fallen victim to my personality's biggest folly...impatience. Had I jumped back in time to do this before my grandfather had been able to give me some pertinent information?

"It's in your blood," my grandfather's voice whispered. Or maybe my queenly powers were answering for me.

"Dragon blood—*my* dragon blood," I murmured in understanding. Ripping the dragon pendant from my neck, I pressed the sharp edge of the dragon's horn against my palm, piercing my flesh. Blood immediately swelled up from the small wound. *But now what? What to do with the blood?*

I instinctively rushed the gate, shoving my hand through while I fed more of my fire magic into it as well. Angry Rider faces peered at me, some of them grabbing at me, but none of them made contact. An intense burning in my hand began as a bright white light spread from my palm. The light kept building until—a sonic boom exploded into the air, throwing me backwards. I couldn't hear or see anything. I had no idea if what I had done worked, or simply made things worse.

After what seemed like an eternity, I blinked the gate back into focus.

Relief and shock swelled through my system, curling numbness around me. The only thing in front of me was a completely open gate. No more Riders.

I did it! I saved the world!

And yet...

I'm alone now. Completely alone.

Overwhelmed, I covered my face with my hands and allowed myself to weep. I was the only witness to the birth of the new world, so to speak. I'd saved my friends and family, and they would never know. I'd sacrificed Khol and my son, and they wouldn't even miss me because they would never know me either. In fact, Liam technically didn't even exist anymore. I'd erased my son from this world.

And I still had so many questions—questions like: How could I be queen with all this power when my birth mother would never be able to give it to me? How could there be two dragon queens at the same time with the same powers? Maybe I just wasn't ready to understand like my grandfather had told me. And time didn't exist in a straight line. Perhaps that's what he meant when he said I would exist outside this bubble of time, being distinctly separate from it. It really was the only explanation I had.

But what about Jenna and Jeremy? Would they still find each other in this version of reality? Would they still be happy? And Bryn—would he get the chance to truly be happy like I wished for him? I fought the urge to check on them because I knew in my heart that I wouldn't be able to see them without wanting to involve myself in their lives. I had to start over too, and to do that I had to let them all go. Besides I'd given them all I could, and I had nothing left.

And what about the humans? I now knew more than anyone else how irrevocably flawed they truly were. How long would it be before they destroyed themselves? As a whole, they were striving to fill something in themselves, even if it was a long ago genetic memory, but something that could never be filled, and they would and could never know that. They were broken in ways that I could never truly understand.

Maybe, in the end, my sacrifice would all be for nothing.

Leaning back on my elbows, I stared up at the sky. "What do I do now?"

I just saved the world and I had no friends, no family, and nowhere to go. I laughed, thinking of the middle name my mom had given me...Joplin. And hadn't Joplin said that freedom meant there was nothing left to lose? How ironic that those words held so true for me now. The possibilities of where I could go and what I could do were endless. I was completely free for the first time in my life. Maybe I was exactly where I always was meant to be. How could I argue with a middle name like Joplin to guide me?

Just then a familiar prickling of power ran over my skin, and I gasped as Khol appeared in front of me. "How?" I rasped.

Khol stared down at me and tilted his head, smiling, before dropping down on one knee. "We have a new queen. I did not expect that. I have been asleep for a very long time. Your power called to me, awakening me in an instant, I was helpless to resist—"

Understanding donned on me. This version of Khol had no memory of me, but it didn't matter—he was still mine. He would always be mine. Jumping to my feet, I fisted his shirt, and pulled him up to me. "Shut up and kiss me—because you're mine," I growled.

Khol's illuminated gaze flashed with lust, and he stole my breath as he took control of my mouth without question. After all, wasn't it the way of the dragon?

In that moment, as Khol's lips ignited my blood, just like his kisses always did, I saw my son. I would get him back. My own voice whispered in my mind as if I was hearing another version of myself speaking—telling me what I would have with this Khol—what I had truly chosen when I stepped through that purple door into the past.

With my powers, sometimes it's like I exist in the past, present, and future all at the same time. I am only now—and not the now of this moment—but of every moment from the beginning of time until the end of eternity. I am eternal and yet I do not exist. It's enough to drive me mad—and it probably would—if not for Khol. Lord Kholkikos, ruler of the rua arach... my love, my world, my Anam Cara. He taught me that sometimes it's not who you want to love, but rather who you have no defenses against not loving. He never gave up on me, never let me go, and he will always find me no matter where I am. In any time, and in any place, his heart will seek out mine, and I will be defenseless not to love him with everything that I am. Khol just isn't a part of my soul—he is my soul—and he always will be—even after all others turn to dust.

Acknowledgments

I have a whole list of people that deserve to be thanked here, and with that in mind, I was going to simply use my original acknowledgments from the first version of Open Gates buuuut ...I'm currently in the process of moving and all of my books are in boxes. I would rip all those bad boys all open to find my copy of the old Open Gates but let's face it, that seems like entirely too much work and I'm already stressed from all the packing as it is.

I would rather list no one here than risk accidentally leaving someone out. So to avoid such a catastrophe, I'm simply going to thank all of the readers out there that have given my books a chance. You mean the world to me. Thank you.

About the Author

Ava Wixx escaped into books at a young age and decided to stay there. It was only a matter of time before she was driven to create her own fantasy worlds from fear of running out of places to explore.

Reader, writer, dreamer ... Ava only toils in reality when absolutely necessary. She lives in North Carolina with her husband, and spoiled mini-poodle.

(If you want up-to-date info on book-y things then visit Avawixx.com and don't bother with the social media. Because let's face it, Ava is an online slacker and she signed up for some accounts but never actually posts.)